Gratified

Omega Queen Series, Volume 12

W.J. May

Published by Dark Shadow Publishing, 2021.

This is a work of fiction. Similarities to real people, places, or events are entirely coincidental.

GRATIFIED

First edition. November 20, 2021.

Copyright © 2021 W.J. May.

Written by W.J. May.

Also by W.J. May

Beginning's End Series
Beginnings

Blood Red Series
Courage Runs Red
The Night Watch
Marked by Courage
Forever Night
The Other Side of Fear
Blood Red Box Set Books #1-5

Daughters of Darkness: Victoria's Journey
Victoria
Huntress
Coveted (A Vampire & Paranormal Romance)
Twisted
Daughter of Darkness - Victoria - Box Set

Great Temptation Series
The Devil's Footsteps
Heaven's Command
Mortals Surrender

Hidden Secrets Saga
Seventh Mark - Part 1
Seventh Mark - Part 2
Marked By Destiny
Compelled
Fate's Intervention
Chosen Three
The Hidden Secrets Saga: The Complete Series

Kerrigan Chronicles
Stopping Time
A Passage of Time
Ticking Clock
Secrets in Time
Time in the City
Ultimate Future

Kerrigan Memoirs
Chronicles of Devon
Chronicles of Angel

Mending Magic Series
Lost Souls
Illusion of Power
Challenging the Dark
Castle of Power
Limits of Magic
Protectors of Light
Mending Magic Box Set Books #1-3

Omega Queen Series
Discipline
Bravery
Courage
Conquer
Strength
Validation
Approval
Blessing
Balance
Grievance
Enchanted
Gratified
Omega Queen - Box Set Books #1-3

Paranormal Huntress Series
Never Look Back
Coven Master
Alpha's Permission

Blood Bonding
Oracle of Nightmares
Shadows in the Night
Paranormal Huntress BOX SET

Prophecy Series
Only the Beginning
White Winter
Secrets of Destiny

Revamped Series
Hidden
Banished
Converted

Royal Factions
The Price For Peace
The Cost for Surviving
The Punishment For Deception
Faking Perfection
The Most Cherished
The Strength to Endure
Royal Factions Box Set Books #1-3

Royal Guard Series
Guardian

The Chronicles of Kerrigan
Rae of Hope
Dark Nebula
House of Cards
Royal Tea
Under Fire
End in Sight
Hidden Darkness
Twisted Together
Mark of Fate
Strength & Power
Last One Standing
Rae of Light
The Chronicles of Kerrigan Box Set Books # 1 - 6

The Chronicles of Kerrigan: Gabriel
Living in the Past
Present For Today
Staring at the Future

The Chronicles of Kerrigan Prequel
Christmas Before the Magic
Question the Darkness
Into the Darkness
Fight the Darkness
Alone in the Darkness
Lost in Darkness
The Chronicles of Kerrigan Prequel Series Books #1-3

The Chronicles of Kerrigan Sequel
A Matter of Time
Time Piece
Second Chance
Glitch in Time
Our Time
Precious Time

The Hidden Secrets Saga
Seventh Mark (part 1 & 2)

The Kerrigan Kids
School of Potential
Myths & Magic
Kith & Kin
Playing With Power
Line of Ancestry
Descent of Hope
Illusion of Shadows
Frozen by the Future
Guilt Of My Past
Demise of Magic
Rise of The Prophecy
Deafened By The Past
The Kerrigan Kids Box Set Books #1-3

The Queen's Alpha Series
Eternal
Everlasting
Unceasing
Evermore
Forever
Boundless
Prophecy
Protected
Foretelling
Revelation
Betrayal
Resolved
The Queen's Alpha Box Set

The Senseless Series
Radium Halos - Part 1
Radium Halos - Part 2
Nonsense
Perception
The Senseless - Box Set Books #1-4

Standalone
Shadow of Doubt (Part 1 & 2)
Five Shades of Fantasy
Zwarte Nevel
Shadow of Doubt - Part 1
Shadow of Doubt - Part 2

Four and a Half Shades of Fantasy
Dream Fighter
What Creeps in the Night
Forest of the Forbidden
Arcane Forest: A Fantasy Anthology
The First Fantasy Box Set

Watch for more at www.wjmaybooks.com.

OMEGA QUEEN SERIES
GRATIFIED
USA Today Bestselling Author
W.J. MAY

Copyright 2021 by W.J. May

THIS E-BOOK OR PRINT is licensed for your personal enjoyment only. This e-book/paperback may not be re-sold or given away to other people. If you would like to share this book with another person, please purchase an additional copy for each recipient. If you're reading this book and did not purchase it, or it was not purchased for your use only, then please return to Smashwords.com and purchase your own copy. Thank you for respecting the hard work of the author.

All rights reserved. No part of this publication may be reproduced, stored in or introduced into a retrieval system, or transmitted, in any form, or by any means (electronic, mechanical, photocopying, recording, or otherwise) without the prior written permission of both the copyright owner and the above publisher of this book.

This is a work of fiction. Names, characters, places, brands, media, and incidents are either the product of the author's imagination or are used fictitiously. Any resemblance to actual person, living or dead, events, or locales is entirely coincidental. The author acknowledges the trademarked status and trademark owners of various products referenced in this work of fiction, which have been used without permission. The publication/use of these trademarks is not authorized, associated with, or sponsored by the trademark owners.

All rights reserved.
Copyright 2021 by W.J. May
Gratified, Book 12 of the Omega Queen Series
Cover design by: Book Cover by Design

No part of this book may be used or reproduced in any manner whatsoever without written permission, except in the case of brief quotations embodied in articles and reviews.

Have You Read the C.o.K Series?

The Chronicles of Kerrigan
Book I - *Rae of Hope* is FREE!

BOOK TRAILER:
http://www.youtube.com/watch?v=gILAwXxx8MU

How hard do you have to shake the family tree to find the truth about the past?

Fifteen year-old Rae Kerrigan never really knew her family's history. Her mother and father died when she was young and it is only when she accepts a scholarship to the prestigious Guilder Boarding School in England that a mysterious family secret is revealed.

Will the sins of the father be the sins of the daughter?

As Rae struggles with new friends, a new school and a star-struck forbidden love, she must also face the ultimate challenge: receive a tattoo on her sixteenth birthday with specific powers that may bind her to an unspeakable darkness. It's up to Rae to undo the dark evil in her family's past and have a ray of hope for her future.

Find W.J. May

Website:
https://www.wjmaybooks.com
Facebook:
https://www.facebook.com/pages/Author-WJ-May-FAN-PAGE/141170442608149
Newsletter:
SIGN UP FOR W.J. May's Newsletter to find out about new releases, updates, cover reveals and even freebies!
https://www.wjmaybooks.com/newsletter

Gratified Blurb:

USA Today Bestselling author, W.J. May, continues the highly anticipated bestselling YA/NA series about love, betrayal, magic and fantasy.
Be prepared to fight... it's the only option.

There is nothing worse than a friend turned enemy or a love turned sour.

When Evie and her friends find themselves stranded alone against the Carpathian army, they think all hope is lost. But the fates are ever-changing, and an unexpected ally comes to their aid. New friendships are forged as the old are tested. As their quest to fulfill the prophecy comes to a close, each of the three must search within themselves to see if they have what it takes.

A realm divided cannot stand, but can such ancient grievances ever be mended?

A change is coming, but only time will tell if it's for the better or the worse.

Sometimes, it just takes a leap of faith...

BE CAREFUL WHO YOU trust. Even the devil was once an angel.

The Queen's Alpha Series

Eternal
Everlasting
Unceasing
Evermore
Forever
Boundless
Prophecy
Protected
Foretelling
Revelation
Betrayal
Resolved

The Omega Queen Series

Discipline
Bravery
Courage
Conquer
Strength
Validation
Approval
Blessing
Balance
Grievance
Enchanted
Gratified

– NEW – Beginning's End Series

Check the excerpt at the back of Gratified to see what's coming!!

Chapter 1

"I heard you were assembling the four kingdoms. But I seem to remember...there used to be five."

Ellanden froze on the edge of the mountain, staring in astonishment as a legion of vampires materialized on the slope in front of him. It was the kind of sight you couldn't tear your eyes away from, even more shocking than the angelic wings trembling with anticipation at his sides.

The Carpathians were still sleeping fitfully just a little further down the alpine ridge, their faces flickering into illumination by the light of a dozen small fires. *They* were supposed to be his biggest problem. The monstrous horde of creatures that had imprisoned them in the peaks.

He'd never imagined that instead of facing one army...he'd find himself facing two.

"Are you unwell, sweet boy?" Diana tilted her head appraisingly, concerned by his apparent inability to speak. "Or have we merely surprised you?"

The fae took a faltering step in the opposite direction, towards the edge of the cliff.

"You frighten him," another vampire remarked thoughtfully, his dark eyes drifting slowly over the young prince. "Hear the way his pulse quickens."

There was a murmur of affirmation by the others, but the sudden and celestial appearance of the fae had surprised them as well and the entire group was standing unnaturally still.

How is this happening? The princess stared across the ravine with the rest of them, hands clamped over her mouth. *You were just standing beside me. How in the world could this be happening?*

"Yes, his heart races," Diana murmured, examining his wings with a tilt of the head. "But his shock could not exceed our own...what an enchanting sight."

The distant firelight glinted off her fangs, and the fae leaned further towards the abyss.

Even from so great a distance, it was impossible to miss the gravity of the situation. Even if the young prince were to leap into the sky, carried away by those fantastical wings, the vampires were faster. No sooner would his feet leave the cliff than he'd be pulled straight back down again.

Ellanden knew this for certain. His best friend had tormented him for years.

"I don't understand," he breathed, stepping back once again. Despite the dizzying drop, he kept each movement slow and fluid—the way one didn't agitate a snake. "Why are you here?"

There was another whisper of movement, but Diana only smiled.

"As I've told you...we've come to help." Her gaze rose over his shoulder to the monastery on the other side of the ravine. "We've travelled for days, following the path of the dragon—"

There was a sudden clattering of stone as the heel of his boot dipped over the cliff. He caught himself quickly, but the incriminating sound remained—echoing slowly into silence.

Diana stood there until it was over, staring into his eyes.

"Peace, child. We mean you no harm."

Sure.

The crowd gathered in the courtyard of the monastery sucked in the same tortured breath, seeing from a helpless distance how *very incredibly easy* it would be for her to do just that.

And even if the queen showed restraint...what of the rest of them?

There was a reason the younger vampires had been given a curfew during their untimely visit, kept under lock and key within the depths of their mountain home. Even now, some of them were regarding the fae with an almost manic light in their eyes. As if they would throw their bodies straight over the cliff—if only to taste his blood on the way down.

"But if you don't mind me asking...what was your plan?" Diana continued. "To carry the bridge to the sanctuary, lead your family to freedom?" Her eyes twinkled as they drifted to the horde of Carpathians camped further down the slope. "Did you forget about them?"

Even now, the brutes were stirring in their sleep. A new day was breaking over the side of the mountains—chasing away the shadows with the first golden traces of dawn.

"We cannot remain stranded on that peak," Ellanden breathed, answering without making the conscious decision to do so. "Someone had to—"

"Someone had to grow the wings of an angel and leap into the night sky?" Diana finished with a twinkling smile. "I love the Fae," she said to a vampire beside her. "They're so whimsical."

...and vampires are impossibly detached.

There was no time for such discussion, as the surreal encounter had left everyone hanging on the same suspended breath. But the initial surprise had started to fade and Ellanden threw a reflexive glance down the slope, wondering what the queen meant when she said they'd come to help.

Diana watched every movement, eyes glittering in the faint morning light. "These people...they have driven you here?"

It was utterly foreign, the carelessness with which she spoke of them. The monstrous horde that had slain so many in their path. She didn't even bother to look.

Ellanden nodded slowly, tensing as a handful of vampires began weaving their way through the crowd, coming to stand beside her. These were not strangers, not entirely. He and his friends had been at their mercy before. He wasn't keen to find himself in the same situation now.

"And you are unable to leave?"

He nodded again, poised on the edge of the cliff.

"What are they doing?" Dylan breathed.

Like a too-distant reflection, he was hovering at the farthest point of the monastery—hands twitching compulsively, like he could reach across all that space and grab the fae back.

Aidan merely stared across the ravine, every muscle in his body locked into place.

There was a fleeting moment when Diana seemed to register him as well. Her eyes flickered across the great canyon, coming to rest on precisely the place where the vampire stood.

Then she turned back to the prince.

"Fly away with your bridge, little bird. But grant me one request." She lifted her gaze once more, staring directly at Aidan. "Make sure they are watching."

Ellanden didn't need to be told twice. Without another word he sprang backwards into the air, flying in a direct line back to Talsing. He crossed the divide in a matter of seconds, but didn't re-hang the bridge as he'd planned. He simply carried it up to the roof where his family was gathered.

Landi—

The second he was within reach, Dylan seized him right out of the air—dragging him backwards over the ramparts and securing him with a strong arm flung across the chest.

The fae hardly noticed, his entire body trembling with delayed shock. "...there are vampires."

The ranger let out a sharp breath. "I can see."

One couldn't fault him for surprise. The princess still couldn't believe it herself. The clan of immortals had moved like a shadow—pouring over the mountain like the breaking of the tide.

The Carpathian army hadn't even awoken.

That was something Diana aimed to remedy now.

"Come out, come out, wherever you are..."

The quiet sing-song drifted over the mountains as she wandered away from the group to the body of a fallen soldier. She spared not a glance for the corpse itself, a victim of Aidan's rampage to eliminate the enemy archers. She merely took the helmet from his head.

Then she walked to the post that once held the bridge...and started banging.

Never had Evie witnessed such a chilling spectacle. There was nothing particularly ominous or threatening about it. Quite the contrary, it was slow and leisurely. Almost childish. But she found herself frozen without a hint of breath, flinching with dread at each reverberating *bang*.

There was movement behind them in the courtyard as the students and warriors who resided in Talsing opened their eyes. There was movement farther down the mountain as the Carpathians stirred to life as well. They looked around in obvious confusion, trying to locate the source of the noise before pushing slowly to their feet when their eyes fell upon the vampire horde.

This...will not end well.

The friends clustered together, staring in silence across the divide with a rising sense of dread. After a few seconds, Asher stepped closer to his father.

"What is she doing?"

Aidan never took his eyes from Diana. "She's making amends."

There was a rushed assembly from the Carpathians—a hasty gathering of those who'd been elected to lead. They couldn't have said much, especially as voices tended to carry. Only a moment later, the biggest of the bunch sheathed his sword and took a step forward.

A man who no doubt still had traces of royal blood on his shoes.

Why put away the sword?

The others stood in unending silence, startling in their skin every time the helmet clanged against the broken metal. There was no reason to keep it going, but Diana felt no hurry to stop. A wraithlike army of immortals loomed up behind her, picking out faces in the early morning mist.

Then, all at once...the banging stopped.

In a way, it was even more jarring. The quiet that followed seemed doomed from the start, just waiting for something to break it open once more.

The Carpathian stared a moment longer, then took a step forward.

"I see you found our missing helmet," he said with forced civility. "Thank you for that."

Diana tilted her head slightly, then dropped it over the side of the cliff. It took ages to fall, echoing in slow silence as both armies stared each other down.

"You have others, I hope?"

By now, most everyone residing in Talsing had gathered on the roof of the monastery to watch. In a frightening way, there was a strange thrill to it. Two such opposing forces. It was a spectacle that could only be enjoyed from a distance. Venture too close, you wouldn't survive.

The Carpathian never flinched, not since that initial sound had startled him awake. There was something practiced and very steady in his eyes. But there was something else there as well, an emotion the princess didn't think his people capable of until that very moment.

For the first time in his life...the man was afraid.

"My lord will be most pleased that you've come round," he said quietly. It was both a subtle threat and a subtle plea. "After all...you have some of the most to gain."

In a flash the princess understood the reason for the banter, the same reason he'd sheathed his weapon when every instinct was screaming to keep it drawn. This was not a battle he could hope to win. Not even in full regalia, with the entire Carpathian army standing behind him. There simply wasn't a way to defeat such a large force of vampires. He could only pray they hadn't come to fight.

The Queen of the Vampires only smiled. "Some of us have more to gain than others."

SEVEN HELLS!

There was no more talking, no hint of a transition to ease the way.

No sooner had Diana spoken than the clan of immortals swept down from the mountain, overwhelming all who came before them with savage fire blazing in their eyes.

Even from so great a distance, it was a gruesome thing to behold. While the Carpathians were hacking away with swords in armor, the vampires had nothing but the clothes on their back. Some of them weren't even wearing shoes. But it didn't seem to make a difference. What others did so well with weapons, the immortals did even better with their bare hands.

...with their bared teeth.

Evie watched in horror as a vampire leapt upon the back of a Carpathian infantryman, hovering there for a moment with the hint of a smile before tearing out the side of his neck. A spray of blood flew into the air, showering those who stood around them. But the vampire was already gone—spiriting away to his next victim before the first had even struck the ground.

He was hardly the only one.

While some vampires preferred not to linger, materializing for a fleeting moment before vanishing without a trace, others appeared almost irritated with the inconvenience. These strode right through the center of the churning crowd—striking out every so often to behead an opposing soldier or simply reach through their armor and eviscerate whatever lay beneath.

The princess spotted Eleazer marching in the center, the elder they'd attacked with a dead snake. A little further down one of the women who'd been tasked with guarding them during that fateful visit was laughing aloud, spinning in a bizarre kind of dance as she knocked them over the cliff.

It was the laughter that echoed loudest, amidst a chorus of metal and screams.

But the poison, Evie thought suddenly. *Some of the weapons are poisoned.*

The Carpathians seemed to remember the baresmain at the same time.

With surprising speed, they kicked open their stores and loaded a volley of arrows—firing without discrimination towards the center of the advancing horde. A chorus of hisses rose up in reply, as though someone had poured a flagon of bitter ale onto a fire.

Some of them were strong enough that it was no more than a nuisance. A few simply caught the arrows and snapped them in their hands. Still others lost their balance entirely, falling like dark feathers over the side of the cliff. But it only took a moment for the vampires to find the poison.

Their retaliation was both swift and severe.

"Seven hells," Ellanden muttered, grimacing as a company of archers was submerged in the toxic barrels. They struggled only a moment before going frightfully still. "It's too much."

Evie nodded in silence, gripping her father's sleeve without realizing. The laws of man didn't apply in times of war, but there were still certain images that couldn't be unseen.

A casual flick of immortal fingers that resulted in a separation of face from jaw. A charging infantryman literally torn down the center by a pale-faced girl a fraction of his size.

The general *loss of limbs*.

Carpathians were hulkish in strength—they had been known to beat their victims beyond the point of recognition—but there was something unnervingly playful about vampires.

There was nothing overtly militaristic about the way they approached a battle. No tactics, or weaponry, or even a general formation that might apply. Once the order had come from their queen, they'd simply moved in the general direction—leaving a fantastic trail of carnage in their wake.

It wasn't a cause for celebration. It wasn't even a cause for pride.

It was just...natural. Vampires were bred to kill.

Evie flashed a quick look at their own resident immortals, both perched with abnormal attention on the very edge of the roof. Their fangs were bared, but their bodies weren't moving. From the first scent of blood they had frozen to perfect statues, forgetting even to breathe.

"Look at how many are still coming," Dylan murmured, clutching both his daughter and the fae as he peered across the ravine. While the first waves of Carpathians had been struck down with ease, a ceaseless supply was flooding out of the trees. "It must be their entire army."

The princess followed his gaze before glancing back at the vampires.

It was the most savage and brutal clash she could imagine—the collision of two great nightmares that had terrorized the realm for centuries on end.

Best-case scenario: they knock each other off the mountain.

But is it the best-case scenario when one of them might be willing to fight on our side?

While she couldn't see Diana amidst the fray, the queen's soft-spoken pledge rang fresh in her ears. They were here to help. And while those simple words were open to a broad interpretation, each

Carpathian the vampires killed was one less that the friends would have to deal with themselves.

...even if they were bloody *terrifying*.

She turned her face as there was a chorus of fresh screams, leaning into her father's cloak.

Even if the Carpathians did somehow turn the tide, she wasn't at all certain the vampires wouldn't find a way to rise from the shadows—clawing their way straight out of the misty ravine.

But the Carpathians were going to lose this battle. And, given the number of them who had already fallen, there was a decent chance the Kingdom of Carpathia would never fight again.

There was a sudden shifting in momentum, a collective retreat the remaining soldiers didn't seem consciously aware of themselves. Every human impulse had been stripped away, save the primal instinct to flee. Even that would be done at the vampires' mercy.

This from a people not particularly known for their mercy.

The princess saw Diana then, standing not far from the bridge where she'd started. There was a pile of bodies littering the ground around her, but the queen was untouched.

She stared after the fragments of the army, considering whether to give chase.

A few of the younger generation had already started—streaking through the forest like a host of spirits—easily outpacing anyone who crossed in their way.

But after a moment she turned instead to the sanctuary, speaking in a quiet voice that somehow carried across the length of the ravine.

"Aidan...might I have a word?"

Chapter 2

Evie didn't know what to call it.
A favor?

As the sun slowly rose over the mountains she'd stood with the others on the monastery roof, watching with detached horror as two dark kingdoms collided...and only one remained.

It was a moment that would shape the course of history. Done without premeditation, done on a whim. Done in the service of some larger agenda, though for the life of her she wasn't at all sure what that meant. There had been no answer from her own people. Diana's words still hung on the air, echoing in the deep canyon while those in the sanctuary gathered in a hasty rooftop debate.

"You cannot let her into the monastery," a shifter said bluntly, folding his arms across his chest. He'd been one of those elected to speak at Michael's funeral. Spirited away from a volatile village at a young age, he was a child of Talsing through and through. "She is a *vampire*." He stressed the word like everyone else hadn't been watching. "Such a creature may not set foot inside."

Aidan raised his eyebrows ever so slightly, while Asher clenched his jaw and lowered his eyes to the ground. Neither said a word. But as it turned out, neither had to.

"And since when do you decide who is allowed entry to this place?" Petra asked sharply, her eyes never leaving the distant cliff. Her signature spear was already in hand, folds of fabric from her brother's cloak wrapped round the grip. "Lucky for you, Michael didn't have such standards."

The shifter glowered in silence, but very few of those gathered behind him seemed to think he was wrong. They had seen what the vampires had done. Some vague, repressed part of them might even have been grateful. But they had *seen* what the vampires had done.

They weren't eager to let them inside.

"They defeated the *entire* Carpathian army," Ellanden said softly.

Though one of the youngest people present he was still the crown prince of two separate kingdoms, and his opinion carried the according weight. Perhaps even more so because the greatest risk if the vampires were to cross that great divide would be to his own person.

Having spent recent time with the clan, he was acutely aware of that risk. Even as he said the words, his hands tightened around the ladder—aching to throw it into the ravine and eliminate the possibility before it could even be discussed. But he, too, had seen the vampires.

They were owed a debt of service. And, despite his misgivings, he could not forget.

"Surely we can't just leave it at that," he continued, glancing from person to person. "I don't relish the thought of them setting foot in these walls any more than you do, but it is a remarkable thing they've done. At the very least, are they not owed a chance to speak?"

Asher smiled ever so slightly, while the shifter flushed with rage.

"And will *you* speak to them?" he demanded, pointing across the divide. "You with your prized eternal blood? I'm surprised they didn't rip you to pieces the second you touched down!"

There was a chance he might have said more, but Dylan's sword whipped out the second he was finished speaking—touching lightly to the base of his neck.

"I understand your anger," he said quietly. "It's easy to be angry when at heart we are nothing but afraid." The blade twisted just a hair. "But you will apologize to the fae and speak to him no further. Because I, too, was *very* surprised he was not murdered when he touched down."

The icy words stopped the conversation in its tracks, sobering all those heated tempers as everyone remembered those breathless, terror-stricken moments before the fight. The ones where they'd watched from afar as the fae stood alone before a swarm of vampires, waiting for one of those shadowy figures to fly forward at any second and snuff out that celestial light once and for all.

After a few seconds the shifter mumbled something, then swiftly departed.

Two sets of protective hands appeared on his shoulders and Ellanden bowed his head, those angelic wings still raised in the air beside him, the bridge still held tightly in his hands.

"Don't hang it."

Evie blurted the words before she could stop herself, flushing with embarrassment as each person in the circle looked her way at the same time. A part of her agreed with the fae, a part was even ready to recant, but she had seen something more than a gruesome fight on a distant peak.

She had seen the look in Asher's eyes as he watched the watched the fight as well.

I cannot lose him. I cannot make it so easy for him to leave.
He was tempted to stay with them already.

"The other kingdoms would never agree to such a thing," she continued hastily, trying to save face. "We should thank them for what they've done...then send them on their way."

If only it was that simple.

Aidan turned to her in surprise, but he seemed to interpret her stammering request as nothing more than the aforementioned fear. It was a kneejerk reaction to such violence, one he'd seen many times. Even now, she had yet to release the edge of her father's cloak.

"Sweetheart, try to see reason," he said kindly. "Ellanden is right, the clan has done us a great service. And you have to know I'd never let any harm come to—"

"It isn't unreasonable," Dylan interrupted under his breath. "You have no idea what Diana has come here to say, only that she's brought an impossible number of your kind along with her. It isn't unreasonable to find a middle ground, to wait until Katerina is back on her feet..."

...and able to set them all on fire.

He'd trailed off without *quite* saying it, but the message was clear.

While a great many people seemed grateful for the attempt, Aidan regarded him without a hint of emotion—a bizarrely neutral expression that seemed to say a great deal all the same.

Dylan faltered for a moment, then nodded quickly at the ground. "Or we can adhere to your judgement. Whatever you think is best..."

In truth, the vampire wasn't entirely sure what was best. When he gazed over the ravine towards his people, there was no comfort or certainty to be found. Yet there was something oddly compelling about Diana's soft request. A second later, he found himself staring into her eyes.

"There are people here who have never met a vampire," he said abruptly. "People whose safety is very important to me. Who will come with you?"

The princess glanced around in confusion before realizing that he wasn't addressing the rest of them, but Diana herself—speaking as though they were standing in the same room.

The queen lifted her hand, and a trio of immortals appeared at her side.

"Just the three."

Innocent enough, except the princess happened to know the three in question.

A pair of towering men, and a woman with cheekbones sharp enough to cut glass. Evie distinctively remembered her smile when the others had grabbed Cosette.

Ellanden stared over her shoulder, then backed away a step. "Wait...*him*?"

All at once, the princess recognized Andrei as the man who'd been leaping from soldier to soldier. As if the entire Carpathian army was playing a game, but only he knew the rules.

From the look on his face she was willing to bet Ellanden recognized him as well—not only from the battle, but as the same man who'd offered him protection in exchange for blood.

The fae went unnaturally still, remembering his reverent attention back in the meadow.

"What did you expect?" she muttered, staring across the divide. "He and Eleazer were part of the queen's council." *Maybe you shouldn't have invited them to come inside.* She glanced at him again before lifting her shoulder in a careless shrug. "Maybe he's forgotten you."

Not likely.

The fae shot her a cold look, but held his silence.

"Is this acceptable?" Diana asked, still waiting for a reply.

Aidan considered a moment, then nodded curtly. "Landi," he said quietly, "tie the bridge to the post."

The fae nodded faintly, but his feet wouldn't seem to move. Perhaps if it hadn't been that *particular* vampire. He was on the verge of recommending they wait for Katerina after all, when a pair of warlocks appeared from nowhere—taking the rope from his hands and walking it down themselves.

"Are you sure about this?" Dylan asked under his breath, watching as they secured it and the four vampires drifted across the bridge. "I don't need to tell you what's at stake."

The pair locked eyes for a moment before Aidan turned away.

"I know *exactly* what's at stake."

For the second time that day, there was total stillness on both sides of the ravine. Each group watched in perfect silence as the small fellowship crossed slowly to the other side.

Although they'd just decimated an entire army, it was the vampires who looked the most in control. The smaller group clustered within the monastery stood for only a moment, watching their incremental progress before coming apart at the seams.

"I cannot stay for this," another shifter muttered under his breath, backing away at the same time. Five others went with him. "We will be in the armory...sharpening blades."

Because that worked SO well for the Carpathians.

Petra watched as they left, but did nothing to stop them. Aidan stood calm at her side, never taking his eyes from his childhood friend. The others tried to mimic his calm, but it eluded them. By the time the vampires were halfway across the bridge twelve more had departed, leaving only a few.

"These wings," Ellanden breathed, shifting uncomfortably, "I don't know how...I don't know how to make them go away."

Dylan glanced towards him, staring a fraction of a second at the shimmering ivory feathers before turning his eyes to the front. "Keep them. They may prove useful."

Hardly a vote of confidence.

For her part, the princess simply wanted to run. She wanted to pull her mother from her sick bed, force the lingering poison from her veins, and soar into the horizon on a pair of fiery wings before the vampires could make it to the other side of the bridge.

That's when her uncle decided to make things worse.

"We should go down and meet them," he said quietly, heading towards the steps. "There will be no one else to receive them. And it is a sign of respect."

The others stared at him incredulously, tensing when he turned back around.

"I must have forgotten the way, Hale." His voice took on a sharper edge as he stared past the others to the ranger. "You lived here long enough. Perhaps you could show me."

Dylan met his gaze, but was spared from having to reply.

"We'll go down together," Petra announced, cutting her way through those who remained by the tip of her spear. "You know what they say about guests...best to scare them from the start."

IT WAS A SOLEMN PROCESSION that made its way down the monastery steps, waiting in the courtyard as the vampires finished crossing the length of the bridge. The door was unlocked, but not open. The princess could hear them approach, but that was the extent.

It was enough.

Her eyes closed as those footsteps got closer and closer. Not until later would she realize even *that* was an intentional courtesy, as vampires were usually quiet as ghosts. Again and again she shifted her weight, feeling her father standing tall beside her.

How many times had she wished for them, when they were stranded in the shadow of that horrible mountain—eating apples from the nearby orchard and praying to be released? His presence should have been a comfort now, but she found herself even more afraid.

She had seen how quickly the vampires had swept down from the peak. Now that the bridge was hung, she knew exactly how quickly the entire lot of them could streak across the ravine.

The monastery would be overrun in seconds. There would be no hope for reprieve.

This is a mistake—

Then all at once...the heavy gate swung open.

"Aidan."

So much love and loss, so much history tied up in a single word.

It escaped Diana like a breath, somehow different from every time she'd said it before. The rest of them paused, caught off balance, and even the vampires standing behind her froze of one accord.

Aidan stared a moment, then took a step closer. "You speak as though we've been parted for ages," he murmured, tilting his head with what might have been the trace of a smile. "It has only been five years."

She smiled openly in return, stepping closer as well. "A lot can happen in five years. You should know that best of all."

The princess waited for them to embrace. Even in royal circles, after a long absence, the custom still remained. But the two vampires held their ground, regarding each other thoughtfully.

It must be so strange, Evie thought, staring at them with riveted attention. *For how many centuries have they known each other? In how many places and in how many times?*

A kind of smile passed over her uncle's face, something genuine and natural he did not often use with guests. Diana's eyes twinkled in return, and for a split second the princess was convinced the two were somehow having a conversation the rest of them were unable to hear.

"But I forget my manners."

The queen's gaze swept over the rest of them, lingering on certain faces before coming to rest on one. An unfamiliar deference came over her, muting the smile she'd worn before.

"Am I now addressing the lady of this house?"

Evie followed her gaze to Petra before looking back with a start. *How did she know?"*

Michael had died only a few days before, and in all likelihood the vampires were halfway across the realm when it had happened. Talsing had no contact with the outside world. There was no way to receive news. Perhaps she had simply smelled the lingering smoke from the funeral fires.

The general's eyes glinted like cool glass, reflecting the whispers of sun.

"Only four days have passed since I buried my brother," she answered without inflection. "I can still feel the dirt of it on my hands. If you have come here looking to harm his legacy and these people he loved so well, please be certain, child…I will wash that feeling clean with your blood."

I should hang that as a plaque outside my bedroom door.

There was a hard note of silence.

"I wish no harm to anyone within these walls," Diana answered carefully, staring right in the woman's eyes. "I come armed with nothing but a proposition."

Dylan folded his arms, shielding his daughter from sight. "And what might that be?"

He had met the queen before. Had fought alongside her. But there were no smiles between them. The only reason he wasn't holding a sword was the love he felt for Aidan and the fact that, though the queen had taken his daughter hostage, she had also allowed her to leave.

"Yes…a lot can happen in five years," Diana murmured, staring at the king with a sympathy just as unfamiliar as the deference before. "Even more can happen in ten."

Bold words. Especially considering that in the last decade there had been no greater possible threat to the safety of the realm than the unchecked and unfettered presence of vampires. They had taken advantage of the monarchs' absence, and seeped into every inch like a slow-moving plague.

Villages had been sacked, forests had been rendered uninhabitable. There wasn't a child in the four kingdoms who didn't peer frightfully into the darkness each night as they climbed into bed.

And yet...there she stood.

Dylan bore the weight of her stare without flinching, lifting his chin as he awaited a reply. But before she could give it Aidan took a step forward, staring her over with a look of surprise.

"Something's changed," he breathed, more to himself than anyone. "What is it?"

A silence fell between them.

"*Tell me*, Diana."

The queen only smiled, turning to the boy at his side.

"Why don't you ask your son?"

Chapter 3

When the friends were little, Evie had convinced the others to help 'borrow' the prophesized jewel from her mother's crown. Having discovered that it could grant immortality, she'd determined that with some slight modifications it could speed up the aging process as well—hastening the royal trio past their inconvenient adolescence and straight into adulthood where they belonged.

Ellanden needed no convincing. The moment she announced the plan, he jumped right on board—declaring the logic to be sound. Asher was a slightly different story.

The poor vampire tried to caution the others, but they wouldn't listen. He'd 'accidentally' knocked over a vase to alert the guards, and the fae smacked him across the mouth. When it came time to actually steal the crown from the queen's chamber, he'd been posted as lookout in the hall.

...only to come face-to-face with the dragon herself.

He hadn't screamed—that was the only thing for which his friends ever gave him credit. He hadn't given them up either, but seeing as they were quickly discovered anyway they forgot that act of loyalty and only remembered the look on his face. It was quite extraordinary. A complete loss of color paired with a visible panic that seemed almost to lift him off the ground.

This was much the way he looked now.

"My son," Aidan repeated blankly, glancing at the young man by his side. "He told me what happened at the Kreo camp, and I am grateful to you for releasing him unharmed...but why would he have any idea why you've come?"

Now it was Diana's turned to be surprised.

"You didn't tell him?"

Asher stared into the middle distance, away from his father's gaze.

"I gave you my word," he said softly.

There had been many moments of dissonance since the children returned home. Many spikes in pressure and quickened heartbeats, and silences so long and grating they almost made the friends wish they were back wandering in the woods.

This was not the worst of these, but it came close.

"...Asher?"

Aidan looked not to the queen, but to his teenage son. A boy who had only once lied to him—a betrayal that spanned over ten years and one they were still working through to this day.

But some betrayals cut deeper than others, and Asher had no intention of breaking that silence now. Without a single glance at anyone, he turned on his heel and walked back into the monastery—leaving a ring of shell-shocked people standing in his wake.

That's one way to handle it.

"Explain yourself," Dylan said sharply, placing a quick hand on Aidan's shoulder. At this point, he wasn't sure what he was protecting—the delicate temperament of an adolescent vampire or their precarious position with the queen. "Diana, why have you come?"

The woman stared at each one of them before resting her attention on Aidan. Her eyes stirred with a flicker of anticipation, perhaps even a hint of fear. But her voice never wavered.

"I have come to join with the rest of the kingdoms to fight against this new darkness. I have come to claim my seat on the High Council, to defend my homeland and to stand by your side."

Just a few quiet sentences spoken in a single outpouring of breath, but empires rose and fell in such moments. It was a speech the rest of the realm had been longing for since the dawn of time, praying so ceaselessly that the warm sentiment had faded and become brittle to the touch.

Where some prayed, a solitary man had worked—planting the seeds of such unity in the minds of others, repeating the words for so many centuries it was as if he'd breathed them to life.

They were oddly foreign to him now, with only one rising to prominence.

"Homeland," Aidan repeated, almost too quietly to hear.

Diana's eyes warmed, though her voice was even and soft. "All those times you came to us, preaching words we were not yet ready to hear. Year after year, decade after decade, and in the end...it took only your absence for the message to take hold."

She paused a moment, then took his hand.

"There are things I need to tell you."

Their eyes met in the rising dawn.

"There is a place in the mountains I want very much for you to see."

"DID YOU KNOW ABOUT this?" Dylan demanded.

Evie and Ellanden shot each other a quick glance, both being dragged by the wrists.

They had left the vampires in the courtyard with Aidan and Petra, retreating inside the monastery under the guise of checking on the injured queen. Needless to say, the conversation had peaked when Diana had confessed the immortal stronghold beneath the mountain. Even the young fae had decided it might be better to slip away with his extended family than linger in the aftermath.

Bet he regrets that decision now.

Evie shot her father a quick look, then decided to lie.

"Of course not!" she blurted without thinking, refusing to meet his gaze. "I'd be surprised if it's even true. You know vampires—famous liars."

Very good hearing, too...

She cast a nervous glance outside, while her father glared down at the top of her head.

Seeing as his daughter had apparently been held prisoner in said stronghold, it was highly unlikely the place had somehow slipped her mind. His guilt-stricken nephew was no better.

"Just when I think we're done with the secrets," he muttered, yanking both teens out of the way as a troop of shifters stormed past. "Just when I think you've told me everything—"

"I *did* tell you everything," she insisted. They came to an abrupt stop, alone in the deserted hallway, and she felt the sudden need to clarify. "I told you *almost* everything."

He stared at her then, waiting in silence for her to continue.

"It wasn't...it wasn't our secret to tell," she finally managed, glancing at Ellanden but finding his eyes fixed on the ground. "The only reason the queen let us go in the first place was because Asher swore that he would keep the mountain to himself, and that if he ever came back it would be alone. I had *no idea* she wanted a place on the High Council, only that things were slowly changing with the vampires. Things that might one day make it possible for them to have a home."

Even as she spoke, she remembered the look in Asher's eyes when he'd seen it. The tender longing that had softened his face as he spoke of it later at the fort.

It had been that tenderness that had brought them together for the first time. A promise of home and a sharing of blood as their two bodies tangled together beneath the stars.

That seems lifetimes ago. So much has happened since then.

"I want to cut her to pieces for taking you to that place," Dylan muttered, hand tightening reflexively on the hilt of his sword. "It's a miracle that any of you made it out in one—"

He stopped short in exasperation, batting feathers away from his face.

"Ellanden, can't you do anything about those?"

The fae blushed to the roots of his hair as the wings drooped. The glorious sunlit image had diminished, and it now looked as though he'd strapped a lifeless bird to his back.

"...sorry."

Deprived of one target, the king quickly zeroed in on another.

"You're sorry," he repeated in a dangerous voice. "How convenient you should feel that way already, for I had thought to make you *very sorry* myself." His eyes flashed as he remembered the fae's improvised leap from the roof. "Did you know that I vowed to protect you before we left? I swore it to your panic-stricken father, gave him my word. Did any of that occur to you before...*this*?"

He gestured furiously, and the wings seemed to wilt beneath his punishing gaze.

"I was trying to help—"

"You are an arrogant boy playing loose games with the hearts of the people who love you the most," Dylan snapped, bearing down on him.

Such postures had grown more difficult since the fae had grown in height, but Dylan had mastered the art of them. By now, he needed neither elevation nor proximity—the dynamic was encapsulated fully in his eyes. That being said, he'd never managed to stay angry with his nephew for long.

"Lucky for you, arrogance has never been a sin in this family," he said stiffly, giving one of the wings a playful flick. "You may be a thoughtless prat, but you're in good company."

Evie grinned in spite of herself as Ellanden dropped his eyes with a smile.

Nowhere else in the realm would such reckless bravery be reduced to adolescent antics. In no other family would such an argument have ever come to pass.

No wonder Seth thinks we're strange. I think we're rather strange myself.

"Now come," Dylan said abruptly, making his way further down the hall, "and we will speak on it no further. In fact...I see no reason that we need ever tell your father at all. We'll amend the story, say it was an errant pigeon that carried the bridge."

The fae was quick to hide a grin, murmuring some obedience that sounded like, "Yes, Uncle," but while the two men continued down the corridor the princess suddenly held back.

"Aren't you coming?" Ellanden asked, glancing over his shoulder. "Your mother won't like you wandering by yourself with vampires inside the monastery walls."

Evie's heart quickened as she began backing away.

"Only a few more vampires than usual," she said lightly, trying to keep her expression clear and unsuspecting. "I'd like to grab some breakfast, so I'll come by to speak with her later."

Dylan nodded briskly and continued walking. Ellanden stared a second longer before following him—glancing curiously over his shoulder every few steps.

The princess didn't see either of them. She was already hurrying down the familiar maze of corridors, her unruly heart pounding like a drum inside her chest.

There were a few more vampires than usual.

But there was only one she wanted to see.

THE PRINCESS WALKED quickly through the crowded halls, pretending not to notice the tension, wondering in absentminded fragments of thought how much license the vampires would be given if they were truly permitted to stay. While Petra might have shut down the shifter who'd declared the sanctuary should close its doors entirely, she couldn't imagine much leeway being allowed to those already within the monastery walls. Vampires were not easily cold, did not mind the rain, and spent most of their lives out in the open. If she had to guess, she might imagine they would be confined to the courtyard—with all conversations and counsel coming to them. But she wasn't guessing, she wasn't imagining, and she wasn't concerned with anything that extended beyond the next door.

The love of her life was somewhere within these walls. Even if they'd stopped calling each other that. Even if he was preparing to leave. His world had been turned upside-down, and she would not leave him floundering by himself in the wreckage. She would make herself available—a quiet listener, a supportive hand. Whatever it was that he needed.

But as it turned out, Asher already had company.

"—just assumed the warlock was opening old wounds." Aidan's voice drifted into the hall. The princess froze where she stood, gazing with wide eyes towards the crack in the door.

Two vampires were standing in the center of the room, not at all naturally but as if some giant hand had placed them there by mistake.

"I assumed he was repeating things he'd said to you on the battlefield," Aidan pressed when he got no response. "But you knew of this place long before."

Evie eased back, but caught herself in the same moment—staring with unblinking attention at the sliver of a room. Even so far away, she could feel the tension between them.

But when Asher finally answered, it was only to ask a question of his own.

"Why did you never tell me what happened?"

His eyes lifted painfully to the man who'd raised him, the only father he'd ever known. Such devotion there was between them, though it was only by a quirk of fate they'd even met.

Another few minutes, and he would have burned with the rest of his clan.

How often must he think of that, quantifying it in his mind? How do you calculate those minutes, when the terms are life or death? The buckling of a saddle? An unexpected flood to delay one's journey on the road?

Aidan took a moment to steady himself—this from a man who'd needed very few such moments over the course of his life. His hands tensed involuntarily before he forced them smooth.

"You speak as though I was keeping it from you, Asher. But that wasn't the case. You knew there was an attack, you knew I rode up at the end of it—lifted you onto my horse."

He paused, as if there might be some new danger lurking in the words.

"Why on earth would I subject you to anything more than that? You didn't remember your clan, you didn't remember your parents—"

"*I didn't remember my parents?!*" The tension shattered, replaced with a trace of hysteria as Asher stared into his eyes. "I remember my parents just fine!"

The words echoed between them, cold as anything that had come before.

"I remember my father's cloak and my mother's smile! I remember the smell of them burning, the screaming of royal mounts, the smoke from a dozen fires stinging my eyes!"

He paced with sudden purpose to the window, lifting a hand to the ledge like he might take a page from his friend's book and jump. But he only stood there, staring at the distant peaks.

"My entire family...slaughtered by royal decree."

It was a small mercy that he was facing the glass. He never had to see the look that washed across Aidan's face. It was worse than anything Evie had seen at a graveside or in the infirmary, or in the sudden cold after battle. It was the purest form of sadness. A grief that knew no cure.

Finally, when enough time had passed, Asher turned around.

"You ride up too late to save them, then take me to a perfect world. A place where I can stay forever, as long as I pretend not to have fangs. As if that wasn't enough, you drag me back year after year, summer after summer, to the rest of the clans—proving them to be savages, proving that I was better off with you than I was before. They were barbarians, and I hated them. I could endure it only by knowing the time would eventually end, and I would be allowed to go home again."

He stared across the room, never breaking his father's gaze.

"Except I never had a home. Not really. You made sure of that."

Seven hells.

Evie brought a hand to her mouth, eyes shining with tears.

It was as if the very foundations had shifted. Something steady, something she'd always taken for granted, had suddenly moved out of place. If she wasn't so worried about them hearing, she would have grabbed hold of the wall for balance. As things stood, she merely stood there and watched as over fifteen years of love and devotion crumbled before her very eyes.

Aidan spoke slowly, looking as though he'd like to grab hold of a wall himself.

"It was never...it was never my wish to..." He trailed off faintly, clearing his throat before he started again. "I only ever wanted the best for you. I'm sorry...if I failed."

Asher's eyes tightened, but he was no longer able to stop. "The *best* for me," he repeated fiercely. "Growing up amidst people who fear me. Sleeping in beds that were never my own. Falling in love with a girl I would never be permitted to—"

He caught himself, breathing heavily.

"Perhaps you should have left me there with my own people. With my own clan. That way I might have had a family. I might have been accepted. At the very least, I wouldn't be alone."

Aidan stared back in silence, accepting each new accusation like the lash of a whip. When he finally answered, his voice was low and rough—nothing like anything his son had heard before.

"If I had left you, you would have burned with all the rest."

The young vampire stared back from across the room, breathing as though he'd just sprinted up the peak. A part of him was desperate to apologize. Another part was sincere. Still another part was furious that his father could *feel* each one of these emotions just as well as his own.

In the end, he said nothing. He simply moved on.

"You should accept Diana's offer." He turned back to the window, a clear dismissal. "You doubt her intentions, but you didn't see what I saw. It could be our salvation."

Or the most bitter defeat.

NEEDLESS TO SAY, THE princess didn't end up comforting Asher that morning. She found herself walking in the opposite direction instead.

So that's how he feels...

In a strange way, she felt as though she should have been expecting it. They *all* should have been expecting it. Since they were just children, running carefree around the various palaces and castles of the four kingdoms, their happiness had always been doomed to expire.

Blame our immortal parents. It's hard to think of such things when you're promised endless time.

The arrival of the vampires had electrified the ancient monastery. And despite her own novelty people paid little attention as she wandered the stone hallways, pausing to look at pictures, pausing again to stare out the windows before finding herself in the last place she expected.

Michael always loved the library.

She pushed open the door with the tips of her fingers, peeking through the crack to make sure no one was already inside. Most of the students were content to work in their chambers or shared classrooms. Considering the care with which Michael had tended to his books, they got relatively little use. Perhaps that was the reason she'd spent so much time there. It had always been one of the first places she would go upon visiting the monastery, ever since she was a child.

The books and manuscripts of a dozen centuries stretched up before her—rising in an endless tower to the morning sky. A rickety wheeled ladder had been anchored at the base, but it didn't cover a fraction of the required height and was more of an irony than anything else.

Michael didn't need a ladder. The man had wings.

Her gaze fell on a shadow in the corner.

And speaking of...

"Ellanden?"

There was a gasp of surprise, then the fae glanced down towards the entryway—still holding a pair of books. The table on the ground level was already covered in them. Historical anthologies, medicinal texts...anything that could help to cure his beloved witch.

"How did you get here so quickly?" she asked, running a finger along one of the spines as he leapt down from a higher level. "I thought you were with my parents."

"Your parents are terrifying," he replied, landing beside her. "I left them as quickly as possible. They make me miss my own parents," he added suddenly, glancing at the table.

There was a chance the ranger's words had struck a nerve.

"What about you?" He moved on before she could delve deeper, looking her up and down. Searching for clues. "I know you weren't going for breakfast..."

She merely shrugged, trying to burn the image of the two vampires from her mind. "I see you got rid of the wings."

A rather transparent diversion, but it happened to have been a rather unwelcome part of the fae's morning. He glanced compulsively behind himself, as if worried they'd come back.

"Oh...right." His lips parted uncertainly before curving into a hasty smile. "I did what anyone would do. Stood upon a great precipice, centered the magical forces within myself—"

"He held his palm over a candle until the pain shocked him out of it."

The friends glanced towards the door with a start as Asher strode into the library. He saw their looks of surprise and smiled in spite of himself, coming to stand by their side.

"I heard it from my room."

I can't believe it.

No tears, no flailing fists, no homicidal profanities echoing behind him. If Evie hadn't been watching from the hallway, she never would have known that anything was wrong.

"Great minds think alike," Asher continued softly, glancing up towards the rafters. "I always loved this place. Whenever we'd come here it was one of the first places I'd go."

The others shared a quick glance.

"Was your father very angry with you?" Ellanden asked tentatively. When the vampire merely stared, he hastened to clarify. "For not telling him about the mountain?"

Asher opened his lips to reply, then glanced away with a shrug. "He was angry enough."

Seriously?

"Speaking of angry..."

In a flash the vampire blurred across the worn stone, smacking the fae upside the head the way a parent might discipline a misbehaving child.

"I don't care the reason, I don't care what kind of misguided notions might be swirling around that demented head...you must *stop* jumping out of windows, Ellanden. Give me your word right this second, or I'll chain the two of us together until the prophecy is complete."

There was a beat of silence.

"It wasn't technically a window—"

The vampire struck him again.

"Seven hells, Asher—"

"Big, *thick* chains." The vampire held up his hands to illustrate, eyes flashing a dangerous glare. "I'll fasten them to your ankle. We all remember how well you liked that the last time."

Ellanden tensed in spite of himself, remembering their unfortunate sparring match in Belaria. Fortunately, such logic was immediately countered with that infernal immortal pride.

"You accuse *me* of theatrics, but you're the melodramatic one," he muttered, keeping an eye on the vampire at the same time. "Chains...honestly, Asher, see reason. I would never have jumped if there wasn't an infinitesimal chance that I might have grown wings."

"Listen to what you're saying!"

"And as I recall," the fae continued, raising his voice, "those wings happened to save not only my own life but the lives of everyone trapped in this monastery as well. So I think a collective *thank you* is actually in order—"

"Do not test me on this," Asher threatened. "I haven't made it this far just to watch you accidentally kill yourself by jumping off a cliff. It was bad enough back at the fortress—"

"Enough!" Ellanden shouted, throwing up his hands in a burst of infantile rage. "You *cannot* be furious with me for every little thing! We are still family, whether you like to admit it or not, and sooner or later you'll have to start loving me again."

The princess stared between them with the beginnings of a frozen smile, unable to believe the fae would say such a thing. Unable to tell how much of it had been serious.

Asher stared at him as well before dropping his eyes with the hint of a grin. "That's true enough, I suppose."

The fae glanced between them, wary but pleased the yelling had ceased.

"At any rate, I'm not the only one doing stupid things. You didn't get angry with Evie for dive-bombing those giants. Or even earlier, when she froze up with the demon."

A strange look passed over the vampire's face as Ellanden continued chattering.

"—looked like an idiot, just hanging in the Kasi's hand. It's a miracle the thing didn't kill you, but for the life of me I can't imagine how you managed to live down the humiliation—"

"I felt that," Asher interrupted suddenly, looking directly at Evie for the first time. "When the Kasi was holding you...you weren't afraid. You were...relieved?"

Both men towered over her.

"*Relieved?*" Ellanden repeated, forgetting his earlier teasing. A rather dangerous look came over him, like the demon would have been a mercy. "Tell me he's wrong, Everly. If this is some fresh nonsense about the prophecy—"

"He *is* wrong," she said quickly, taking a step back. "I wasn't—would you stop looking at me like that! I wasn't relieved I was about to die."

I don't want to die. I can't believe I'm going to die.
I can't believe this is how we're spending the time that remains.

"Then what was it?" Asher pressed softly. "I wasn't wrong, Evie. There was a moment when you thought it was over, and the only emotion I could feel was—"

"Seven hells!" The princess threw up her hands in exasperation, vowing to murder them both. "You want the truth? I was relieved that I wouldn't have to get married."

A pang of silence echoed in the room.

Because that's sure to make things less awkward.

Asher froze in astonishment, then dropped his eyes. His face was completely clear of emotion, but she could have sworn his lips curved with the hint of a smile.

The fae was a different story.

He started innocently enough, nodding along—relieved that it wasn't something more sinister. Then he played back the words and went perfectly still.

"You'd rather get *mauled by a demon* than marry me?"

Shit.

Evie bit her lip, trying to mitigate the damage.

"The thing is...phrasing's really important. And that's not quite what I—"

"You're the worst." He gathered up his books a moment later, knocking into her shoulder as he headed for the door. "You're the meanest person I know."

Asher was shaking with silent laughter as she hurried after him.

"Ellanden—"

"You say the meanest things."

It was a fight that could have put the others to shame. One that would no doubt have wreaked havoc on Michael's beautiful library. But they would never know, because a second before the fae could reach the door it flew open and an agitated shifter stepped inside.

"They've decided to accept the vampires. We leave at first light."

Chapter 4

There was no time for questions, none of those endless council meetings that had made each of the friends secretly question if such logistics outweighed any benefits to sitting on a throne. It was a historical decision, but it had come from nothing more than a simple discussion in the courtyard.

Dylan had carried Katerina out of her room to speak with Diana. Petra and Aidan were standing side by side, just as they had in the days back in the rebel camps.

They'd spoken for only a few minutes before coming to an agreement.

And just like that, the plan was set.

"I still can't believe this is happening," Evie murmured, hitching a bag over her shoulder as she tugged at the sleeves of a borrowed dress. "I thought they'd at least want to sleep on it."

Any supplies the group had brought from the High Kingdom had been lost when the dragon plunged into the forest, and despite their royal blood they were using crude weapons and hand-me-downs—anything the people of Talsing had to spare. They'd done their fair share of complaining, but each of the friends secretly rather liked it. It reminded them of their time travelling the woods.

"There isn't time to waste," Ellanden replied, running his hands appraisingly over a gifted bow. "Although I'm surprised we weren't included in the conversation. This is *our* prophecy. You'd think the rest of them would be at least slightly interested in what we had to say."

Asher walked up beside them, slipping a pair of daggers into his belt.

"The prophecy may be ours, but the realm belongs to our parents." He flicked a clasp along the quiver, reminding the fae to tighten the strap. "You're not Lord of the Fae yet."

It felt a bit counterintuitive, but it was true. As none of the friends wore the crowns of their respective kingdoms, the decision was not theirs to make. With the exception of one.

"Ellanden...come speak with me a moment."

The trio glanced over the moment they stepped outside, to see Dylan waving them closer from the center of the courtyard. The rest of their parents were standing beside him, along with Diana and Petra. The remaining vampires were hovering listlessly by the iron gate.

The fae approached cautiously, the slender bow lashed to his back.

"You've packed?" Dylan asked rhetorically, glancing over his shoulder.

Ellanden glanced at the others, then nodded. "We were told you had reached an agreement."

There was a swift look among the circle he wasn't meant to see.

"We have reached an agreement," Katerina told him, holding on to Aidan for balance as her legs trembled with fatigue. "The decision was unanimous. But not all of the kingdoms had a voice in the discussion. Two were not represented—your father's and your mother's." She looked at the others before turning back to the fae. "We're asking you to speak on their behalf."

It was phrased casually, almost as an afterthought, but Evie suddenly understood the weight of what might happen next. Two kingdoms had not yet decided. Two out of four.

If the prince chose to speak against the accord, it could not come to pass.

Ellanden's eyes flashed between them, nervous to be put on the spot. While he had spoken testily about their exclusion, under no circumstances had he actually expected to be consulted.

Katerina flashed a warm smile, nodding as if anything was permitted and there was no way to go wrong. Aidan nodded patiently beside her, wearing a similar expression. But it was Dylan who put an arm around his nephew's shoulder, lowering his voice as if the rest were mere prying eyes.

"I have discussed this matter with both of your parents many, many times," he said quietly. "I feel confident in what they would say. The unification of the realm is the dream of all its people. Every creature, in every land. When you were born there weren't four kingdoms. There had always been five." He paused, allowing the boy to gather his thoughts. "But moments like this will be recorded. Our words will be weighed and tested—ascribed to us for years to come."

He paused again, staring Ellanden in the eyes.

"You understand why you must make the decision yourself?"

The fae nodded in silence. He certainly looked ready to do so. But at the last second, his eyes drifted over the bridge to the vampiric horde camped on the other side.

"...what will they eat?"

There was a compulsive movement from those lingering by the gate as Katerina looked down with a start. "Excuse me?"

"We are marching to the western shore, but that will take time. Once we arrive, we will need to wait even longer as the rest of the army joins us from across the land. There will be thousands of people camped in a relatively remote area, without any customary way for a vampire to feed."

He turned back to his uncle, never losing that steady calm.

"I will agree to your accord whole-heartedly— as the entire realm is longing for peace—but I will not do so until I have assurances that the vampires will be sated enough to distract them from their longing for the blood of my people. If that isn't the case...then no such agreement can be made."

Dylan's arm vanished from his shoulder. It was replaced with a look of respect. "Diana?"

Her eyes twinkled and she nodded slowly.

"While it physically pains me to give you the satisfaction," she intoned, glancing at Aidan, "I suppose the clan can survive on the blood of animals for that long."

The trio by the gate soured with the same expression. Across the mountain there rose a resentful hiss. But not a single vampire said a word against her.

"At any rate," she continued lightly, "we can drink freely at Blackstone."

...Blackstone?

"You mean the mountain?" Evie blurted, unable to pretend not to be eavesdropping for a moment longer. "You wish to return to the mountain?"

Asher's gaze jumped from person to person, but he kept his opinion to himself.

"It's settled along the path we'd take anyway," Dylan explained. He'd been hesitant to visit the vampiric homeland for a great many reasons himself, but each had been quelled by Aidan's soft-spoken request. "Your mother isn't yet well enough to fly, and I'm suspecting you're not either. A few extra days to cross the grasslands and we'll—"

"A few extra days in the wrong direction!" Ellanden protested, unable to believe they were considering it. "A few extra days in a journey that will already take weeks! We haven't the time to spare. Freya might be awake by now—"

"Your witch?" Andrei interrupted with concern, appearing from nowhere. The others continued talking, oblivious to the intrusion. "I do hope she's all right. Did something happen?"

Ellanden froze where he stood, lowering his voice to a hiss.

"Must he *always* be here?"

Asher tried not to smile. "He's her third in command."

"Can't he be replaced?"

Evie glanced between them with a grin. "You realize that he can *hear* you, right?"

"Come now, angel," Andrei inserted kindly, "let yourself see sense. There's no need for such hostility—least of all towards me. As I've assured you before, I am one of the only people here who wouldn't harm a hair on your lovely head."

He's never as comforting as he thinks.

Ellanden seemed to agree.

"I'll just be inside," he called to the others, casually backing towards the sanctuary, "breaking in this new bow..."

Evie stared after him before turning to Asher with a faint grin. "These accords are off to a great start already."

THE NEXT FEW HOURS were spent in preparation.

While the vampires would be travelling ahead with the small group that had departed from the High Kingdom, Petra would take up her brother's mantle and lead the warriors of Talsing along the same trail. Without the aid of a dragon, they would be forced to move at a mortal's pace. But although she hadn't the power to create a portal, the general had several magical tricks up her sleeve to ease the way. The two groups would reach the western shore at approximately the same time.

If we all make it there in one piece.

Evie perched on the steps of the courtyard, watching as the people of the monastery hurried back and forth. She understood now Aidan's very first words to Diana, that most of them had never encountered a vampire. There was an instinctual protocol, one that protected both sides.

One that was completely foreign to the people of Talsing.

"Excuse me?"

There was sudden movement by the fountain as an anxious-looking laundress approached one of the three unoccupied vampires. A laundress who was apparently far braver than the cowering shifters watching from inside. She cleared her throat nervously, clutching a bundle in her arms.

Evie tensed instinctively, straining to see the vampire in question. It was the woman with the impossible cheekbones. The one whose face made a casual appearance in every child's worst dreams.

Cicely—that's what Asher called her.

The vampire raised her head slowly, staring without a shred of expression on her perfect face.

"I thought...I thought you might want these." The woman shoved the bundle towards her without thinking, retracting her arms just as fast. "It's not much, just a few blankets and extra cloaks that we keep in case of emergencies. Not enough for everyone I'm afraid, but...hopefully it helps."

Cicely blinked slowly, then tilted her head. In all likelihood, she thought the woman was touched with a slight bit of madness. Why else would she have thrust ill-fitting clothes into her face?

"Hopefully it helps?" she repeated blankly.

The princess slowly pushed to her feet, propelled by a sudden chill in her veins. No one else had seen the little exchange—they were still busy making travel arrangements.

Look up...somebody, look up...

The laundress blushed and paled at the same time. A bizarre combination that made her look rather splotchy, like someone had held her face to a fledgling fire.

"It's just—" She caught her breath, wanting very much to retreat but finding herself unable to move. "I figured you probably left in a hurry and didn't have a chance to take much with you."

The vampire tilted her head again, lips curling back with a frightening smile. "So you brought me these scraps...how considerate."

Oddly enough, there was a chance that she meant it. At any rate, she didn't throw the fabric back in the woman's face. She stood up instead, towering almost a foot taller.

"But I have no need for your clothes," she continued, fixing the woman in that snakelike smile. "Is there anything else you'd like to offer?"

Not good.

Fortunately, Diana glanced over that very moment—making a strange sound in the back of her throat. It was almost too quiet for a mortal to hear, and only the princess' shifter blood had brought it to attention. But the vampire stepped back immediately, receiving the clothes with a bland smile.

"I'm sure we'll find use for these."

The women parted ways a second later, leaving Evie and Diana staring at the fountain where they'd stood. Their eyes met in the emptiness and the vampire flashed the faintest of smiles before returning to her conversation—leaving the princess casually quaking in her boots.

It's fine. Everything's going to be fine.

She amended that a moment later.

I'm going to find Mom.

Injured or not, it was hard to spend any time with the Damaris queen without imagining her throwing waves of dragon fire or tearing through the skies. All her life, Evie had leaned hard into the image—weaponizing it against her friends and seeking solace behind it at the same time.

That being said, Katerina was most certainly still injured.

"Hey...how are you feeling?"

Evie breezed quickly across the courtyard then came to a sudden stop where her mother was propped up on a bench beside the outer wall. A thick blanket was draped over her knees—an appeasement for her fretting husband—but despite the added warmth she was still shivering. Dark circles bruised the hollows beneath her eyes, and her already-thin frame was dangerously waifish.

Still, she greeted her daughter with a smile.

"You hiding from that scary vampire?" she teased.

The princess froze, then glanced reflexively over her shoulder.

"No... I mean, I have no idea what you're talking about." She hitched the cloak higher around her chin, resisting the urge to peek again. "Maybe you've started hallucinating."

Katerina laughed quietly, shivering in the breeze.

"Maybe you're right." She fluttered her fingers with a mischievous wink. "But I had my eyes on her all the same. This place needs all the washerwomen it can get."

Evie grinned in spite of herself, but it faded just as fast.

"Can you..." she asked hesitantly, lowering her voice. "Can you use the fire?"

It didn't seem likely. Despite the queen's fearsome reputation, baresmain was an unrelenting poison and her body had withstood all it could take. Yet who would dare underestimate a dragon?

Katerina kept a careful smile, staring into her daughter's eyes.

"Of course I can."

The princess nodded automatically, then hesitated, and then went very still. Her mother's voice had carried, but perhaps that had been the point. Each of the vampires on the distant mountain knew of the queen's deadly power, and not one of them doubted that she could incinerate them on the spot. They weren't close enough to see her trembling fingers, the sickly pallor to her skin.

So I'm not the only one worried about this new alliance.

A familiar voice rang out behind them.

"Well, this is a lovely sight." Dylan swept gracefully across the courtyard, lifting his hands as if to frame the image before lowering them with a radiant smile. "How are my girls?"

Evie stifled a grin as he swept back her mother's hair with a tender kiss.

It didn't matter how many years her parents had been together, they still looked at one another like it was the first time—lit up with the glow of love's first embrace.

He took his time, long enough to make Katerina laugh, then slapped a quick kiss to his daughter's forehead as well. "A pale imitation, but I love you nonetheless."

The princess laughed, yanking herself free.

"I'm doing just *fine*," Katerina said with a hint of dread, craning her neck like he might be hiding something behind his back. "Well past the point of that ghoulish medicine, you sadist."

He lifted a hand to his chest, feigning innocence.

"I have no idea what you're talking about. I've brought you nothing but tea."

Evie's nose perked up with the scent as a woman from the kitchen walked out with a steaming mug, bowing with reverence before placing it in the hands of the queen.

"What is that?" she asked suddenly, skin prickling with dread. "Dad, what is—"

"It's Beligorne tea," he answered without looking, stroking Katerina's hair and steadying her with his other hand. "I wouldn't be surprised if you've never heard of it. We drank it all the time when I was growing up, but it's not so easy to find now."

The princess backed a step away, feeling rather sick herself.

Never could she forget such an aroma—she'd lived in a cloud of it for over ten years. It was the same brew Therias used to drug her and her friends in the cave.

"No," she said faintly. "I've never heard of it."

There was sudden movement in the courtyard as Aidan and Diana swept together across the stone. They were soon joined by the others, all carrying weapons and satchels for the trip.

"That's everything," the vampire declared, throwing a glance towards the iron door. "We scoured the remains of the Carpathian camp and took everything that could be useful. There's a limited amount we can carry with us, but if we're careful it should get us to the western shore."

"If we're careful," Diana repeated with amusement. "When did you get so cautious?"

Aidan flashed a quick look.

"When I had a son," he said plainly, turning to face her. "A son who will be travelling with us, along with two other children I happen to hold most dear."

He hadn't asked a question, but it rang between them all the same.

In a flash, the queen's smile faded into something more serious. "They will be safe, Aidan. I've already given you my word. At any rate, it isn't a tremendously long journey—"

"It spans across most of the realm," Evie argued as the rest of them joined her. "We're in the eastern mountains, heading to the western coast. How could it be any longer?"

Did I actually just interrupt the vampire queen?

Dylan squeezed her arm, pulling her backwards. But Diana only smiled.

"It's true we have many leagues to travel, but my people move at a faster pace than you're accustomed to, sweet child. The journey will not take weeks. We will reach the shore by the next moon."

An impressive declaration. But it raised some logistical questions.

"And how will the rest of us keep pace?" Ellanden asked hesitantly.

Under normal circumstances, the fae would rather cut off his own arm than admit such a limitation. But despite his peoples' breathtaking speed, there was no denying vampires were faster.

"I can run alongside you," Aidan volunteered, "like we did before—"

"When you broke my wrist?" the fae reminded lightly.

"You couldn't help him anyway," Dylan interrupted. "I need you to carry Katerina. I'd do it myself, but I couldn't keep pace as a man—I'll need to shift."

"I'll shift as well," Evie said quickly.

While she highly doubted she'd be able to sustain a transformation as a dragon—even if she wasn't shot out of the sky—there wasn't a doubt in her mind that she could shift into a wolf.

Which still left the fae.

"I could carry you," Asher suggested tentatively.

Ellanden shot him a look that could melt ice. Several hyperbolic alternatives jumped to mind, but before he could say any of them an unlikely voice came to his aid.

"Could you not simply fly?" Andrei asked with a smile. "Those wings of yours have already seared into memory, but I for one wouldn't mind seeing them again."

Disconcerting as this statement was, the fae latched on like a raft.

"Yes, I could! I could fly." He said the words carefully. It was still unfamiliar, and he had yet to recreate the magic since that day. "Of course I could fly. I should have thought of it."

There it is.

Such was the imperious nature of every fae. Those who loved from a distance looked on in wonder. Those privileged few who knew them better only rolled their eyes.

Andrei smiled again, as if witnessing the adolescent musings of a young god.

The others continued their discussion, gesturing out towards the mountains with wide sweeps of their hands. Asher discreetly pulled the fae aside.

"Truth: can you do it again?"

Ellanden considered another moment before lifting his eyes to the sky. "It may involve jumping from a window..."

Chapter 5

I've missed this...

The princess threw back her head with a euphoric howl—a lone point of color amidst the wraithlike shadows that loomed on either side. At first, they had frightened her. If it wasn't the pure speed with which they moved, it was the absolute silence with which it was done. Not a single sound to mark each footfall. The fur on her back had bristled. Every instinct was screaming to run.

After a few days, they had become just another part of the scenery—cold and lovely, and moving too fast for detail. As if her journey through the woods was bolstered by a chilled breeze.

And such a journey it was!

Diana hadn't been exaggerating in the slightest when she spoke of the fundamental difference in speed between humans and vampires. The only way one stood a chance at keeping pace was to avoid being human at all. The moment the princess had crossed the bridge, pausing on the other side to wave farewell to Petra, she'd handed off her cloak and satchel to Asher then embraced the less civilized side of her heritage—transforming into a spirited Belarian wolf.

There was nothing like it. Legs stretching out beneath her, lean muscles contracting then springing as one. The world blurred out of focus yet sharpened at the same time. Highlighting patches of scent and bursts of color. In some ways, she preferred it even to flight.

She howled again and picked up her speed, trying to keep pace with her father.

Given their current mission—the fact that they were but a small portion of a larger army spiriting away to meet the rest—she probably should have been more careful. Kept those invigorated sounds to herself. But despite the vampiric swarm moving around her, she didn't have a hint of fear.

So the enemy heard her howling? Let them come! Let them see how they fared against a company of vampires.

Besides, she was a Belarian princess. The latest heir in a royal line of wolves.

And she had never run alongside her father.

Where are you?

He was much faster. She should have foreseen this. Lupine form was a shimmery reflection of one's human state. The coloration, stamina, and approximate size. Her father was lean and agile, but there was a strength and speed to him that she couldn't hope to match.

Not that it wasn't delightful to try.

With another exhilarated bark she stretched out her legs, streaking like a crimson arrow through the long grass. She sensed rather than saw him running ahead of her. Always within sight of her mother, always within springing distance of his daughter. A position that made it relatively simple for her to charge up behind him, throwing herself upon his back with a playful growl.

Take...THAT!

There was a murmur amongst the vampires. Glittering eyes flashing in the dusky light.

Dylan shook her off involuntarily, casting a glance over his shoulder without ever breaking his speed. For a split second, he looked on the verge of chiding her—a prospect made infinitely more terrifying when coming from a wolf—but such spirited antics were much harder to resist after one had shifted. The King of Belaria was no exception. He was rather known for such antics himself.

His eyes twinkled, and without a hint of warning he dug his claws into the ground and threw himself straight backwards—knocking his shell-shocked daughter straight off her feet.

They tangled together in a blur of yips and snarls, wolfish profanities that would have made the princess' governess slap her straight across the mouth. She struggled and strained, but there was very little to be done. Warriors with decades' more experience had tried and failed to get the best of her famous father. In the end, she decided to go limp—letting out a long and petulant whine to catch the attention of her mother. For good measure, she feigned injury at the same time.

There was a flickering of laughter as the vampires around them slowed their pace. A moment later Aidan appeared suddenly beside them, carrying the Damaris queen in his arms.

"Is someone tired of running?" he teased, eyeing her newfound limp with a twinkling smile.

Dylan took a playful bite at him, then shifted back in a blur of color—taking his cloak from the vampire's hands. "Someone has a death wish. But we can hardly begrudge her a bit of fun."

He winked at his daughter, rubbing her affectionately behind the ears.

They'd been running for four days. Four days at a speed and duration the princess didn't know how she could possibly sustain. Shifting in general was still a relatively new process, and even at peak performance the speed of a vampire outmatched the speed of a wolf. The clan had slowed down substantially to allow her and her father to run beside them. They'd cut short their hours and taken unnecessary breaks at night. But no one could deny they'd made remarkable progress. In only a few days, they'd travelled weeks of distance as measured by a mortal pace.

And there's a chance it's killing me...

With an undignified *oof*, the princess flopped onto her side—legs splayed out like a pitiful carcass as she closed her eyes and drifted immediately to the verge of sleep.

"Darling, look what you've done," Katerina chided, swinging herself to the ground and kneeling beside her daughter with a smile. "I thought we agreed not to attack the children."

Dylan nudged her unfeelingly with his boot. "I remember no such discussion."

The queen ignored him, peering up at Aidan instead. "Shall we make camp for the night? I know there's another hour or so left of daylight, but we started so early this morning..."

The vampire took one look at his defeated niece and instantly agreed.

"Of course." He waved his arm, catching Diana's attention, then shaded his eyes—squinting towards the setting sun. "Ellanden!"

A shadow fell over them as the Prince of the Fae drifted down from the heavens, looking for a place to land. He'd been told to stay as low as possible. A dragon had been shot out of the sky, and the others didn't know what similar threats might be lurking in the woods.

He had agreed when asked, then decided to compromise—gauging how high the average vampire could jump, then staying carefully out of reach.

The others watched as he circled lower, those angelic wings catching the sun's fading light.

"I wish Tanya could see this," Katerina murmured.

Dylan gave her hand a squeeze. "She will."

A sudden gust of wind swept over them—blowing back their hair as the fae touched down in a fluttering of wings. The others engaged in obligatory applause (having been scolded the first night for not doing so) and the princess lifted her head with a tired *yip* as his feet touched the grass.

"Did you *see* that?" he cried, flushed with excitement and unable to catch his breath. "It was the highest I've gotten yet! Oh—must we stop? I could stay up there for hours!"

Dylan chuckled under his breath, placing a steadying hand on his shoulder. "You've already been up there for hours, and as I recall you made a promise not to stray up so high. At any rate you need to eat something, Ellanden. You'll wear yourself out."

The fae scoffed as if such earthly concerns were beneath him, lifting his gaze to the heavens.

"You don't understand...I was made for better things. And I'm not hungry," he added off-handedly before amending it just as fast. "Actually, I'm starving. Give me some bread from your pack, then I can go up again."

The king laughed once more as his nephew reached for his satchel—remembering a young boy learning to ride a horse who used to say exactly the same thing. He slapped at the fae's wrist, about to say as much, when his daughter let out another impatient, wolfish whine.

"Sorry, darling—of course."

Despite the princess' exhilaration in running, she didn't relish the subsequent nudity every time she was forced to stop. And her clothes were currently disappearing into the woods.

"Asher!"

She followed his gaze further into the forest, where the young vampire was still streaking through the trees. The last few days had brought a slight change in perspective. They'd covered more ground than she would have thought possible, at speeds she could never have imagined. Once she'd gotten over the initial thrill, it was easy to see that Asher had always held back. Checking his strength, adjusting his pace. Tempering all those extraordinary parts of himself in order to seem more human. He was relishing the newfound freedom as much as she was—replacing that perpetual control with complete abandon and surrendering to his true nature for the first time.

She could see only glimpses of him now. Dark eyes and a little smile creeping up his face.

No wonder he hates living with us mortals.

"Asher!" her father called again.

The vampire cocked his head then spun around in the opposite direction—doubling back towards them through the trees. Less than a second later he was there—all flushed skin and wild eyes.

"What's wrong?"

Aidan stared at him a moment, taking in all the signs the princess had seen as well before gesturing to the pack slung across his shoulder. The two hadn't spoken since that painful morning at the monastery. When the older vampire had tried, his son had mysteriously disappeared.

"Evie needs her clothes."

It took Asher a second to change tracks. Then he glanced at the crimson wolf by his feet.

"Of course. Sorry...I didn't realize we'd stopped."

He swung the bag off his shoulder, rooting around inside, then surrendering it sheepishly to Katerina—who quickly located an emerald cloak. The men discreetly glanced away while she held it up, allowing her daughter to shift back and dress in relative privacy. Having travelled countless months as the only shifter in a company of men, she was well-familiar with the problem herself.

"You should eat something as well," she said softly, fastening the clasp beneath her daughter's chin. "You've been running on adrenaline for days, but that takes a toll."

"We can all rustle up something together."

The group turned to see Diana walking towards them, with Eleazer and Cicely just a few steps behind. It was Eleazer who had spoken—lips thinned into a humorless smile.

"Perhaps a tasty rabbit," he said dryly. "Or a field mouse. You like those don't you, Cicely?"

The woman said nothing, though a chill emanated from every step.

Evie gave her a wide berth, but smiled in spite of herself.

Despite the vampire's surly exterior, she'd taken a liking to Eleazer ever since he'd stopped her from falling into a pond. They'd been standing on the bank with the others, listening as Katerina and Diana spoke, when the rain-soaked ground had given way beneath her feet. He'd barely glanced up from the conversation, but his hand flashed out and caught the back of her cloak—setting her on the ground with the utmost care. He'd since ignored all her shows of gratitude—acknowledging her presence only to say that, no, he didn't like flowers and please would she leave him alone.

Maybe I'll find him a rabbit, just as a joke...

"You really think there are any animals left?" Aidan teased, flashing an indulgent smile at his niece. "This one's incessant howling probably frightened them away for good."

"That was for Ellanden," she explained with a grin. "You know how distractible he is. I had to give him a way to follow along, otherwise we'd lose him to a rogue canary."

The fae gave her a shove, unable to keep from grinning.

It had been that way since they'd left the monastery. Good-natured teasing, breathless smiles. There was something undeniably cathartic about running oneself into the ground, gulping endless breaths of the clean forest air. It was a welcome change from all those lovely palaces and castles, all those gilded tables full of diplomats and councilmen subtly inserting themselves into their lives.

It was almost enough to make the trio of friends forget they were barely speaking to each other. That they'd been alternating between moments of the purest tenderness and spikes of bitter and divisive grief—unable to find a solid patch of ground in between.

"So it's true, then," Cicely interjected, as bored with their adolescent teasing as she'd been with everything else. "You really mean for us to drink the blood of animals?"

Dylan lowered his eyes to the ground, keeping all inflammatory comments to himself.

"As a sign of good faith," Diana replied calmly, eyes sweeping the trees, "we can let the younger ones hunt for the rest of us. They've never done so before."

...not animals.

Evie fidgeted nervously, but Ellanden's head snapped up at once.

"We could go as well," he volunteered quickly, itching to test out the limits of his bow. "In a different hunting party, of course. Asher, Evie, and I could head—"

"Absolutely not," Dylan interrupted. "You are not to leave my side. Not for a second."

The fae opened his mouth to protest, but never got the chance.

"Not for a second," Aidan repeated sternly. "It isn't open for discussion."

It was one thing when the fae was up in the air, but things were entirely different when he was on the ground. The younger members of the clan had been told to stay clear, but the temptation of eternal blood was enough to overwhelm even the most aged and experienced vampire.

His uncles were taking no chances, protecting him every moment in between.

"That's...great," he said listlessly. "Family bonding. *Again.*"

"It's better than being eaten," Evie said sweetly.

He flashed her a cold look. "Thanks."

They watched as the vampires drifted away to give the order, calling down a group of immortal teenagers perched lazily in the trees. There was some murmured discussion, followed a raucous cheer as the younger generation caught scent of a bear. A second later, they were gone.

"How are we to form an alliance, when we can't be left alone?" Ellanden asked softly, staring into the trees. "How can our two peoples live in peace...when one craves the blood of the other?"

The others glanced over in surprise, thrown off balance by the change in tone. A rush of feeling swept across Aidan's face, but it was Katerina who answered—taking the fae by the hand.

"You model it for one another. Such tolerance doesn't come through force of will, it is a lesson that must be learned." She glanced once more towards the vampires before handing him a satchel. "Why don't you and Asher set up the tent?"

An innocuous way to end a rather pivotal discussion, but the message was clear. The two boys gave each other a bracing look before walking in silence towards a patch of level ground.

Evie stared after them, lost in thought.

Sometimes it seemed like only yesterday they'd set out on their great adventure—a trio of friends who'd loved each other since childhood, ready to take the world by storm. Never could she have imagined the dangers they'd face, or the people they'd meet along the way. Never could she have imagined the twists and turns of their journey, or how many years would be lost in between.

Never could she have imagined they'd end up here.

Engaged to one, in love with another.

Knowing all the while that I'm going to die.

She'd done her best not to think about it. The number of tiny calamities that had happened since that moment in the dungeon had helped a great deal. It was only in times like these—the quiet moments in between activities—that she found herself staring wistfully at the others. Memorizing faces, playing back memories. It was only in times like these she allowed herself a moment to grieve.

They would do such magnificent things, her darling boys. Such magnificent, breathtaking things. Things that would shock the world yet come as no surprise. Each one was destined for greatness. She'd known it since they were children. She believed it even more watching them now.

Since the day he was born, Ellanden had been ready to wear a crown.

It ran in his veins like a drug—the ethereal refinement of his father's people, the hot-blooded magic of his mother's desert tribe. Never had she seen such an exquisite paradox. The man was cold and imperious, but loved with the heat of a nova. He was arrogant to the point of clinical instability, but would be the first to laugh every time he went wrong. He would rather leap off a cliff than admit he'd lost in a round of sparring, but she'd once watched, spellbound, as he'd knelt spontaneously on the bank of a river and sang a blessing upon the creatures residing beneath the tide.

He ruled with his head, led with his heart, and if all else failed...he turned to the stars.

And Asher...what can I say about Asher?

The boy was a bridge—a connection between two worlds. At home in neither, yet belonging to both. It had been that way since he was just a child, cringing from the savagery of vampires, turning a nomad into a father, preaching fair labor practices on the castle steps.

After shifting to a dragon the first time, she had teased him that he'd yet to reveal his great power. It didn't strike her until later that he wouldn't see the obvious sarcasm in the joke.

The man was a lens, reflecting the potential in everyone around him. Projecting a better version of the future for the rest of them to take hold.

He was their salvation.

Even if he didn't see it yet. Even if he never quite did.

Of course, those weren't the things that she'd remember. Her memories would be simple.

A flower twirling between long fingers. The sunlight catching in his hair. The tiny smile that pulled at his lips when they were together. The feel of his heartbeat as he looked into her eyes.

Stop thinking about this. You'll start to cry.

The princess blinked quickly, tightening her cloak as the adults continued talking and her friends went about constructing a tent. Despite the strange assortment of company, there was a decided levity to the proceedings—one that probably had a great deal to do with the sound of laughter echoing through the distant forest as the young vampires chased after the bear.

In actuality, a single animal would never be enough to satiate the clan. They could find a dozen, and still have to search for more. Of course, they were having too much fun to realize this.

"—forget sometimes, they are still children," Diana was saying, looking bizarrely normal as she spoke with Aidan, wrapped in the folds of a silken shawl. "Some are merely in their teens."

He nodded thoughtfully, glancing towards the trees.

"And how many more reside at Blackstone? I was shocked to see the number you had already brought with you, I can't imagine there are many more."

The queen smiled as another chorus of laughter rang through the trees.

"Merrick was always so exclusive," she answered. "Unless one had been alive for centuries, he wouldn't even consider allowing them to stay. But with the arrival of the children..."

She trailed off, turning her head.

It took a moment for the princess to realize what was different, to understand the layer of tension that had settled in the air. The woods had gone abruptly quiet. All the laughter was gone.

...what happened?

Silence was never a good thing when dealing with a vampire. It was something equivalent to other people's screams. This one stretched on several seconds, each one longer than the last.

Eleazer froze in the middle of the clearing. Cicely and Andrei pushed to their feet.

Then came the screams.

The rest of them whirled around just as the vampires raced back into the clearing. A pair of tent poles collapsed behind them, clattering to the ground. Evie stared with bated breath at the trees, unable to believe any such reaction could have been caused by a common bear. That's when she saw the bear they'd been chasing had led to something bigger, something that was chasing them instead.

Her mouth fell open as the ground beneath her trembled.

Please say no...please say this isn't happening...

A second later, a dozen giants came storming through the trees.

Chapter 6

What the heck does one call a large group of giants? A pack or a herd? A coven—though that seemed offensive to witches. And vampires. A clamor, that would be more accurate. Or perhaps an inevitability, for there was something inescapably final about it. That was the silly question looping in Evie's head.

There was very little time to process, and even less to prepare. By the time the princess had registered the panicked return of the teenage vampires, the woods behind them tore open and at least a dozen thundering giants burst into the camp. Their only salvation was that the giants were just as surprised as the rest of the camp was. They paused for a split second—the space of a single faltering heartbeat that pulsed behind the princess' eyes.

What can we do?!

It was near impossible to combat a lone giant, let alone upwards of ten. And these were not the more 'civilized' breed that had uprooted her wedding. These were forest-dwellers—cave-dwellers—creatures that roamed the wilderness with optional clothing and yesterday's dinner in their teeth.

The one in the center let out a fearsome bellow, and the princess saw with a grimace the bear the vampires had been chasing. The poor creature had somehow found an even worse fate.

Stop looking at the bear and THINK of something!

Diana took a bracing step backwards—one of the few people not stumbling for balance though the ground was shaking beneath her feet. Her gaze rose to the monstrous brutes, each large enough to demolish the ancient forest. So many she was unable to see the horizon on the other side.

A muscle twitched in the back of her jaw, and her lips thinned into a line.

...she doesn't want to fight them.

In a way, it was the most terrifying thing to happen yet. A vampire's willingness to engage was a true litmus test of whether or not a battle could be won. Above all things, they were survivors—the proverbial canaries in a mine shaft. And if they didn't want this particular fight...?

But the queen had made a promise. And Aidan was watching her as well.

Their eyes met ever so briefly in that moment of stillness, sharing a look the princess found impossible to describe. Then she lifted her hand with a piercing yell and waved the clan forward.

Sealing the alliance of the five kingdoms with an offering of immortal blood.

"Look out!"

The princess raised her head just as the giants stepped forward—lifting their meaty hands to greet the shadowy tide pouring across the forest floor.

There were some on both sides who would argue they knew what would happen next. Those who had met a vampire would swear that tide would overwhelm everything in its path—the way a jar of spilled ink left nothing around it untouched. Those who had stood in the shadow of a giant would see it quite differently. Waiting with grim certainty for those thick-muscled arms to tear straight through that cold immortal beauty, leaving nothing but porcelain pieces in their wake.

They would both be right, and they would both be wrong. Because neither side was quick to dominate, both were locked in the fight. And Evie had never seen a fight so bloody.

"LOOK OUT!"

The same voice cried out again before choking silent in a gurgle of blood. There was no way to tell who it was. By the time the princess whirled around there was nothing but wet, folded grass where they had stood. She stumbled blindly towards it anyway, then raised her head in fear.

I have no weapons close enough to reach.

That left a single option.

I need to shift.

The moment she thought the words, her body made it so—ripping itself apart and stitching together so seamlessly that only a second later a crimson wolf sprang up in her place.

It was perhaps the only thing that saved her.

While the chaotic picture remained the same her reflexes quickened, her adrenaline spiked, and her ability to see what was happening sharpened tenfold. She watched with perfect clarity as a vampire charged up the leg of the nearest giant, wielding a flaming log from the fire that he intended to smash into the creature's eye. He got only as high as the knees before another beast appeared from nowhere, capturing him in the flash of a hand and lifting him into the sky.

The flaming branch fell to the ground.

The pieces of the vampire followed soon after.

By the gods...

She turned and looked for her parents, who were standing at the edge of the camp near the fire.

Her father's instinct had been the same as hers. The urge to shift was almost overwhelming, and the drive to fight ran deep in his blood. But his wife was in no condition to be left on her own, and he didn't dare release her. Instead of charging into the fray he was holding her against his chest, yelling something above the clamor to Aidan and making wild gestures with his hand.

The princess could understand just a single word.

Her own name—shouted at the top of his lungs.

I'm here!

Unable to reach him, she threw back her head with a piercing howl. His face changed the moment he heard it, eyes sweeping the clearing until he saw her standing amidst the wreckage.

"Come here!" he cried, still holding the injured queen. A sea of bodies tangled between them, but their eyes locked in the center. "Run to me—come here!"

Even if she could barely hear him, it was impossible not to understand his request. While one arm supported Katerina, the other was frantically waving her forward—summoning her away from the battle and into the relative safety of the distant trees. Her mother was shouting as well, no doubt with the same message. But with a heavy heart the princess shook her head.

She had no grievous injury, had not taken someone under her care. And while she had no idea what a single wolf could do against such creatures, of one thing she was terribly certain.

I can't go with you. I need to fight.

She howled again—an answer, an apology. Then she whipped around and streaked towards the nearest giant, losing sight of her white-faced parents in the writhing crowd.

Her friends were already busy at work.

While Asher and his father were fighting together—working with a team of vampires to attack the giants from the ground—Ellanden found an archer's perch inside the tree-line and picked a specific target, firing a dozen arrows straight into its eyes.

There was a blood-curdling howl as it reached for its face, thick drops of blood falling like rain on the ground. The fae reached for more, but his quiver was empty. He grabbed a silver knife instead, spiriting into the trees and coming down a second later upon the creature's back.

There was another howl and Aidan yelled something his nephew was unable to hear, making a furious gesture that read very much like *get back on the fucking ground.* The prince obeyed a moment later, but only after burying his blade with the arrows—leaving the creature furious but blind.

He flipped to the grass with a look of triumph, but the giant was far from defeated.

No sooner had his feet touched down than a shadow fell over him—large enough to block every trace of light from the sky. Ellanden let out an involuntary breath, taking a split second to get his bearings and debate where to run, when the decision was suddenly made for him.

Faster than sight, a vampire seized him by the wrist—pulling him to safety as the giant's massive boot flattened the ground where he'd been standing just a moment before.

It barreled off in the opposite direction, leaving the two immortals standing alone.

"I hurt the bone," the vampire said abruptly, feeling the damage through the skin. He released the fae with a strangely impassive expression. "I'm sorry."

Ellanden took a second to catch his breath.

"Don't apologize," he panted, shaking from head to toe. "You saved me...thank you."

There was a curt nod, followed by a lingering look. Then they headed in different directions.

No more stalling—just pick one and go!

Evie let out a feral cry, then charged into the fray.

The giants were even bigger than she remembered, striking her with a sudden memory of the one who'd kidnapped her and her friends and trapped them in a swinging cage. They hadn't been able to find a way to defeat it any more than the fearless clan was having any success fighting these ones now. The most they'd been able to do was set its cottage on fire and try to escape.

But her fire was weak and inconsistent from the poison. It was the very reason she'd decided to shift. And while she could no longer hide in the trees, perhaps there was something better.

The ravine!

Her eyes flashed towards it before returning to the giant. It was a quirk of geography, a sheer drop in an otherwise steady forest that ended in a quarry of rocks below. In all likelihood, the others had yet to realize it was there. They had been intending to sprint straight past it. It was only because of her wolfish antics that they'd decided to stop there at all.

Without thinking she darted to the nearest vampire and sank her teeth into his sleeve, giving a sudden tug as she tried to direct his attention to the drop.

In hindsight, it was an incredibly stupid thing to do. She was lucky not to lose a hand.

He whipped around with fangs still bared and grabbed hold of her neck before catching himself in surprise as he detached from the bloodlust long enough to realize who she was. A look of sheer consternation came over him as he tried to free his sleeve, casting a quick glance behind him.

"What are you doing?" he demanded. "Our queen did not order a retreat."

The princess shook her head, biting his sleeve once more and pulling him to the cliff.

She was lucky. This time, he followed.

He lingered only a moment, his eyes sweeping over the side to the jagged rocks below. A faint smile pulled the corners of his lips before he flashed her a genuine smile.

"You mortals aren't so useless after all."

...jerk.

He was gone in a flash, streaking from one of his brethren to the next, pointing occasionally over his shoulder to where the crimson wolf was standing beside the cliff. There was no reason to lower his voice or mask his intentions. Giants may have been the pinnacle of brutality and strength, but they shared an equally stunning deficit in terms of higher thought. The idea caught the vampires like wildfire, leaping from head to head until she was staring back at a sea of ivory faces.

Some were torn and broken. Some were stained with blood. But a ghostly smile filled each one as the sun dipped behind the mountains and slowly surrendered to the light of the moon.

She could see the faces of her friends among them. Asher was standing within arm's reach of his father, while Ellanden was twirling a dagger in his fingers—dripping a slow trail of monster blood.

Each of them gave her the slightest of nods. Diana went so far as to smile.

"It's a good idea," she said softly as the fight raged on behind her. "I can see no other way."

Exactly.

To linger on solid ground was suicide. The bodies of many vampires were already strewn across the forest floor, but the giants had yet to lose a single comrade. The only solution was to find something even bigger than the beasts themselves to end the fight once and for all.

Something like gravity.

Just, uh...let me get out of the way first.

The princess beamed back at them, then realized all at once that she was standing directly in their intended path. She skittered nervously towards the others as the vampires turned and resumed the fight once more. This time with a purpose. This time with a strategy in mind.

Unlike the Belarian wolves, who had swarmed over the giants foolish enough to attend her wedding, the vampires had a slightly different strategy in mind. Instead of driving the beasts towards the cliff, they lured them towards the edge—backing closer and closer in such a convincing show of defeat that the princess half-believed them herself.

They would leap up in an apparent attack before letting themselves get swatted back to the earth—all with various degrees of pretense and pain. The only commonality the two species shared was a frenzied reaction to blood, so they allowed themselves to bleed a little as well. Limping, and tearing, and crying out as the rest of the clan continued fighting with all their strength.

Slowly, the 'weakened' ones were targeted. Slowly, the giants ventured forth.

Then, at the last possible second—

YES!

The princess let out a triumphant cry as the clan attacked in perfect unison—striking the beasts in a coordinated blow that left nine of them tumbling off the cliff. Another reached out to grab them and ended up falling as well—fingers scraping the rock as he plummeted to the ground. A series of nauseating sounds echoed from the quarry, but the final two giants had found their balance.

And they were out for blood.

"Get down!"

Faster than the princess would have thought possible the larger of the giants made a sudden reach for the ground, snatching up the same vampire whose cloak she'd bitten just a few minutes earlier. There was a terrible moment when it simply held him, staring down at all those pale faces while the rest of his companions choked their final breath. Then he lifted the immortal with a grin.

...and bit off his head.

Evie froze where she was standing. The vampires froze as well. On the other side of the clearing Katerina covered her mouth with a quiet gasp, still held in her husband's arms.

The body swung lightly from its fingers like a ghostly doll—perfect from the neck down. It dangled there a moment before the giant tossed it over the cliff to reside forever with the rest of the fallen. But the head was a different prize. The giant stared right at Diana and swallowed it.

The queen took a step forward, lips curling back to reveal a set of deadly fangs.

A quiet hiss rattled from her throat, lower and rougher than any the princess had heard before. In a flash, Andrei and Eleazer were standing beside her. Cicely was nowhere to be found.

"Give me a sword," she said softly, extending her hand.

Evie glanced around the clearing in surprise. As a rule, vampires didn't often fight with weapons. The concept was a bit too superfluous for everyone involved. But that didn't mean they never travelled with blades. Andrei reached for the nearest corpse and swiftly disarmed it.

"Did you enjoy that, giant?" She stepped slowly forward, dragging the tip of the sword on the ground. "Did you enjoy the taste of his blood?"

The heat was still rising from a host of immortal bodies. The heavy stench of bloodshed was rising from the earth. But none of that seemed to matter. From the second Diana started talking, the rest of the world melted away—until there were only two people left standing.

The queen and the giant.

Soon there would only be one.

"Answer me, beast." Her eyes glinted in the fledgling moonlight, cold as those distant stars twinkling up above. "Or is that beyond you? Do you not have the power of speech?"

The giant answered in kind—ripping out a young sapling and hurling it towards the vampire with a vengeful screech. A silent scream caught in Evie's throat as it careened through the air. But Diana simply gauged the trajectory and waited, staring at the creature as the tree breezed over her head.

It tumbled over the cliff behind her, landing with a shocking lack of sound on the pile of bodies gathered just below. The queen allowed the branches to settle, then lifted the blade again.

"Such a simple creature...it's time to join your friends."

A whisper of air, then she was gone—vanishing into the night itself, like all those wingless phantoms men learned to fear as a child. The princess' eyes flashed around the clearing, searching for the silver glint of the sword. But she didn't see it again until the fight was already over.

And Diana was plunging it deep into the giant's skull.

Seven hells...

In no possible version of the world could Evie imagine the strength it must have taken to drive it down so far—penetrating skin and bone without ever splintering the blade. Of course, the queen didn't bother to remove it. The second the light faded from the creature's eyes, she landed lightly upon the grass—not sparing a glance for the final giant as she headed into the forest.

"Finish it."

Just two words, that's all she said. But a collective hiss rose up from the remaining vampires as they circled around the solitary target, pale fingers and spiked fangs glowing silver in the night.

At that point, any sane creature would have fled. But 'sane' had never been a word used to describe giants, and this one didn't intend to change that now. If anything, the hopelessness of its situation seemed to have made it even more dangerous. It threw back its head with a ferocious cry, stampeding across the clearing in a wild trampling of boots.

When there were eleven other giants doing exactly the same thing, that had been a much more difficult challenge to avoid. But now the vampires merely drifted aside, ebbing back and forth like the waves of a lake as the creature flailed in the middle, forever imprisoned in that ghostly ring.

"Not so difficult like this," Eleazer said conversationally, turning to a young woman standing by his side. The princess recognized her from their time spent in the mountain—a pale-faced beauty with a mess of wild hair. "But faster than you'd suspect. How might you approach?"

Evie stared at them in amazement, unable to believe her eyes.

He's turning this into a lesson. He's teaching her how to fight.

The girl was hardly alone. No sooner had the elder spoken than the rest of the teenagers they'd met in the stronghold appeared from nowhere, following his every gesture with their eyes.

It was utterly bizarre, like watching a lion bring its cubs on a first hunt. Ironically enough, the princess had plenty of memories with her own parents doing the same thing. Teaching her to fire a bow, positioning her fingers around a knife handle. It was then that she amended her first assessment.

He's teaching her how to stay alive.

It was one of the most difficult things to understand about vampires, the duality that left one side just as fragile as the other was strong. For as skilled as they were at killing, they lived in a world just as intent upon taking their lives. They needed to learn such things if they wanted to survive.

Evie stared after them for a moment. A part of her was morbidly interested in how the ill-timed lesson would play out. But her shoulders sank with a tired sigh and she found herself slinking in the opposite direction—towards her parents and Diana, waiting together in the trees.

I have nothing to wear, she thought vaguely, scanning the clearing for any remains of her tattered pack. *Not even a cloak, much less a dress.*

Fortunately, her father was just as familiar with the logistical perils of shifting himself. The second he saw her coming, he took off his own cloak—tossing it towards her in the grass.

"Have you ever seen so many?" Katerina was asking.

Although she had tried on many occasions to insert herself into the battle, her unyielding husband had stopped her each time. While it was a clear admission that the queen's powers were still recovering from the grip of the poison, that no longer seemed to matter. One arm was firmly around Dylan's neck as the other beckoned for Asher and Ellanden to join them.

"So many," she repeated under her breath. "I didn't know they travelled in bands so large."

Evie lifted her head, tying the cloak beneath her neck.

So it's a band of giants.

"No," Dylan replied softly, staring towards the ravine. "I've never seen such numbers." He flashed a quick glance at his daughter. "Not since your wedding."

Diana broke from her trance.

"Wedding?" she repeated in surprise. "You and Asher have wed?"

An awkward silence fell over the clearing.

Both Asher and Ellanden had been trudging across the grass, but they paused upon hearing the words—flashing each other a bracing look before reluctantly continuing forward.

"It's complicated," Dylan muttered, raking back his hair.

The queen didn't wish to press further, not with the blood of her people still soaking the ground. Her eyes swept the trampled glade before she let out the softest of sighs.

"Merrick was right," she murmured, still wrapped in the tattered folds of her shawl. "You let yourself care for something...and it bites you in the hand."

A hundred yards away, Aidan froze where he was standing—looking away from the remains of the final giant as the adolescent vampires around him let out a celebratory cheer.

"We knew this would happen," Katerina muttered, lost in her own world. "It was clear at the hidden palace, Kaleb has a horde of beasts at his disposal. My mother warned us more would come."

Diana turned to the others once again.

"Your mother," she echoed. "The same mother who's been dead for fifty years?"

It was a pivotal moment—one that felt almost insignificant, given the weight of what they'd just done. The others shared a look, but there was no need to debate amongst themselves.

The vampires had proven themselves. It was time they proved themselves in return.

Katerina let out a sigh, then swung her feet to the ground.

"Perhaps we should start at the beginning..."

Chapter 7

They buried the fallen vampires. That had surprised Aidan. Diana and Eleazer said a few words in remembrance. That had surprised him even more.

Then they set out with fresh purpose to Blackstone.

The skirmish with the giants wasn't the only trouble that plagued the travelers, although it was by far the worst. There was a torrent of rain that resulted in a series of flash floods. On days game was scarce, Ellanden would fly higher into the clouds. At one point near the end they ran into a herd of unsuspecting kelpies, who were so caught off guard they actually put up a fight.

But all things considered, they reached the stronghold with relative ease.

Probably because no one in their right mind would cross a horde of vampires.

"Call down the fae."

Evie glanced up in surprise as Diana came to a sudden halt.

For the last few miles, they'd been walking—such a far cry from their usual speed she'd actually shifted back. While at first the princess had worried as to the reason, it soon became clear that they were nearing their destination and the queen wanted more time to gather her thoughts.

They stopped now in a thicket of trees as Dylan lifted his head with a whistle. A few seconds later, there was a rustling of wings and Ellanden drifted down from the sky.

"We're here," he whispered, landing beside his friends. "I saw the top of the peak."

Evie stifled a shiver, remembering the last time they were there.

As if the idea of a vampire stronghold wasn't reason enough to fear, they'd been faced with the strong possibility that they wouldn't be allowed to leave. A possibility that was made all the more frightening when it became clear that, like most immortals, vampires had a loose concept of time.

Apples, she remembered suddenly. *They fed us apples from the trees.*

"Why do you pause?" Aidan asked softly, standing at Diana's side. He may have appeared calm on the surface, but his pulse was racing. "Is there something you haven't said?"

The queen kept her eyes on the forest, not focusing on any particular thing.

"There is much I haven't said," she mused, "but that is not the reason. For a long time now, I've wanted to show you this place. Yet I vowed never to let you through the door."

A look of genuine surprise washed over him. "Why?"

She stood there a moment, then turned with a sad smile. "Because I thought you'd tear it down."

Neither of them could think of anything more to say. They stared a few seconds longer then continued walking to the mountain, closer than before, matching each other's strides.

The royal group fell into step behind them. The vampires kept pace behind that.

One foot in front of the other...

Evie walked between her parents, feeling the grass beneath her bare feet. Her shoes had been lost in the fight with the giants. Along with most of the monastery's blades.

"Do you feel that?" Dylan murmured, glancing around the woods. "Nothing stirs in the air, nor in the trees...there is not a hint of life in this forest. Was it like this when you first came?"

Evie followed his gaze, noticing it for the first time.

She'd attributed all such feelings to the trauma of their circumstance, shivering without realizing the reason. At any rate, she had very little memory of their previous journey.

"When we first came...I was high on snake venom."

Her father gave her an indecipherable look.

There may be some parts of the story I left out.

Faster than the princess would have liked, the group swept in silence through the slender band of trees and came out on the other side—pausing in the shade of the mountain.

Blackstone. It's a fitting name.

All sinister connotations aside, there was nothing particularly unordinary about the peak except the darkened hue to its granite sides, as if the entire thing had been drenched in smoke and the stains had yet to clear. There was grass in the meadow, a breeze blowing from the clouds. Nothing at all to indicate that this particular mountain was any different from any other.

...with the exception of the door.

Evie saw it only because she knew where to look. The others missed it entirely. Aidan's eyes flew straight for it like a magnet, burning with such intensity he was unable to look away.

It was only then she realized how long he must have been aching to see such a place. How many decades or even centuries he'd dreamed of hollowing out a mountain of his own.

When Dylan clapped his shoulder, he jumped out of his skin.

Katerina took his hand instead. "So this is it...a home to all vampires."

She quoted Diana's words to the letter, flashing the queen the faintest of smiles. The two women may not have bonded the first time they'd met, but they'd reached a shared understanding.

"Every man, woman, and child." Diana inclined her head, never turning from Aidan. "But its doors are open to any friend of a vampire as well. Will the rest of you be joining us?"

I'd rather chop off my own arm.

"We shall remain outside with the children," Dylan replied, a bit more quickly than he'd intended. "Though I appreciate the invitation."

Diana's eyes swept over the rest of them, twinkling with a knowing smile. "As you wish."

She snapped her fingers and the vampires that had been escorting them vanished with the breeze. Some disappeared into the mountain, others bypassed it entirely—heading to the settlement Evie knew was somewhere on the other side. At the same time, the queen swiftly made her way to the door, Asher striding along by her side. It took a moment to realize his father was no longer with them.

"Aidan?" Diana turned in surprise. "Aren't you coming?"

He certainly wanted to, it was written all over his face. But now that the moment was finally upon him, now that dream had been made into reality, he found himself frozen in place.

Katerina glanced back towards her family, then took his hand.

"I'd like to see it," she prompted.

Evie's mouth fell open, while Dylan closed his eyes.

He was no longer surprised by such declarations from his wife. Though each one continued to age him to the brink of that borrowed immortality.

Aidan kept his eyes on the mountain, though he gave her hand a grateful squeeze. A second later, the two were walking side by side—towards that tiny crevice and the endless shadows inside.

"If it weren't for the irony," Dylan muttered, "I'd have bought her a leash."

Evie grinned in spite of herself, flashing a look at the fae.

"Michael had a similar idea for the two of us."

Ellanden simply backed away with a shiver, those angelic wings still raised defensively by his sides. While he'd never admit such a thing the fae had spent many nights dreaming about that forsaken stretch of grass, and he was thoroughly horrified to find himself back there now.

"I might just...I might just go for a flight—"

"Exposed in the open, where you're a perfect target?" Dylan interrupted in a dangerous voice. "I don't think so, Ellanden. I think you'll be staying right here with me."

Exposed in the open, where he's a perfect target?

The fae was no doubt in agreement, but he kept such opinions to himself—flashing a strained smile before pacing as far from the mountain as possible and settling in the grass.

Dylan stared after him a moment before turning to his daughter "...snake venom?"

She let out a sigh, kneading the grass with her toes. "It's a long story."

He gestured around the deserted meadow. "We have nothing but time."

<hr />

THE PRINCESS HAD ALREADY taken her father through the story once before, a few days after they'd reunited beside those mighty falls, but there had been several gaps along the way. Strategic edits, moments of such dissonance and recklessness she'd thought it best to keep them to herself.

But kings had a way of ferreting such information out of you.

Fathers were even better.

"So you went into the hut...and drank the contents of a dead snake?"

The conversation had started innocently enough, but now he and the princess were facing each other in uncomfortable silence—their knees touching in the grass.

"Was this something I should have specifically banned when you were younger?" he asked before she could respond. "I assumed some things were a given, but apparently I was wrong."

"It wasn't like that—"

"I only ask so I can do a better job raising the next child," he explained. "The *preferred* child. The one who avoids reptiles in general and promises to never run away."

This is going fantastically well.

"It wasn't nearly as unsafe as you're making it seem. Ellanden was right there with me," she added quickly, as if this offered some absolution.

The king's eyes narrowed. "I'm not surprised."

She lowered her gaze, letting out her best plaintive sigh. When that didn't work, she tossed her hair with an impatient, "It's not like I did it for fun. I was trying to revisit the memory of the shipwreck—find out whatever force it was that kept us alive."

Dylan considered this a moment, eyes never leaving her face. "...and did you?"

She hesitated, then shook her head with a frown. "There were only fragments—nothing was clear. We were sinking, I could see that. The ship was gone and we were beyond hope...but there were these voices."

Most parents would have panicked at the venom. When it came to hearing voices, they would have opened a bottle of whiskey and started making plans.

But Dylan Hale wasn't most parents. And he'd heard stories like this before.

"Voices," he pressed, tilting his head to catch her gaze. "What were they saying?"

"...I couldn't tell."

"Where were they coming from?"

"Below me," she answered, remembering all at once. "From somewhere deep in the water below me, but they weren't dangerous or afraid of the storm. I wanted to get closer. I wanted to find out who they were. But then a shadow moved in the water and everything went cold..."

She trailed off, shivering as if she was still there.

"The next thing I remember, we were waking up five-hundred leagues away."

The story faded into contemplative silence that lasted a lot longer than either person was aware of at the time. After a few minutes, Evie lifted her eyes with a tentative question.

"...do you think it could be true?"

Dylan tensed ever so slightly, considering his answer. "Kreo magic is some of the most powerful in the world, but nothing about it is static. Every spell, every potion, every vision changes, depending on the people involved."

Not really an answer.

He read her impatience with a roll of his eyes. "I'm saying that whether or not that's what actually happened, it's what you were supposed to see. Those voices are important. The shadow in the water..." He shook his head. "It has some significance as to what happens next. What that significance might *be*, is another question."

Again, not really helpful.

This time the king seemed to agree.

"It's why I haven't the slightest bit of patience for the desert people," he continued, shooting a grin at his nephew at the same time. "Always speaking in riddles, parsing metaphors with bits of truth. Michael always liked them," he added suddenly. "Riddles were his specialty."

The princess warmed with a smile before staring down at her hands.

"It's not my only vision," she confessed. "When Seth and I were diving off the cliff, I struck my head in the water. Before he dragged me out, I had a dream or something like it. It was of you and Mom, standing on the bank of a river. The same river where the three of us almost drowned."

Dylan kept his eyes on the forest, but his face went very still. "...you saw the river?"

Evie nodded, wishing suddenly she'd kept it to herself. "You knelt on the shore, dipped your hand into the water. I could see on your face that you knew it was too fast, too cold. That we wouldn't have survived."

She hesitated a split second.

"You cried. I had never seen you cry before."

Another silence fell between them, this one even longer than the first. She kept waiting for him to break it, to either confirm or deny. But he just stared into the woods with an expression so desolate, so completely devoid of warmth, she hardly recognized her own father's face.

"Was that true?" she finally asked. "Did that actually happen?"

Their eyes met for an instant, then he turned back to the trees.

"I went down to the river. It happened just as you said."

...just as I said.

THE SUN DRIFTED SLOWLY across the sky, but the door to the mountain stayed shut.

Dylan channeled his nerves into manic pacing and reckless interrogation of every vampire who wandered across his path. His daughter had watched for a while with morbid curiosity, wishing he would remember the clan had things like staggering numbers and savage-looking fangs, until she realized how easily such fevered energy could be directed toward her. At that point, she quickly left her spot on the grass and wandered off to find Ellanden dozing fitfully beneath the trees.

She opened her mouth to wake him, then caught herself with a smile.

Although exhaustion from the journey had eventually overtaken him, the fae was just as wary as the ranger was himself. He'd kept the wings to be ready at a moment's notice, folding them around his body like blankets as he slept. There was something undeniably beatific about the image.

And something utterly bizarre.

"Oi—wake up!"

The princess kicked him in the legs, then knelt immediately to examine his feathers. She'd wanted to do it from the first moment he'd gotten them, but it had never been the right time. His eyes flew open to see her running one along the edge of her palm, debating whether to pluck it off.

"Hands off," he said irritably, shoving her right back. "They're mine—not yours. If you find yourself lacking such heavenly gifts, then I suggest you sit down and grovel where you belong."

She stumbled backwards with a snort of laughter. "You're going to make a fantastic king."

His face broke into a grin before sobering as his eyes drifted to the mountain. "They're still not back?"

She shook her head. "My dad's having a low-key panic attack. I'm pretty sure I heard him muttering something about 'scaling the peak', but I'm sure he'd deny that if we pressed."

Ellanden didn't want to press. He didn't want to be anywhere in the vicinity. "Let's take a walk."

The two friends wandered into the trees—glancing back every so often to make sure they were still within visual distance of the mountain. After a few minutes, Ellanden closed his eyes with a look of uncharacteristic focus and the wings vanished from his back.

"You're getting good at that," Evie remarked in surprise.

The fae nodded briskly, as if such things happened every day.

"It puzzled me at first how to control it—the whole thing's rather paradoxical. Instead of deriving the momentum from panic and necessity, one must summon a feeling of inner peace." His lips twitched at the corners. "Another irritating quirk of my mother's people."

The princess laughed, remembering her father's condemnation.

"There's a chance he wanted you to hear that."

"He wasn't wrong." The fae came to a stop on a bluff, gazing out over the wooded valley below. "It's so lovely from a distance...I wonder what nightmares are roaming inside."

She glanced over in surprise before following his gaze.

Not a soul could deny they'd seen their share of nightmares. And no doubt beneath the dappled oaks and sprigs of wild violet there lurked even more. It made her think back to the fae's childhood room—every inch of the walls covered in pictures of hellions and monsters. Some he'd drawn himself, others he'd torn from the pages of a book. He'd spent his days plotting against them, and his nights dreaming of his own great adventure—when he would take up the hero's sword.

"A dozen giants," she murmured, shaking her head slowly. "When we set out from the palace just a few months ago...could you have imagined we'd find ourselves facing a *dozen* giants?"

He opened his mouth to answer, then came to a pause.

"A few *years* ago," he corrected, throwing her a quick glance. "But no, I could never have imagined such a thing. I was shocked when fewer than half that many crashed our wedding."

The princess tensed at the words, but he said them so lightly—gazing at the distant trees and absentmindedly massaging his injured hand. She took a deliberate breath and moved past it.

"You needn't have feared. Such creatures are nothing compared to a dragon." She flashed a quick look at the side of his face. "In case it wasn't clear...*I'm* the dragon."

His lips twitched with a hidden smile. "That was you?"

"Not that I need to shift," she continued smugly. "I was the one who pointed out the ravine to the others in the forest. I'm taking credit for those giants as well."

She expected the fae to contest this, but a look of sudden worry troubled his eyes.

"Have you ever seen such a fight?" he asked in a low voice, turning to face her as the mountain loomed up behind. "All of them working together, I can think of no army that could stand against them. And when they defeated the Carpathians...?"

He stilled with an abstract feeling of dread.

"...it's like they were playing a game."

Both friends stood on the edge of the forest, haunted by the same memories and afraid to speak any further at the risk of what they might say. The worst part was that the princess had remembered thinking the exact same thing—disturbed not only by the effortless brutality but also the playfulness with which it was done. Almost a full week later, that eerie laughter was still ringing in her ears.

She stood there another moment, then forced a breath. "I'm glad they're on our side."

They shared a silent look.

"Yes," Ellanden answered in a neutral tone, "I'm glad they're on our side."

They might have said more if there wasn't a sudden rustling in the forest. The branches swayed and the leaves crunched. A few seconds later, a familiar face walked out of the trees.

"Are you two writing poetry out here?" Asher flashed an unexpected grin, shading his eyes against the golden sunlight. "I'm surprised your father let you out of his sight."

The others smiled in return, relaxing in spite of themselves.

It had been one of the hardest things to reconcile since their incendiary return to the land of the living. That natural warmth they shared between them. The one that could thaw any argument, erase all the sins of the past. In the last few weeks it had been tested beyond all measure. And while it may have faltered on occasion the foundation always remained, drawing them back again.

They would find themselves cursing the very sight of each other, but couldn't resist telling little jokes in the aftermath if only to coax a smile. They would find themselves walking on opposite ends of the forest, a clan of vampires between, only to close every day sleeping side by side.

In a fast-changing world, it was small solace. One that left them trembling at the same time.

"I could say the same to you," Ellanden replied, turning to greet him. "Has Diana finished giving the grand tour?"

The vampire shook his head. "No, they're still inside. I imagine it will take some time."

Evie looked at him curiously. "You didn't want to stay with them?"

He hesitated a moment, then cleared his face with a smile. "I've seen it."

...seriously?

The princess raised her eyebrows, but said nothing. She remembered quite clearly the last time he'd set foot in that shadowy cavern—she'd never seen anything like it. If it weren't for the risk that his friends outside were being eaten, he might have stayed forever.

Not that he was particularly concerned at the time.

"How's it been going out here?"

Ellanden rolled his eyes, keeping things light. "Evie's been regaling me with tales of her glory. Apparently, she single-handedly rid the world of giants—courtesy of that flaming lizard she's taken to impersonating."

Asher turned to her in surprise. "That was you?"

"You two are incorrigible!" she exclaimed. "And by incorrigible, I mean *weak* and *small*. You can try to diminish it all you like, but I'm still the only person here who's actually *thrown* a giant."

The vampire blanked, like he'd already forgotten. The fae scoffed in disdain.

"The height of elegance on the battlefield," he replied sarcastically. "It probably came down upon some unsuspecting deer, crushed the thing to a pulp."

"Are you serious—"

"You're a menace, Everly. A hazard to the forest."

A curl of smoke rose from her hands, but she held her tongue.

The friends stood there for a while longer, gazing out towards the horizon, thinking of all the things that were yet to come. In truth, they didn't know which unsettled them most: The fact that they were gearing up for the fight of their lives or the fact that it would soon be over. One way or another, the prophecy would be finished…and at least one of them wouldn't survive.

"Do you think this will work?" Ellanden asked softly, glancing at the vampire. "Do you think it was a good decision to agree on my parents' behalf?"

He wanted so badly to believe it. But the man had literally grown a pair of wings each morning just to keep himself out of reach. It didn't matter how many monsters were lurking in the trees if they couldn't trust the people walking beside them.

Asher hesitated, then dug his hands into his cloak. "I think it will work just as well as the two of you standing before an altar."

And…we're back.

The fae stiffened, then dropped his gaze with a quiet sigh. A moment later he was walking back through the forest, calling a vague excuse over his shoulder. Missing the witch who slept in the castle, missing the days the three of them could speak without one of them wanting to cry.

Evie stared after him before lifting her eyes to the vampire.

"Feel better?"

She turned before he could answer, heading back into the trees. However, a quick hand shot out and caught her arm— gently turning her back around.

"I'm in love with you," he said softly, unable to meet her eyes. "How am I supposed to reconcile it? Even if I understand the sacrifice, even if I understand the reason? How am I ever supposed to reconcile the idea of you marrying someone else?"

She stood there a moment, then pulled her arm from his grasp. "By thinking of someone other than yourself."

Chapter 8

The sun was already starting to dip lower in the sky when the granite door cracked open and a tiny group of people ventured out of the mountain. Katerina looked overwhelmed, blinking rapidly to adjust from that oppressive darkness. Aidan was a little harder to describe.

He stood close beside her and Diana, listening in a daze as the vampire queen spoke at a rapid pace. Every so often he'd nod absent-mindedly. Every so often he'd allow his hand to be taken in greeting as more and more vampires poured out of the cave.

"That's a lot," Dylan murmured with visible unease. "That's more than we thought.'"

He caught his wife's eye and she left the others, heading towards them across the grass.

"Well, it's settled," she announced, grabbing his hand. "Aidan is unsure of the village, but they are coming with us. Many more than Diana had thought would be coming before."

That's good news...right?

Evie cast a bracing look at the peak as more immortals flooded onto the field.

"Even some of the younger ones?" she asked hesitantly.

Not many of the teenagers she'd met before had come to the sanctuary, just five—two of whom had been killed by the giant. The rest didn't seem to be grieving; if anything they looked excited for what was coming next. She watched as they huddled in the grass, talking at rapid speed.

It lasted only a moment, then in perfect unison they looked towards the trio of friends.

One friend in particular.

"When we were here before, Diana gave them a curfew," she added nervously, wondering if there were any similar protections in place. "Ellanden will be flying for most of the day, but what about the nights? At some point he'll need to land and rest."

"I'll be fine," the fae answered quietly, though every muscle was tense with stress.

"Diana has assigned a group of elders to watch over the children, and Ellanden will sleep each night at Aidan's side," Katerina answered, squeezing her daughter's hand. She had recovered slightly from her time in the mountain, though traces remained—making her fingers tremble and her pupils dilate. "I swear...it was stranger than when we met Merrick. And different...very different."

"I should hope so," Diana said, striding towards them with a smile. Aidan and Eleazer were behind her. "Merrick would not have abided our little homestead. But you know that full well."

Aidan merely stared into the distance, lost in thought. For a split second his son actually took a step towards him, his eyes tight with concern. But he caught himself just as fast.

"You haven't said much," the queen continued, looking almost nervous for his approval. "I had thought you'd be pleased."

Aidan glanced up quickly, like one awakened from a spell. "I am...overwhelmed."

His head bowed forward, spilling dark hair into his eyes. The princess was struck again, as she'd been so many times growing up, by how incredibly young her parents and their friends still looked. The abdication of the crown had aged them briefly, adding five years to their lives, but every ounce of that youthful radiance remained. It seemed impossible to imagine how much they'd been through, how much had already happened to them over the course of their lives.

I wonder if people look at us and think the same thing.

"So it's been decided, then?" Ellanden asked, his eyes jumping from one to the next. "The vampires will march with us to the shore? They'll fight at our side, against Kaleb's army?"

They'll take their place as the fifth kingdom?

Dylan shared a look with the others. "That is a question for the High Council...but, yes, I believe so."

An invisible tension settled over the others as each of them wondered how such a proposal might be received, but Evie found herself strangely comforted by the news.

So, if nothing else, we accomplished that.

The vampires would not have established a home if the land had not grown wild enough to allow them to do so. The other four kingdoms would never have been desperate enough to consider the possibility of accepting the fifth. The realm would never had stood a chance at uniting if they hadn't found themselves faced with an enemy great enough to destroy them all.

Now we can face him together. As allies, and perhaps even as friends.

Evie stiffened as one of the boys who'd spoken with them in the mountain caught her eye across the field. He froze as well, gave the world's strangest wave, then vanished into the crowd.

For however long that lasts...

CONSIDERING THEY WERE an eternal people, vampires required shockingly little transition.

No sooner had Diana announced they would be leaving than the clan left their mountain home and gathered in the adjoining field. There were no weapons to sharpen, no horses to gather, and very little to pack. The only thing they took care to do beforehand was feed.

And even that took the princess by surprise.

"Are those...?" Katerina trailed off in amazement, standing on the tips of her toes to get a better look. "What did Diana call them?"

Aidan went perfectly still beside her.

"Companions."

Evie turned in surprise as a different group of people appeared on the distant curve of the mountain, slowly making their way across the grass. Perhaps it was because she'd grown oddly accustomed to traveling with vampires, but each movement appeared disjointed and clumsy. Even the ones who stepped more freely seemed uncoordinated, laboring with every passing breath.

Is this how mortals look to vampires? Is this how I look to Asher?

The vampires glanced up as well, turning in unsettling unison as the villagers made their way towards them. Some of them rolled their eyes, muttering little sarcasms under their breath, while others were genuinely pleased to see them—striding forward to meet them halfway.

"So each of those..." Dylan trailed off, flashing a look at Aidan. He'd had a similar reaction to the villagers' arrangement as the princess had. "Each pair shares a bond?"

It was the queen who answered, strolling up through the grass.

"Half a bond," she replied with a wink. "Less than what you share yourselves. And it was a choice for every person involved." Her eyes swept the distant crowd before zeroing in on someone in particular. "We'll depart in a few minutes, but if you'll excuse me..."

The group watched in amazement as she blurred across the length of the field, reappearing beside a woman standing at the edge. At a glance, they were approximately the same age—both touched with a regal bearing that set them a bit apart from the rest. They met with a smile and exchanged a few simple pleasantries. The woman even threw back her head with a laugh.

Then the two vanished into the woods, walking hand in hand.

"*Diana* has a companion?" Evie gasped in astonishment.

"It would hardly set a good example if she didn't."

The others glanced around as Eleazer came up from the same place as his queen, finished with any arrangements she'd required him to make. He caught their apprehension like a scent on the breeze and smiled, nodding towards the villagers.

"You forget, this was her idea. Diana was the first to bond."

The first to bond. Not the first to feed.

Interesting.

"But not you?" Dylan guessed stiffly.

The vampire smiled again, showing all of his teeth. "Never found a good fit."

He lingered a moment longer, almost as if he was waiting for someone to volunteer. Then he headed in the same direction as his queen, swiftly moving across the grass.

Evie turned back to the villagers, staring in open fascination. She remembered the first time she'd witnessed such an arrangement, between the old man and the young vampire inside the cave. She thought of the easy proximity, the casual familiarity. It wasn't quite a friendship, but something had warmed between them all the same.

"...Father?"

The others continued talking, but Asher had circled behind the rest—stepping into Aidan's line of vision with uncharacteristic hesitation. He dipped his head, looking almost shy.

"Diana's right, you haven't said much. Was it...was it not what you wanted?" His eyes came up then, searching for clues. "You've spoken of this for as long as I can remember, a balance in which we might coexist with the rest. But I had never imagined such a compromise. The first time I learned of the villagers, I thought...I thought you might hate it."

Evie blinked in surprise, staring at them.

She remembered being dubious when Asher had made his promise of silence to the vampire queen, then shocked when he'd kept his word. For how long his father had been travelling from clan to clan, preaching a doctrine of peace and inclusion, it seemed almost criminal to keep the secret of a vampiric homeland to himself. But perhaps there was a different reason for his silence. Perhaps he was simply afraid to be the one to break his father's heart.

The two hadn't spoken since their fight at the monastery, and Aidan didn't say anything to him now. He simply looked back to where the vampires and villagers were mingling in the field.

Several had been content to conduct their 'business' right there in the open, talking amongst themselves and casually rolling up sleeves, until there was a startling flash of fangs. Most of the others preferred to do such things in private—finding a quiet place beyond prying eyes in which to make the exchange. It didn't take long. The vampires didn't take much. Diana and her companion were already coming back from the forest. Most of the others had finished as well.

Now there were goodbyes to be said. Now there were hasty summaries of explanation as one group raised their hands to the other—seeing them off with a wave of farewell.

"They have ties to this place," Katerina murmured, shooting a glance at Aidan. "Lines of emotion that go beyond the mountain. Regardless of the shelter, I think they'd find a way to stay."

And they would be welcome.

Evie looked from afar as an older man rushed out at the last minute, calling out a name and waving something frantically in his arms. The teenagers she'd been watching earlier came to a pause, then one of them doubled back a few steps to meet him—a silent question on his face.

"For the road."

The man offered it between them, and Evie squinted to get a better look.

It's a sweater.

The young vampire froze, staring as if he'd never seen one. His friends were gawking behind him, but the man was waiting with a hopeful smile. After a second of hesitation, he reached for it.

"...thank you."

The vampire blushed, but slipped it over his head—watching as the man headed back to the village. The second he was out of sight the sweater came off again, but the pensive look remained.

His friends were rather less contemplative.

"*Mortals*—what a preposterous idea," one of them scoffed, swatting playfully at the sweater as he walked past. "When was the last time you felt cold?"

The others laughed and headed after him but the vampire just smiled to himself, rubbing the fabric between his fingers. He came when they called for him, stuffing it into his pack.

...there's something you don't see every day.

Evie turned back to the others, only to discover that she hadn't been the only one fascinated by the exchange. Her parents were riveted, looking after the young vampires as they headed into the trees. But Asher was staring with fixed attention at his father, waiting for a verdict.

There hadn't been a hint of movement since the old man had started calling. Every other part of the world had dimmed as Aidan watched in a kind of trance.

Diana looked at him as well, a trace of that quiet anxiety in her eyes.

He didn't notice either of them. He stayed consumed with the pair until the elderly man had vanished over the hillside and the young vampire had returned to his friends.

Only then did a hint of that old light return to his eyes.

Only then did he begin to smile.

THE FIRST NIGHT WAS the hardest because there was trouble right from the start.

The journey had been taxing enough on the friends—each of them pushing themselves to the limit just to cover the necessary ground. But the younger vampires had never experienced such a thing either. Most of them had spent their childhoods elsewhere, and the bulk of their adolescence in the mountain. They were not accustomed to long stretches of travel like their older brethren. Their hearts were racing and their adrenaline was primed when Ellanden swept down from the sky.

"Look out!"

The instant the fae's feet touched the ground, a blistering snarl tore out of the trees just behind him. He was still turning around when a teenage vampire flew towards him—eyes wild with hunger, a pale hand stretching though the air...only to be immediately caught by Diana.

"Seven hells!" Evie gasped, clutching her chest. "Where did you come from?!"

The vampire queen had moved faster than she'd thought possible, just as fast as her uncle did. While the young vampire she'd caught had been in a frenzy, streaking forward in a blur of color and desperate for the fae's blood, she had materialized with a look of perfect calm. Holding him by the back of the neck with a single hand, oblivious to his feet dangling off the ground.

"Oh, *come on!*" he pleaded, whining like a puppy trapped on the wrong side of the door. A kind of mania had come over him, making everything else fade from sight. "*Please,* Diana!"

It was this frantic request more than anything else that froze the princess in her tracks.

He's actually asking permission. He's that far gone.

It had only been a few seconds, but the commotion had already attracted the others.

Katerina and Dylan were both standing by with hands at the ready, while Aidan was tensed just a short spring from the vampire himself. A vampire who was still *writhing*. One hand was still clawing uselessly at the air, while strange, disjointed sounds were coming from deep in his throat.

Ellanden went dangerously pale, backing towards the others.

"Eleazer."

A second later, the elder was there—staring with a detached interest as the boy thrashed and strained, still dangling from the queen's hand like an errant cub.

"Take care of this for me."

The young vampire was transferred between them, still begging without shame as Eleazer dragged him into the trees. His voice carried for long after, striking each of them to the core.

"Eleazer, please—how can you stand it?! We can share him together! He may even live!"

The screaming stopped soon after, but the silence that followed was even worse.

"How will you discipline him?" Aidan asked quietly.

Diana glanced over with a touch of surprise. "Do you think I should?"

She walked away a second later, stunning the friends. They'd expected an apology, or at the very least a flush of shame. Aside from the inevitable tension, they had all been meticulously well-cared for since embarking upon their trip. But the queen was as calm and collected as ever, pausing at the edge of the clearing to look each of the young royals in the eye.

"You will *never* understand it," she said softly. "The insurmountable struggle they face."

Then she was gone, leaving them even more astounded than before. In perfect unison they looked at Aidan, expecting him to provide a voice of reason. But the vampire merely sighed.

"Put on your cloak," he said quietly, draping it over the fae's shoulders. "And take down your hair. Don't make this more difficult than it has to be."

Ellanden stared back in silence, then managed a slight nod—reaching up with trembling fingers to unthread his warrior's braids. They fell loose and wavy to his shoulders, covering his neck.

"You see?" Aidan flicked him beneath the chin. "No harm done."

...not this time.

TWO HOURS LATER, THE friends had yet to get over the shock.

"I mean, I was never in any *real* danger," Ellanden was saying, leaning back against the rocks piled around the fire. "I could have leapt out of reach and flown back into the sky. I was just—"

Asher glanced up with an innocent smile.

"—slower than he was?"

Perhaps he would have been kinder—considering his friend was nearly attacked—if he hadn't been forced to hear different variations of the speech for the better part of the evening. At this point, the fae had looped the words so many times Asher was able to recite them himself.

Ellanden glanced over sharply, then returned his eyes to the flames.

Since they left the royal caravan, it felt as though they'd been locked in a quarrel. Finding themselves on different sides of an argument, when all their lives they'd been fighting together.

Evie glanced between them, perpetually stuck in the middle.

Asher was right, it was easier when we were still at the castle. He wasn't a vampire, I wasn't a shifter, and Ellanden wasn't a fae. We were just people. Not like it is out here.

The wind picked up and settled, making two of them tighten their cloaks as they shivered a bit in the cold. Asher looked on from across the fire, sudden nostalgia softening his face.

"You *were* never in any real danger," he said quietly, scooting closer to the fae. "When Diana told the elders to watch over the others, that isn't to be taken lightly. Their speed is unmatched by nearly anything on this earth, Ellanden. They will always get there in time—"

"Lucky for you."

The trio lifted their heads as two figures drifted towards them, moving at a deliberately slow pace until their faces were lit by the glow of the fire. It was only then that Evie recognized them—the boy who'd given them an unofficial tour of the mountain, and the one who'd accepted the sweater.

Both shot a permissive glance behind them before tentatively settling by the fire.

"And lucky for Sebastian," the boy continued, flashing what was meant to be a friendly smile. "The queen would finally have made good on all her threats and ripped off his head."

Evie cringed into the rocks as Ellanden stifled a shudder—trying very hard not to think how close he'd come to that predicament himself.

"We came to apologize on his behalf," the other boy volunteered. "He meant nothing by it."

...seriously?

Asher glanced at them, positioned between the two groups. "I imagine he's calmed down quite a bit," he said leadingly, casting a pointed glance at his friends. "I also imagine he's nowhere near this place."

The vampires glanced at him with the same puzzled expression before turning back to the others. Although the night was winding down, they were teeming with undeniable energy. Those bursts of adrenaline had always been slower to fade from immortal blood.

"At any rate, we wanted to introduce ourselves," the first boy continued cheerfully. "I'm Daniel, that's Cyrus. Please don't take your earlier encounter as a reflection on the rest of us. We're very excited to be here. Fighting...whoever it is that we're fighting."

The friends stared back in disbelief.

Were they truly so disconnected? Or did they simply not care?

In a flash, Evie remembered the time they'd spent together in the mountain—those listless expressions, the numbers carved into the walls.

Perhaps they simply wanted out of the cave.

"Diana hasn't told you?" Asher asked curiously.

"She told us enough," Daniel replied. "Said it was the latest in a long line of people set out to take over the realm—just like your parents did."

Evie froze perfectly still.

I never thought of it like that.

"She said most of those people tend to come from your bloodline," Cyrus added, glancing at the princess with a little smile. "Families can be tricky...or so I've been told."

Unlikely as it was she found herself smiling in return, recognizing him as the same boy who had left to feed when they were in the mountain. The one who'd come back with an older man.

"I saw you with your companion today," she said tentatively, hoping it was an acceptable topic of conversation. "That must have been an adjustment. Why did you choose him?"

There was a slight shift in momentum as Daniel leaned back with a look of distaste.

"I didn't," Cyrus said briskly. "He picked me."

The plot thickens.

At that point a reckless curiosity took over and the princess ignored her friends' cautionary glances, leaning forward to see him better across the flames.

"He picked you?"

The vampire hesitated before answering. "All the mortals picked their companions...though I was surprised by Samuel," he added suddenly. "I had worried I wouldn't be chosen, as not many would risk a bond with someone so young."

Evie stared in fascination, having never considered such a thing.

"Listen to what you're saying," Daniel said with a hint of irritation. "You were afraid not to have been chosen? They're lucky you're offering such an arrangement at all." His eyes flashed to the rest of them. "No offense intended...we shall honor the command of our queen."

We should turn that into a drinking game.

Cyrus flashed him a look, then nodded along.

"I suppose you're right," he replied softly. "Although it's not an unwelcome feeling...having something to come back to after the fighting is over. *If* we come back."

Evie warmed to him in spite of herself, disarmed by that thoughtful honesty.

"Something to come back to?" Daniel mocked. "Something besides our actual *home*?"

Cyrus pushed to his feet with a sigh, raking back his hair. "Something beyond that hollowed-out rock designed to keep out the rain? Yes, Danny. You have grasped the point perfectly."

Evie stifled a grin as the vampire departed with a murmured goodnight.

In a strange way, it felt very much like several conversations she recalled between Asher and Ellanden—when the fae was being especially stubborn, and the vampire was trying to open his eyes.

Not that Daniel needed help opening his eyes. He was seeing just fine.

A little too fine.

"Do all Fae have wings?"

She turned back to the conversation to see him staring with unnerving attention at Ellanden, fingers drumming against his legs like a kid on a sugar high. The fae had been purposely avoiding the discussion thus far, but found himself trapped with such a direct question.

"Uh...no," he answered hesitantly. "That's just my family."

The vampire nodded slowly, eyes flickering in the light.

"Your family," he echoed. "It's passed through the blood of kings?"

Ellanden tensed, probably at the word blood, then shook his head. "The magic is from my mother's side. I'm only half-Fae."

Daniel opened his mouth to answer, then closed it just as fast. The mere proximity was making his head spin and he involuntarily leaned closer, like a moth to a flame.

"Only half," he repeated in a low murmur, eyes sweeping over every inch. "And yet you are their prince. Is such a thing common? That one could rise to such—"

"*Leave.*"

Both Evie and Ellanden glanced up with a start, to see Asher positioned suddenly in between. They hadn't seen him get up, any more than they'd noticed the way Daniel was leaning dangerously close to the fire—unaware that the tips of his boots had begun to smoke.

The vampire sat back slowly, flushed with shame. "I wasn't going to—"

"If there is even the slightest temptation, then leave." Asher spoke without a hint of compromise, never relaxing his position. "This is not the place where you test those limits."

Evie froze perfectly still, staring with wide eyes.

One hand was braced against the ground while the other was already on the grip of her blade. If it came to a fight, neither would be particularly helpful against the speed of a vampire.

But there wasn't going to be a fight.

No sooner had Asher spoken than Daniel pushed swiftly from the ground and disappeared into the camp. Not bothering to say goodnight. Not daring to glance behind.

The others stared after him, at a loss as to what to say.

"How did you know?" Ellanden finally managed. "How did you know he was going to do anything? I thought we were just—"

"He was keeping you talking," Asher interrupted, lowering his eyes to the fire. "It's an old tactic; I don't think he was even aware of it himself."

How do YOU know it?

Evie flashed him a quick look and decided never to ask.

"You're best in small doses, Landi." She clapped the fae on the back, forcing a reassuring smile. "We've said it for years. Consider this unbiased proof."

He tried to smile in return, but found himself standing instead.

"I should get some rest," he murmured, scanning the camp for his uncle. In the beginning, he had chafed against the required sleeping arrangements. Now they were making a frightful amount of sense. "It will be another long day tomorrow."

The others nodded and bid him goodnight, watching as he headed into the trees. The loose waves of hair made him look younger than he was, somehow more vulnerable to the world around him, and he hadn't gone more than a few steps before he stopped and turned around.

"Thank you...for saying all that."

Asher tensed ever so slightly, meeting his gaze across the fire. "You're my best friend. I'd protect you with my life."

There was a beat of silence. Then the fae nodded, forcing a quick smile.

"Goodnight."

"Goodnight."

He was gone a moment later, leaving the others alone by the dwindling fire. They glanced at each other, then made a conscious effort not to look—remembering their argument on the bluff.

"We should probably get to sleep as well," Asher finally murmured, pulling a blanket from the side of his pack. "You're welcome to have this. Cyrus was right, we don't really get cold—"

"How long can we keep this going?" she interrupted.

The vampire paled, afraid of what she meant. "You mean, the two of—"

"Travelling with a clan of immortal warriors who want to eat our friend."

Asher's face instantly cleared.

"Oh—that." He nodded quickly, trying his best not to look relieved. "We're nearly to the shore... another few days and we should see it."

"And after that?" she pressed. "Ellanden is just one fae, and we're heading towards an entire kingdom of his people. How is that ever going to work? It feels like it's only a matter of time before there's some terrible accident and one of the vampires—"

"They will get used to the temptation," he interrupted gently. "They don't have a choice. Why do you think Diana allowed the others to speak with us tonight? Why do you that think either my father, or Andrei, or Eleazer never stepped in—though they were watching us the entire time?"

They were watching us?

"They need a chance to learn," he continued softly. "To build a tolerance. These things can't happen overnight. And the elders will watch over things in the meantime."

Evie stifled a shudder, picturing the look on Daniel's face.

"...and what if they can't learn?"

It was quiet for a moment, then Asher gave her a coaxing nudge. "I did."

Yes, you did. At only five years old...you somehow learned.

She stared at him without thinking—overwhelmed with feeling. Not a hint of restraint. Then her cheeks flushed and she glanced at the blanket, tracing it self-consciously at the side.

"Are you sure about the blanket? I've seen you get cold before."

He stared back at her, eyes flickering in the light of the fire. "...you could keep me warm?"

She hesitated a moment, then nodded—lying down on the ground. He settled gracefully beside her, hesitating a moment as well before slipping under the blanket with her.

It was difficult at first, a far cry from the way things had been before. Like two statues they lay stiff upon their backs, arms rigid at their sides, staring up at a starry sky clouded with occasional wisps of smoke. The sudden quiet was unbearable. A suffocating stillness that threatened to choke.

Then little by little, it began to get easier. Little by little, they began to get closer.

It happened in fragments. The press of a leg. The brush of a hand. The shy interlacing of fingers beneath the safety of a blanket, where the rest of the world couldn't see.

He pressed a soft kiss to her temple.

She turned her face and began to cry.

Chapter 9

The next few days progressed at a speed the princess wouldn't have thought possible.

Whether it was the reassurance that the journey would soon be over or the trepidation that the fight would soon begin, both sides pushed themselves to new heights of speed. The forest was nothing more than a blur. Any enemies that might have tried to overtake them were left in the dust before they had a chance to mount an attack. By the end of the third evening they were moving so fast that Evie was dizzy with exhaustion, and even the young vampires were struggling to keep pace.

Then, at the dawn of the fourth morning, Ellanden let out a sudden cry. The princess lifted her eyes to see him pointing into the distance, those powerful wings beating at his sides.

He sees the ocean. We're nearly there.

The initial burst of relief cooled to a sudden chill.

From here, the ships will take us to the Dunes. It's the last time I'll be on these shores.

Instant rebellion rose up inside her—stalling momentum and throwing a sudden hitch into her stride. It happened without permission. An involuntary need to protect herself and hide in the woods, where those doomsday fates couldn't find her. Dylan cast a quick glance over his shoulder, wondering if she had tripped, but the others were already slowing down themselves.

"We need to come up with some kind of plan," Katerina called, uncurling her arm from Aidan's neck and swinging her legs to the ground. "The others will be expecting us to return with a company of Talsing warriors. We can't flood into the camp with a clan of vampires instead."

Diana appeared beside her, her two lieutenants standing at her side.

"Was that not the general idea?" she asked lightly, a slight edge to her tone. "Or would you rather we linger in the woods—without the protection of the rest of the army?"

Katerina blushed, but it was Aidan who answered.

"Do not be angry; we must simply be gentle in our approach. The companies of fae should already be within the encampment. Would you risk entering without announcing ourselves, putting the entire clan at the mercy of their archers?"

The queen stared a moment before turning her head.

No, she would not.

A shadow passed over the group as the fae circled above.

"Why are we stopping?" he called impatiently. "We're almost there!"

Dylan waved him down, having shifted back to stand with the others.

"I could go first with Evie," he volunteered. "Tell them what happened to the Carpathians, share our idea for the accords." He paused ever so slightly. "I could tell them about Michael."

The others tensed, then grew quiet.

There had been so much death in the last few weeks, but the hardest ache was that most treasured member of their family who was missing—laid to rest in the place he'd loved the most.

It was a loss that resonated with each of them. It would be felt in the camp as well.

"That's not a bad idea," Aidan said softly. "Cass and Tanya should probably hear that news from you. We can stay here and wait for your return, maybe set up camp among those…"

He trailed off, looking up at the sky.

"Ellanden…what are you doing?"

The prince had started to come down when his uncle called him, but he'd caught himself just as fast—hovering with a strange expression as he stared toward the settlement on the shore.

"There's smoke," he murmured, almost to himself. "Smoke from a funeral pyre."

A chill ran up Evie's spine as she looked towards the sea.

The moment he said the words, she could smell it—drifting along the breeze. It was a specific smell of ash and cedar. One she'd become all too familiar with in recent times.

"They had already burned all the dead," the fae continued, lifting a hand to shield his eyes from the sun. "Why would...?"

A look of horror washed over him, stealing his breath.

"No!"

He let out a scream that carried to the distant seashore, bouncing in echoes along the rocks before losing itself in the waves. His eyes blurred as those mighty wings beat the air around him, tearing through the skies at a speed unmatched by anything that had come before.

"Freya."

Evie said that single word then started running after him. There was nothing else that could touch him so deeply. Nothing else that would cut through him so fast.

The rest of them sprang into pace beside her, even those unfamiliar with the name. Faster and faster they ran, into the salty mist that heralded in the ocean and crossing all the remaining distance between their immortal fellowship and those royal tents. At the end of the tree-line the vampires stopped, leaving only Diana and her generals to continue along with them. But even before they'd made it past the watch tower and through the gates, the princess knew they were already too late.

Ellanden tumbled to the ground just as they reached the base of the pyre, somersaulting violently before rolling to a stop. There was a collective gasp from the people who had gathered, a ring of the most loyal subjects who didn't immediately recognize their own prince.

He was but a fallen angel—bruised and bloodied and covered in dirt. As the wings vanished he clawed himself back to standing, racing forward once again before freezing to a sudden stop.

The girl he loved was lying still on the pyre. Waves of hair arranged beside her, fingers laced across her chest. Her eyes were closed, but there was a freshness and beauty to her face that caught in Evie's heart like a thorn—making her check to see if the girl was still breathing.

But of course she was not.

"No," Ellanden whispered again, shaking as the word tore from his throat.

He took a step closer, then another, staring down at the pyre with a look of such perfect heartbreak the others felt it ache in their own chest. A breath caught inside him, a silent prayer. Then all at once, he picked up the nearest bucket and threw the water onto the flames with a feral cry.

"What are you doing?!" he screamed, grabbing another and dousing the wood. "You would think to *burn* her?! This is nothing more than an enchantment! You would *dare* to lose hope?!"

Those standing closest took a step back, watching through silent tears as the prince let out another cry and kicked violently at the altar. The outer beams fell, one after another, but the thing had been well-built—and while the fire had extinguished, those flames would not lie dormant for long.

Evie shifted back without thinking, hands clapped over her mouth, wracked with silent sobs as she leaned into Asher's chest. It was only then that she saw his parents, watching with twin looks of horror, standing at the front of the crowd. Seth and Cosette were standing just beside them, both of them clad in robes of mourning, gripping each other though they were still as a stone.

"Help me!" Ellanden demanded, a blur of motion in a sea of statues. He grabbed the nearest guard by the sleeve. "Help me with the water! Why was she placed up here in the first place? The wood is too hot and she could still...she could still open her..."

His grip went loose and the man stumbled away from him. The fae hardly registered he was there. With faltering a step, he approached the witch's body—silent tears running down his face.

"...her eyes," he finally managed. "...she could still open her eyes."

Asher quickly passed Evie to her father then ghosted up the steps— cautiously coming up behind his friend and placing a hand on his shoulder. "...Ellanden."

The fae merely stood there, gazing down at the witch.

"How could this have happened? How could she be gone?"

There was a muffled sob as Cosette buried her face in Seth's jacket—shaking violently as he gripped the back of her head. His gaze lifted, crying tears of his own, locking on the princess.

"It happened only a short while before you arrived," he said softly. "She'd been getting worse for days, and her breathing was so shallow. We'd hoped she could hang on until..."

He trailed into silence, unable to say another word.

"Ellanden," Asher pressed softly, "take a breath."

But the fae was in a different world.

He pulled free of the vampire and drifted forward, sinking onto the altar beside the lovely witch. So perfectly she had been positioned, but he pulled her onto his lap, rocking her in heart-breaking silence and pressing teary kisses to the sides of her face.

"Please...don't do this," he breathed, clawing gently at her skin. "*Please*...come back to me."

Asher froze on the platform, casting a helpless look at the rest.

There was nothing he would not do for his friend, but there was nothing he could do to help him now. And in a thousand years, he would never forget the look on Ellanden's face.

"Leave," he finally managed. If he could not fix the problem he would dismiss the crowd, banishing them with a wave of his hand as if he were a great lord himself. "All of you—leave."

The people did as he asked. Fae and shifters, men and the Kreo brethren alike. All of them had gathered to pay respects to the bright-faced girl with whom none of them had spoken more than a few words. The same girl who'd fought beside their monarchs, coaxing one of them into love.

Ellanden didn't notice. His head was bowed.

"You cannot leave me here," he whispered, still rocking her like a child. "It isn't fair to ask, I know that. I left you for ten years. But you cannot do the same to me. I will not survive it."

He kissed her again, eyes blind with tears.

"We were supposed to have forever. I was *made* to love you forever."

...and *that's* when it happened.

In the beginning, it was so slight that no one noticed. There was nothing but a subtle shift in sensation, as if the sun had come out from behind the clouds.

Then there was light.

Painful, beautiful silver light that caught on everything around it. Pouring from the sky like an over-turned vase, spilling over the head of the fae, then further, onto the girl that he loved.

At first it slid over her. All the cracks were sealed, there was no way in. Then like a summer pool shimmering beneath endless sun, it sank abruptly into her body—vanishing without so much as a whisper before making a sudden reappearance...when she opened her eyes.

YES!

The light faded slowly—sharpening and softening the various edges until the smoking altar looked like something out of a dream.

The girl blinked a few times, trying to get her bearings, then swiftly raised her head when she felt the gentle pressure of her lover's arms.

"You're back," she whispered.

Ellanden nodded, then opened his eyes quite suddenly—gazing down without a shred of recognition on his face. His eyes drifted to her lips, trying to convince himself that she'd actually spoken. Then realizing none of that mattered, given that fact that she'd opened her eyes.

"I'm back?" he repeated, then let out a gasp of laughter. "You...*you* are the one who came back. I would have followed you, but there wasn't a need. You came back to me."

He then smiled so sweetly it brought fresh tears.

As his friends and family looked on in wonder he stroked her hair, leaning down with tender kisses, murmuring *my love* again, and again, and again...

The princess took a step back, feeling rather weak.

Since being passed to her father on the platform, he'd been supporting almost all of her weight. She leaned into him now, legs trembling and heart pounding, on the verge of fainting.

"I can't believe it," Cassiel breathed in astonishment, a reflection of that silver glow still shining on his face. "He's only a child...to call down such a blessing...?"

Only a handful of times had such a thing been accomplished. Most were absent from the chronicles of history, preserved only in secret moments of shared devotion that had vanished over time.

But the fae had done such a thing himself only a few years before.

To save the woman he loved. The future mother of his child.

It was only then the princess felt the weight of all those people around her—the ones who'd fled at the request of the vampire but found themselves glancing back mid-step at the edge of the courtyard, their astonished faces awash with that unearthly silver light.

Each one of them had frozen where they'd stopped, staring with scarcely concealed wonder as the Prince of the Fae embraced his beloved...while his fiancée watched from the steps.

"How can we do it?" Evie whispered to no one in particular. "How can I marry him now?"

"You can't," Diana said bluntly. The trio of vampires had frozen like all the rest of them, watching from afar as the world subtly changed. "Haven't you already realized this?"

The princess glanced back in surprise, having forgotten they were even there.

"What do you mean?"

The woman stared at her shell-shocked expression before warming with the hint of a smile.

"There are five kingdoms now, little princess." Her eyes drifted to the curls of smoke still rising from the funeral pyre. "The realm has no use for a marriage that would unite only four."

"IS THAT TRUE?" EVIE demanded for the tenth time. "Is what Diana said true?"

She was standing with the rest of her makeshift family in the largest of the tents, making a concerted effort to lower her voice though the discipline continued to elude her. The only thing that had kept her from shouting at the top of her lungs was Ellanden and Freya curled up together in the corner—lost in their own euphoric bubble, oblivious to the rest of the world.

"I don't know," her mother began diplomatically.

"Then why did she say it?" the princess insisted. "What does it even mean?"

The Damaris queen let out a quiet sigh. "It means, dear one...you will not be marrying Ellanden."

The two glanced over to where the fae was tenderly entwined with his beloved, wiping happy tears from her cheeks and pressing constant kisses to her hair.

Evie's heart warmed at the sight.

"And I'd just grown used to the idea," she said dryly.

Asher was sitting at the far edge of the tent with his aunt—pretending not to be listening, although his entire body had gone very still.

"That's *if* the High Council agrees to the accords," Dylan interjected quietly, rising from his chair to join them. "And the Fae are not certain. Neither are the Kreo."

Evie looked up in surprise.

"But Ellanden already spoke for them," she said defiantly. "He did so for a reason, and he was *well* within his rights—"

"And his parents don't disagree," Katerina inserted smoothly, laying a calming hand on her wrist. "But they serve the people. And their councils feel quite strongly."

...that's understandable.

"That's bullshit!" the princess cried.

Her parents exchanged a long-suffering look.

"Is it?" Dylan challenged softly, glancing towards the newly-resurrected witch before raising a finger to his lips. "The vampires have been a plague upon this land for longer than most people can remember. This *exact* clan slaughtered a Kreo village just a few months past. And the Fae...?"

He trailed off with a worried expression.

"There have already been problems in the camp."

Evie opened her mouth to answer, then found herself staring at the doorway of the tent. In no possible world did she doubt there had already been problems with the vampires. Over the course of their travels with just a *single* fae, the temptation had almost cost Ellanden his life.

And he wasn't even full-blooded.

"Well...how did you stop that before?" she asked petulantly, aware that she'd officially begun to whine. "When you united in the Dunes—vampires and Fae fought side by side."

"My brother stopped it," Aidan answered, sweeping inside the tent. A gust of salt air blew inside with him, fluttering the canvas walls. "Rather, the threat of my brother stopped it."

Evie pursed her lips, trying to imagine the famed vampire for the thousandth time.

"Okay," she began tentatively, "so then why doesn't Diana —"

"Diana is not Merrick," Aidan replied simply. "There is none who is."

Katerina glanced innocently at the ceiling. "That's not *entirely* true..."

But the vampire shot her a look and she fell silent.

"All right, so then what are we supposed to do in the meantime?" Evie demanded, glancing again at the pair in the corner. It didn't look like they would be detaching any time soon, and the rest of the five kingdoms were slowly gathering outside their door.

If there are five kingdoms. If we can reach an agreement with the other four.

Katerina followed her gaze, then pressed a kiss to her cheek.

"We wait for the others to assemble and we come to a decision about the accords."

Waiting and politics. My two favorite things.

"Cheer up," Dylan nudged her with a smile. "It isn't all bad."

"Oh yeah?" she said glumly. "How's that?"

He pulled back the door with a wink.

"...we're at the beach."

EVIE STOOD BY HERSELF on the shoreline, gazing out over the waves.

For the last hour she'd been pacing up and down the sand, listening to the sounds coming from the encampment and watching as sporadic ships pulled into the harbor further down the beach.

There hadn't been any screams—that was a good thing. Aside from an incident the previous evening, all of the vampires had stayed obediently on their side of the camp. Not that the princess was giving much thought to the matter. For despite the growing anticipation, her mind was miles away.

Ten years we were trapped in that cave. Ten years you've been searching for the stone.

Why haven't you already found it?

"You missed quite a spectacle back at camp," Asher called out behind her, stepping onto the beach. "Those teenage vampires were given their first taste of animal blood."

Evie smiled humorlessly, never taking her eyes from the water. "How did that go?"

He pursed his lips as the image floated through his mind. "...it could have gone better."

She let out a sigh and he stepped up behind her, wrapping his arms around her waist.

It had been easier to do those kinds of things since the fae called down the eternal power of some distant star. It had been easier to pretend their relationship was getting back to normal.

Easier...not easy.

"You've been out here a while," he murmured, pressing a kiss to the back of her head. "Is there something in particular on your mind?"

She sighed again, leaning back into his chest.

"Why isn't Kaleb just flying to the Dunes? A regular-sized dragon could never manage the journey, but he's *much* bigger than that. Why not just fly there and fulfill the prophecy himself?"

Asher tensed involuntarily, then shrugged. "Maybe he already has the stone."

She shook her head. "He doesn't. I would feel it."

The vampire glanced at the top of her head but didn't contest it. He was growing frightfully aware of the fact that his girlfriend had a connection to this man that others did not.

It gave him nightmares. It drove her to the beach.

What are you waiting for...?

"And take a look at *these* two love-birds!"

They glanced around as Freya and Ellanden strolled towards them across the sand, moving at a far slower pace than usual—most likely because they were still ridiculously intertwined.

The fae kissed the side of her neck, flashing a roguish grin.

"When there are pressing affairs of state? You two should be ashamed."

Asher rolled his eyes with a grin as Evie laughed in spite of herself.

The fae had only brought his witch back from the dead the previous morning, but already there had been an inalterable shift. No longer was he willing to play along with his council's idea of matrimony. No longer was he willing to tolerate the faintest whisper from anyone else. Truth be told, a part of him would have welcomed the challenge just so he could rage—just so he could fight.

...not that he was capable of physically separating himself from the witch.

"They need guidance, darling." Freya ran a finger along his cheek, leaning back into his arms with a grin. "Not everyone can be as gifted a politician as you."

"Is *that* what you did before?" Asher lifted his eyebrows. "Politics?"

The fae shrugged. "My version of it."

The two men shared a quick look, then glanced away with matching grins.

After seeing the fae throw his body onto a smoking funeral pyre, the vampire's perspective had y changed inalterablas well. The past grievances had been laid permanently to rest—with *relief*.

He'd missed his friend.

"It's getting busy out there," Ellanden continued, cocking his head towards the camp. "Petra arrived this morning—the warriors of Talsing are camped beside the Fae."

"How many came?" Evie asked curiously.

"Almost four hundred. More than she'd promised."

Freya ignored all talk of military endeavors, just as she'd done since the moment she opened her eyes and discovered she'd almost been set on fire. But she did perk up with sudden interest at the ships mooring in the harbor, standing on the fae's boots for a better view.

"Are those your ships?" she asked excitedly. "The ones from Taviel?"

Ellanden hitched her onto his shoulders for a higher perch.

"Some of them," he replied, pointing a bit further. "But *those* are the real prize—they're called *sirizat*. Immortal war ships from the olden days."

At that point, Evie and Asher perked up as well.

"Really?" Asher asked excitedly. "Have you ever sailed on one before?"

The fae shook his head.

"I've only seen them in paintings." He cast a sideways glance at his eager friends. "But seeing as they technically belong to my father...shall we take a look?"

With a lot more enthusiasm than any of them had felt the last few weeks, the four friends hurried across the sand—fast as their legs could take them. The warriors of the Fae, as well as Kreo and shifters from different parts of the realm, were busy loading cargo. However, each of them bowed their heads with respect as the young royals rushed past, staring after them long after the fact.

"Good morning!" Ellanden called as they neared one of the warships. "I didn't see you here yesterday—did you just get into port?"

A windswept fae who'd been coiling a length of rope dropped it immediately on the deck, lowering his eyes and pressing a fist to the opposite shoulder in acknowledgment.

"Yes, Highness. Lord Aerin commands this vessel and two others."

Evie watched him curiously, trying to place the name.

"He's one of their most respected generals," Asher murmured in her ear. "He's got a seat on the High Council, and commands several companies of archers famed for their unparalleled skill."

"I remember that," she whispered back. "But didn't he...?" She trailed off, flashing a quick look at the sailor. "Wasn't there some tragedy with his men in the Western Mountains?"

"You are correct, Your Highness," the fae interrupted quietly, having overheard the entire secret conversation. "I'm afraid he is famed for that as well."

She shook her head incredulously, having visited the range before.

"But I've seen those peaks. What could have even reached them?"

The fae flashed a sad smile.

"Giants," he said simply.

Needless to say, that was the end of her questions.

"I would be happy to give you a tour, my lord," the fae continued, suppressing a smile as his eyes swept over the young prince and his eager friends. "Or perhaps you would like to wander."

Ellanden flushed, but couldn't suppress a grin.

"Actually, I was thinking—"

"Your Grace."

The friends turned as another fae swept suddenly across the deck, sinking into a low bow with the tips of his fingers pressed together. Five or six others mimicked the deference behind him, those bright immortal eyes lowered in respectful submission to the deck.

"It is an answer to many prayers to see you again," the fae murmured, crossing himself in a gesture the princess had never seen. "The lights in the citadel were lit every day until your return."

Ellanden tensed in surprise, then motioned for them to rise—murmuring some words in his native tongue that brought a smile to every face. When they left, silence lingered in their wake.

"I keep forgetting there are people who haven't seen you yet," Asher murmured.

Freya nodded thoughtfully, while Evie's face screwed into a sudden frown.

"The lights were kept burning every day?" she asked incredulously. "For *ten* years?"

Ellanden shrugged casually, though his eyes followed the man. "I'm rather well-liked."

There was a beat.

"But what if you had never come home?" she pressed, unable to let it go. "What if you'd died or something? They'd just keep going through candles? How many candles *is* that—"

Asher clapped a hand over her mouth.

"Can you dwell less on the practicality and more on the degree to which I am adored?" the prince demanded, levelling her with a haughty glare. "I should build myself a statue. Let them all gather around it and sing songs of my return..."

Freya clapped a hand over *his* mouth.

Then the friends continued their exploration of the ship.

Considering the size, it didn't take long. Because while the vessel was certainly impressive, carved of smooth white wood and ivory, there was just one thing they *really* wanted to see.

There it is...the captain's wheel.

Evie spotted it first. Leaving the rest of them behind as she bolted across the deck and grabbed hold, she struck an obligatory pose while the others clapped their hands in sarcastic applause.

"You're being a child," Ellanden reprimanded before shoving her aside. "It's my turn." The same fevered enthusiasm swept over him like a drug, transforming him from prince to pirate before their very eyes. "I love it," he declared with a boyish grin. "I'm stealing it for myself."

Asher leapt onto the platform behind him. "You have enough nice things. Give it to me—a gift to repair our broken friendship."

The fae chuckled before turning to him abruptly. "Done."

There was a pause.

"...*what?*"

"*Say that again?*"

"*Yeah—what?*"

"Not this particular ship," Ellanden amended, "as it already belongs to Lord Aerin. But I will give you another. I agreed to marry your girlfriend...a ship is the least I can do."

The vampire stared at him, stunned.

In moments like this it was always hard to tell whether the fae was being serious. He had a tendency of blending reality and whim. But there was nothing but honest sincerity in his eyes.

"You truly mean that?" Freya asked incredulously, torn between amusement and utter exasperation. "You're giving him a ship?"

The fae shrugged his shoulders. "Seems fair."

Evie bit the inside of her lip, eyes flashing with rage.

"Let me get this straight," she began in a dangerous tone, "because Ellanden agreed to marry me even though the idea made both of us physically sick...he's atoning with a ship?"

There was a pointed pause.

"Are you saying I'm worth the value of a ship?"

Asher shot her a quick look, then chose not to answer the question directly. He looked at the ship instead, running the tip of his finger along the wheel.

"...seems fair."

Unbelievable!

She threw up her hands in disgust, preparing several choice profanities to let them know how she felt on the subject, but before she could start a horn sounded in the distance and the friends lifted their eyes. Four separate battalions were making their way out of the forest and into the camp. Two were of Belarian shifters, another was from the High Kingdom, and the fourth...?

"Are those warlocks?" Evie asked in surprise.

Since her disastrous attempt at a wedding, warlocks had been generally shunned by the rest of the royal army. It wasn't technically their fault, they simply belonged to a group of people who tended to be swayed either way. Kaleb had many warlocks fighting with him as well.

They were *terribly* effective.

"It's a good thing," Asher replied after a moment's hesitation. He remembered all too well his last encounter with a warlock. The memory woke him up in the night. "Warlocks are powerful, and that many will bolster our numbers. At any rate, they should have a say in the accords."

Evie frowned to herself, thinking back to the pair of teenage warlocks they'd seen practicing magic at the Kreo camp. Just a few hours later they'd been torn to pieces.

Are you sure about that?

"When is the High Council meeting?" Freya asked, twisting round to look up at Ellanden.

"Tonight," he said flippantly, pressing a kiss to the tip of her nose. "I care not. No matter what they decide...everything is going to be fine."

The others smiled along with him, wanting very much to believe that.

But they weren't sure it was true.

"An accord to unify the realm," Freya murmured thoughtfully, fluttering her fingers over her lips. A second later she lit up with excitement as she looked at two boys. "Hear me out...why don't *you two* get married?"

Asher and Ellanden glanced at each other then froze.

"What?"

"What?"

"It makes perfect sense," Evie chimed in eagerly, liking the idea even more now that she'd been valued at the same price as a ship. "Together you represent the vampires, the Fae, and the Kreo! Three out of the five kingdoms—that's not bad!"

The men glared stiffly, then headed back inside.

"Come on—at least consider it!" Freya giggled, running after them.

Evie was right on her heels. "You could adopt me and Cosette!"

Chapter 10

The friends spent the rest of the day gleefully ignoring the apocalyptic events stirring inside the camp, delighting in each other's company instead.

It had been too long that they'd been separated, this from a group of people who'd bonded together hard and fast. Freya soon went inside to sleep—as she repeatedly told the rest of them, it wasn't easy coming back from the dead. But Seth and Cosette took her place, wandering with the others along the shoreline, sneaking inside for food, then slipping away unchallenged once again.

"I will never understand royal life," Seth remarked, popping a honeyed grape into his mouth as they strolled along the wet sand. "The other day I saw a knight of the High Kingdom stay bent at the waist for almost ten full minutes because the lord he was bowing to hadn't noticed him, yet the princes and princesses of the land are allowed to nick food from the kitchens like common thieves."

"No one *allowed* us," Evie said authoritatively, though some wiser part of her suspected this wasn't true. "We made off with this stuff through nothing but cunning and raw skill."

"The kitchen maid actually bowed as you crept past," Cosette inserted tentatively.

"The others are in training," Seth continued, "preparing for battle, sharpening blades—yet we can do this." He kicked at the sand, misting it into the air. "There is no sense to any of it."

"We *shouldn't* be doing this," Asher replied, almost more conscious of the rules than the others. "I imagine the only reason they aren't calling us back is because…because of the…"

The rest of them fell silent, but Ellanden flashed a bright smile.

"Did something happen?"

There was a tittering of laughter as they moved past it as one.

The conversation had been like that for a while, ebbing and flowing like the movement of the tides. Too much had happened in too condensed a time to dwell on any particular thing, no matter how extraordinary, and yet they were all aware the most pivotal moments were still coming.

Somewhere across that expanse of sea, the rolling Dunes were waiting. And somewhere in all that sand was a prophesized stone. One that could either bring salvation to the people working frantically in the camp behind them...or sentence them all to a grisly and premature death.

Hence the avoidance. And the grapes.

"I don't know why you're listening to Asher anyway," Cosette continued, smiling with delight as the foamy surf rushed over her toes. "He belongs to no royal house. That protocol you lament doesn't cage him the way it does the rest of us."

Seth nudged her with a grin. "Because you were so caged by royal protocol, working on that fishing trawler..."

The others laughed, but Evie stopped in her tracks—white as a ghost.

She didn't know why she hadn't thought of it earlier. She didn't know why some part of her had genuinely believed that things might be fine. But despite the strong probability that she would no longer be forced to marry Ellanden, that didn't mean Asher was a suitable candidate either.

His father had abdicated all authority to Diana. Even if the accords were successful and the vampires were to gain official recognition as one of the five kingdoms, even if the queen were to tire of the crown and appoint a successor—it would be someone of her choosing, not the son of an old friend. Melkins had said it himself. The laws were set, old as time. A prince had to marry a princess.

And no matter which way the dice fell...Asher was no prince.

"Evie? You coming?"

She glanced up to see the others staring curiously at her a bit farther up the beach, completely oblivious to the quiet heartbreak that had frozen her to the spot. An aching tension pulsed deep in her chest, like the tightening of a cord. But she flashed a quick smile and hurried to join them.

It doesn't matter anyway. Asher can marry whomever he likes. I'll soon be dead.

It was another of those insurmountable things the friends were refusing to talk about.

One that was getting harder and harder to ignore.

"Jokes aside," Seth pressed curiously, still holding Cosette's hand. "I see no flowers in that camp, only arrows and blades. The two of you are no longer getting married?"

"We can't," Ellanden said shortly. "It's that simple—we can't."

...can't we?

"My father wasn't so certain," Evie said hesitantly, unwilling to press in case she received an answer she didn't like. "He thought it depended on certain variables."

"Then *your* father should have asked *my* father," the fae replied smugly. "When one of the Fair Folk surrenders a piece of their heart, that love is bound forever. The Council would not *possibly* force me to marry. It stands directly opposed to everything our people believe."

The prince had always been convincing, enough so that his friends had learned to tread carefully and look for a bluff. But the magnitude of what had happened atop the funeral pyre couldn't be ignored, and in spite of herself the princess found herself glancing at Asher.

The vampire had been perfectly silent every time the subject arose, lowering his eyes carefully to the ground as he listened to what the others had to say. He had been dubious at first, then trepidatious. But for the first time it looked as though he was beginning to hope.

"Wasn't it also illegal?" Seth asked innocently.

That careful silence shattered as the others broke into soft laughter—glancing back towards the remains of the pyre. It had been all but dismantled, only the foundation was still intact.

Yes it was forbidden, what the fae had done. Unforgivable some might say, considering that he had called upon the ancient powers on behalf of an outsider. Evie hadn't been alive when a similar discretion had been made atop the roof of her childhood home, but having grown up under the stern gaze of Leonor—head of the Fae's Council—she was guessing it hadn't gone over well.

Of course, it helped a great deal that Tanya had shortly after given birth to Ellanden. The Council could hardly begrudge the woman her life—not when she was carrying the crown prince.

"Uh...yes, *technically*," Ellanden admitted, glancing not at the pyre but towards a particular tent. "But I happen to know the king. I also happen to know he broke the same law himself."

It was perhaps the greatest difficulty Cassiel had encountered upon becoming a father: finding the credibility to discipline his son for sins he'd frequently committed himself.

Dylan and Katerina had the same problem.

"Why all this talk of marriage?" Ellanden asked with sudden suspicion. "Is that why you became Evie's beta? To make yourself eligible to marry Cosette?"

The little princess' eyes widened in horror as she quickly reclaimed her hand.

"Would you stop talking?" she hissed. "He wasn't thinking anything of the sort—"

"It will never happen," Ellanden said plainly—oblivious as ever to the effect his casual words were having. "The Fae care not for the politics of wolves. You were a cutthroat and a thief—"

"Stealing from a bunch of drunks so my little sisters didn't go hungry?" Seth interrupted viciously, eyes flashing with quiet rage. "I sleep just fine at night, thanks."

"Enough," Ellanden said irritably, avoiding the vampire's chiding look. "Don't make this about anything other than the fact that I don't like you. I happen to be very fond of your sisters."

They continued walking in silence before the fae spoke up again.

"But the fact remains—"

"Are you serious, Ellanden?!"

"...punch you right in the throat..."

"Shut the hell up!"

"The fact remains," he continued, raising his voice, "in order for you to stand a chance you'd need to be something more than a beta."

"By the gods, Ellanden," Asher muttered beneath his breath. "Sometimes—"

"You know I'm right," the fae interrupted hotly, continuing down the sand without a hint of concern. "It's a good thing we're coming up on a time of battle."

Seth flexed his hands, resisting the urge to drown the fae beneath the waves.

"Why?" he muttered. "Because I might die and solve everyone the political headache?"

The prince glanced over his shoulder, eyes dancing with the hint of a smile. "Because there is no greater way to prove oneself," he said quietly. "No greater way to swiftly make your up the ranks."

The others stared at the back of his head in surprise. Cosette released the handle of her blade, and even Seth forgot his eternal hatred of the fae—looking profoundly touched.

...then *profoundly* embarrassed.

"If we make it through this, I would like to send you to a healer," he murmured, falling into step beside Ellanden. "Someone needs to properly examine what's happening inside your head."

Ellanden nodded absentmindedly, kicking at the sand. "Many have tried..."

The others hurried to catch up, then continued their endless walk—pacing from one end of the camp to the next before coming to a sudden pause as a metallic clattering rang over the shore.

It's the blacksmiths, Evie realized. *They're using the time to forge new weapons.*

"So the others are preparing to fight Kaleb's army," Cosette began softly, "but what of the stone? While they fight...we'll be searching the Dunes?"

Asher shook his head, frowning with concern. "I don't yet know. I think they're hoping to kill him before that's necessary."

...that's not how prophecies work.

Evie stared a moment longer, showers of sparks reflecting in her eyes. Then she turned to Ellanden, determined to lighten the mood. "I thought *you* were supposed to marry Cosette."

The fae went blank. "...what?"

"You made a promise to that giant. You were going to marry her in a birdcage."

There was a split second of silence, then each of them burst out laughing once again. The vampire and the fae continued striding down the beach—Cosette wedged inescapably between them—but the two shifters hung back, standing side by side.

"Royal protocol..." Evie finally quoted, casting him a faint smile. "Does this mean you're officially disenchanted? Done with the glamor of royal life?"

The shifter smiled in return, folding his arms across his chest. "I've simply realized there is no glamor at all." His eyes flickered to the camp as the smile faded slowly from his face. "They're just people. Scared, brave, ordinary people."

Evie tilted her head, following his gaze. "Not so different from your village," she murmured, remembering the tight-knit group she'd met in in the woods. "Do you ever want to go back?"

"Every day," he said without pause, staring towards the mountains. Then his eyes travelled a bit further, to the lovely fae walking along the beach. "But my love is here, and my friends are here. My entire life seems to have led me to this moment."

He flashed a quick smile then headed after them.

"How could I turn back?"

The princess stared after him before her gaze drifted to distant clouds on the horizon.

...exactly.

TIMES OF PARTICULAR stress had a way of bringing out the best in people. Past friendships and alliances were made new, old prejudices and grudges dimmed beneath a stronger light. Like a stone kept long underwater, all the superfluous edges were worn away to reveal something smooth and elemental. Free from the barbs and distractions that slowed things down. It was the purest form of fellowship, a unification to strip away the baggage and reveal the true potential of one's character.

...in theory.

"It is OUT of the question!"

Leonor stood in the middle of the Council tent, a company of fae beside him, a trio of vampires in front of him, abandoning all grace and poise as he shouted at the top of his lungs.

"We have already gathered here to fight against one enemy! I will not place our people in further jeopardy by inviting another to walk straight through the gates!"

The rest of the camp had been apprehensive for the duration of the day, wondering what would happen in the nightly discussion.

Each ventured their own whispered opinion, whilst simultaneously begrudging that it would be hours longer before they knew the decision for themselves.

They had been wrong. The 'discussion' could be heard quite clearly.

"I say again—it is out of the question!"

The princess cringed as the fae's voice shook the tent, rattling each person inside before losing itself in the night air. She had never heard him so angry. Not even when she and Asher had cut Ellanden's hair on his fifth birthday. Never once had she heard him yell.

"Haven't we done this once before?" Dylan muttered, standing a deliberate distance from the commotion. "I'm having the strangest feeling of déjà vu..."

Aidan glanced at him testily, keeping a similar distance. "You could always *help*."

"...after you."

It had been difficult enough to explain why a clan of vampires was camped outside in the forest. The proposal that they be allowed a seat at the table was a step too far. It had been a toss-up as to which of the kingdoms would protest the loudest, but the Fae were quickly taking the lead.

"My lord," Leonor said pointedly, finding Cassiel in the crowd, "you cannot *possibly* condone such recklessness. We are on the eve of battle. We should dispense with this nonsense and prepare!"

Cassiel shifted uneasily, making a quick sweep of the room.

Like the other monarchs, he was standing near the back—letting the various councils take the floor and debate to their hearts' content. But the debate had turned into nothing more than a verbalistic slaughter, the vampires were losing patience, and tempers were wearing thin.

"You're right," he said softly, "we are on the eve of battle. And it's a battle that I intend to win." He paused ever so slightly before finishing, "I'm not sure that is possible without the clan."

A fresh commotion swept over the tent as Leonor's face went cold.

"You heard what happened at the monastery," Katerina reasoned, raising her voice to be heard above the crowd, "a single battle in the mountains—but it will change the realm for decades to come. I'm not saying that things have always been easy between us, or that there are things for which both sides don't need to atone. But in order to do such a thing, we must—"

"Things for which *both* sides need to atone?" a Belarian general interrupted in surprise. It was one of the only forums in which he could parley directly with his queen, but he had no qualms doing so now. "How many towns were overrun with vampires in the last ten years? How many times were we forced to defend our territory, to drive them back? Belaria is *soaked* in the blood of their victims!"

"How many clans were exterminated?" Diana asked in a soft voice. Although she had been the target of countless attacks, she'd only spoken a handful of times. "How many of my own people were slaughtered by royal command?"

She lifted her eyes, staring calmly at the general.

"Or perhaps you do not count them. Because we are not people in your eyes—merely animals to be hunted down for sport."

Aidan made a compulsive movement towards them, but caught himself just as fast. For as long as he'd been the one arbitrating this very discussion, it had progressed to a place beyond his stewardship. He had brought the people to the table. What happened next was out of his hands.

"Take a seat, Matthias," Dylan commanded quietly, flashing the general a look.

The man obeyed immediately, but four more sprang up to take his place. A dozen new voices rang out in the tent—each more vengeful and adamant than the last.

In an act of desperation, Evie turned to the woman at her side.

Of all the people in the world...my hopes fall upon Miranda Cartwright.

"Do something," she hissed. "You are the head of my mother's council, and her wishes are clear. Do something to make our position known."

The councilwoman studied her a moment before turning back to the rest.

"Your mother's wishes and the position of *this* Council are not always the same," she said quietly. "I will follow her commands to the letter, but this meeting was a call for debate. I must advocate the *Council's* position until the very moment that command is given."

Evie flashed a secret glare. "And what is the Council's position, then?"

The woman paused again, weighing her words carefully.

"That sometimes it is more important to keep an old ally than to make a new." Her gaze drifted through the crowd, coming to rest upon Leonor. "The Kingdom of the Fae is revered for a reason. They are an ancient people who have long safeguarded this realm, often at their own peril. I have nothing but respect for their opinion. If they are against this accord, I will honor their wishes."

Evie looked at her again, trying to hide her surprise.

Sometimes I forget she's not actually terrible.

She considered this for a moment.

...it makes her even worse.

A fresh chorus of descent rang out, and she let out a soft sigh.

For the better part of an hour, they'd been standing in the tent with not a hint of progress to be seen. The men stood with their council. The shifters and Kreo lamented their dead. The fae continued shouting as the vampires stood their ground—accepting each censure and accusation without flinching. On the surface, they were nothing but calm. But Evie had a terrible suspicion that they were taking notes, memorizing the names and faces of everyone who spoke against them.

To save for a rainy day...

"Your prince has already made the decision," Diana finally interrupted, losing what remained of her patience. "Had he not granted his permission, we would not have travelled all this way."

The room quieted immediately as fifty pairs of eyes settled on the teenage fae. He'd been standing along the edge of the tent with his parents, and looked mortified to be called upon now.

He shot Diana a look of betrayal, then stepped reluctantly towards the center.

"She's telling the truth," he said quietly, almost shyly. "I spoke on my parents' behalf and gave the clan my word. And I would do it again," he said a little stronger. "They have already laid waste to the Carpathian army as nothing more than a show of good faith. We *need* them fighting beside us. Is it not the dream of every person in this room to unify the realm?"

Cassiel's eyes shone with pride, but Leonor stepped between them.

"You mean well, dear one, but that is a dream that died long ago."

"Is it?" Aidan challenged abruptly, stepping forward as well. "Because I seem to remember a similar group of people coming together in a place such as this, agreeing to set aside their differences and make the world a better place than it was before. A dream that took all *five* kingdoms."

Leonor's expression softened, but he didn't relent.

"I do not cherish the memory of your brother, Aidan. But I *am* grateful for what Merrick did. Without his aid, every person in this room would have been lost in the Dunes."

He came to a pause, glancing around the tent.

"But what have the vampires done since? Time and time again, we find ourselves in this position—them standing before us like errant school children, offering a gesture of help so that we might forget their past sins. You wish to safeguard the future? We ought to kill them where they stand. Avenge the blood of all those sisters and brothers who cry out for it from beyond the grave."

There was a cry of assent from the crowd, but it was echoed almost immediately by a chilling hiss from the distant forest. The vampires had not been permitted inside the encampment but could hear the argument just as well as those listening on the beach.

Tensions were rising, people were reaching discreetly for blades. What had started as a heated discussion could have ended in tragedy. But then something very strange happened.

"I understand."

Diana left those standing beside her and walked slowly to the center of the room, weaving through all those silenced voices of dissent until she and Leonor were eye to eye.

"I understand your anger," she said softly. "And I understand the desire for revenge. Just as I understand that such an alliance could never be perfect. For in a thousand years, my people will never escape the craving for your blood. And your people will never stop fearing that hunger."

She stared at him a moment, then shook her head with a pensive sigh.

"Were there ever two such peoples as different as ours?" she murmured. "Creatures of dark and light." A faint smile warmed the edges of her face. "I am asking you to find something in between."

She did not ask for such a thing directly, nor did she wait for his reply. It was a decision that had already been made in the hollow of a mountain, far away from the distant shore.

"Whether or not you accept our alliance...my people will fight this enemy. Even if such a venture is hopelessly outnumbered. Even if such a thing means our death. I have brought us here to stand for something that will outlive us all. I only ask that we stand together."

Every voice in the room fell silent. Every hand went loose upon their blades.

There was a suspended moment when Evie was sure that eternal doubt had lifted, when she looked around the room and saw the same irrepressible hope she'd learned from her uncle reflected in a sea of new and uncertain eyes. For a suspended moment, she saw a glimpse of things to come.

But such moments are like candles in the breeze, extinguished just as quickly.

"Then you will perish," Leonor said softly. "There is some justice in that, I suppose."

"WAIT!"

The meeting ended as abruptly as it had begun—not with a resolution but with the sudden departure of all parties, until only the vampires remained. The young monarchs had stayed with them, trying to restore balance, trying to keep even a hint of that hope alive. But Ellanden had raced outside after Leonor, and his friends were running close behind.

"Leo—*wait!*"

The elder paused in his tracks then turned. In all his countless years, the young prince had been the only person permitted to call him such a thing. He saw him now just as he'd been as a boy, with the wind in his hair, the light in his eyes, and the flush of adventure in his cheeks.

"You cannot be serious," Ellanden panted, coming to a breathless stop. "You heard what Diana said in there. You heard her promise. She's going to fight—we cannot let her fight alone!"

The councilman stared back at him, then let out a tired sigh.

"Yes, I heard what she said," he answered softly. "And I've heard such a thing before." He shook his head, gazing out towards the darkened sea. "Since the dawn of time, vampires have been making such promises. In all those years, not a single promise hasn't been broken by the spilling of innocent blood."

"But this time could be different," Ellanden insisted, grabbing his arm when he started to walk away. "You didn't see the home they built. You didn't see their companions."

A crowd had begun to gather, one made of mortals and immortals alike.

Such a talk shouldn't be had on a public beach, but while the elder statesman was keenly aware of it the young prince was caught in a wave of emotion—speaking without thought.

"That is enough, Ellanden. I've made up my mind."

"But you need to *listen*—"

Asher ran up behind him, pulling him back.

"Do not let your temper get the better of you," he cautioned under his breath. "He isn't wrong to be skeptical, and people are starting to stare."

Perhaps it was the sight of a vampire whispering persuasions into the fae's ear. Perhaps it was the fact that the councilman had spent the last weeks making preparations to bury even more friends. But he found himself turning on Asher in absolute rage. A boy he'd known as a child.

"It's no wonder you say such things," he snapped. "We let that soulless creature into the palace and it's poisoned you since it arrived. I should have done a better job of protecting you."

Asher went pale and took a step back, while Ellanden lifted his head in shock.

"What are you...?" He trailed off in astonishment. "You can't be talking about Asher."

"You've always been too close to that vampire—"

A fist struck him in the face.

Holy crap!

Evie's hands flew to her mouth as the crowd behind her fell instantly silent. At the same time, the tent flew open and those who'd been speaking raced outside.

Asher was white as a sheet, but Ellanden's eyes were blazing.

"Does anyone else have something to say about my friend?"

He threw an arm around the vampire's shoulder, challenging the rest of the crowd. At a glance it looked almost casual, but there was something deliberate in the way he was standing. Hair swept back, neck carelessly exposed. At this point, Evie wasn't sure whether it was intentional.

But the point was clear.

Not a word was spoken on the shoreline. Not a word was spoken in the trees. Just a few seconds later everyone dispersed without prompting, leaving only a handful on the beach.

Leonor gave the prince a long look before turning on his heel.

Cassiel stood a moment longer before taking off after him.

In the end, only the friends remained—each of them as astonished as the moment it had happened, unable to understand how anyone else had the wherewithal to leave.

Asher was perfectly frozen, standing beneath the fae's arm. "You shouldn't have done that."

Ellanden stared down the beach, the nightly fires flickering in his eyes. "...but I did."

Chapter 11

Evie didn't go back to her parents' tent that night. She went to Asher's instead.

She had no idea what she was going to say to him. At several points, she'd almost chickened out and headed right back across the sand. Then the image of his face drifted through her mind.

I still can't believe that happened. I can't believe Leonor said all that.

...I can't believe Ellanden punched the idiot, too.

The night had been difficult enough for the young vampire, listening to hours upon hours of his childhood protectors calling for the death of his people. Replacing the idea of an alliance with a vengeful cry for blood. At several points along the way she'd cast him a secret look, wondering how he was taking it. Wondering why his father didn't discreetly force him to leave.

But the two men had stood in silence, listening to the rounds of heated voices with the same distant expression in their eyes. Distant and sad. Although the night had ended quite differently.

What could he be thinking? she wondered nervously, weaving her way through the tents until she found the correct one. *How could he possibly—*

But she wasn't the only one who'd gone to check on the vampire. The fae was already inside.

Not that he was particularly helping matters...

"—should have guessed Diana would put me on the spot like that. Just goes to show, no act of kindness ever goes unpunished. Fortunately, I'm a gifted public speaker and I managed to steer things back on course, *again*, before those blasted shifters piped up and ruined everything—"

The fae had clearly been speaking for a while, and he'd chosen to do so from the comfort of Asher's own bed. The vampire was standing in the corner, watching as his friend tossed a dagger absentmindedly into the air, catching it by the tip as he continued to monologue.

"—exact same thing as at the monastery, and I don't care what Uncle Dylan says, I don't agree that it *does* help things just because we're on a beach. If anything, it adds a kind of manic backdrop that makes everything feel unnecessarily time-sensitive and heightened and..."

The fae finally came to a pause, glancing towards the corner.

"What's the matter with you? You haven't said more than three words since I arrived."

Evie lifted a palm to her forehead, while Asher made a habitual prayer for patience. For years, it had been the bulk of his communication with the heavenly spirits.

He'd yet to receive a satisfactory reply.

"I feel like you should be a bit more concerned with my feelings."

"I feel like you should be a bit more concerned with my hand," the prince countered, flexing his fingers. "We're about to head into battle. How am I supposed to grip a blade?"

He lifted his eyes with a grin, only to see Asher's remote expression.

"Why are you making light of this?" he asked softly. "Ever since Freya came back, you've been acting as though the world's problems have been solved and there's no reason not to smile. I understand your relief. If it had been Everly on that pyre..." He trailed off, unable to finish. "But we are on the brink of something, Ellanden. Something that's bigger than all of us, and my people will be left to face it on their own. You heard the crowd, calling for the death of all vampires—"

"Exactly," Ellanden interrupted, sitting upright on the bed. "The death of *all* vampires. As if there aren't levels of divergence. As if you're all cut from the same cloth."

There was as pause.

"...but we are."

"You're not."

"Yes, we are," Asher insisted with sudden vehemence, as if it was a point of distinction he'd long wanted to make. "We are all vampires, Ellanden. You should have seen those who resided in the mountain. They were exactly like me—"

"I saw those outside the mountain. They were nothing like you."

"You're wrong."

"Asher, they were nothing—"

"You accuse the Council of ignorance, of being deliberately blind to the truth—but since we were children you've done the same to me. Labelling me as some kind of exception, as though it would make it more palatable that I'd been allowed into your home."

The fae stood up slowly, a strange expression on his face. "Why are you speaking like this?"

"Because you're wrong!" Asher cried. "I am *exactly* like those vampires! They are my people! We *are* cut from the same cloth. They look like me, move like me, have all the same impulses—"

"You don't act on them," Ellanden cut in quickly, "and that's *precisely* the kind of divergence of which I speak. We all have impulses. You think I don't have them myself?"

"Not to kill people."

"*Often* to kill people."

"Do not make jokes!" Asher cried in exasperation. "This is serious!"

A sudden silence fell over the room—holding them both in perfect stillness. It was exactly the same as back in the Council tent. Only, for whatever reason, this one felt more serious.

It wasn't between enemies. It was between friends.

"They are what they are," the vampire said softly. "They are what they were born to be. And the rest of the world, including all *your* people...would kill them for it. If my father hadn't taken me when I was young, I would have grown up right there alongside them. Thinking the same things, doing the same things. If you and I hadn't grown up as friends, we might have met on opposite ends of a sword. I'd be just another vampire and you would kill me for it. It's only through a quirk of fate we ended up on the same side. It's probably the reason my father was slow to saddle that horse."

Ellanden stood there in silence, looking as though he'd been struck. His lips were slightly parted, but the ground had shaken so violently he couldn't think of a single thing to say.

"I believe your father is a good man," he finally answered, quiet as a grave. "I believe he came as soon as he could. And for what it's worth, Asher...I think you believe that, too."

The vampire's wish had come true. The fae was no longer smiling.

It looked as though there was a good chance he would never smile again.

"You chide me for speaking as though you are different from the rest of them, for not lapsing into generalizations like I'm living in some kind of denial...but I *know* you, Asher. Since we were children, you've walked around with the inherited guilt of an entire race of people. Punishing yourself and limiting yourself for crimes you didn't commit."

He took a step closer, eyes glowing in the light of the candles.

"Everything they were saying in the tent tonight, everything that happened on the beach in those moments after...none of it is your fault—"

"My *fault*," Asher quoted in exasperation. "You speak as though being born a vampire is something that happened to me. Like a curse or an illness. You shy away from generalizations because you see nothing but evil in the fundamental essence of *what I am*. I often address you not as a person but as a Fae. It doesn't bother you. You take pride in what you are. But all my life you've tried to shield me, to mislabel me, as though I could not possibly have pride just the same."

His fangs came down, glinting.

"This is what I am, Ellanden. There is nothing wrong in it."

The fae lowered his eyes to the ground, as if he was having trouble looking at them straight on. He searched a moment for the right words, weighing each one with utmost care.

"Yes, it's what you are. And I see nothing inherently evil in being born a vampire. But you must admit there's... After everything that's happened, we haven't ever..."

Asher took a step closer, forcing him to meet his gaze.

"What?" he demanded. "Just say it!"

"I refuse to be frightened of my best friend!"

The two stood in perfect silence in the center of the room, without moving, without even breathing. There were just inches between them, yet in a terrible way they'd never felt further apart.

"There were times on this journey when I was truly afraid of you, Asher. Times I realized I had never allowed myself to see precisely what you are. You almost *killed* me. It almost *broke* us."

Ellanden paused, searching for breath.

"No one has stood more of a chance than you and me. We grew up as brothers. You're asking the realm to welcome a new alliance, but if the two of us can't make it work—"

He caught himself then, unwilling to say any more.

For a long while, they stood without speaking.

Both were thinking how much easier things had been when they were lost in the woods, toiling on some impossible adventure, danger always nipping at their heels. It was a different kind of battle now between them. They didn't always find themselves on the same side.

"What would you have me do?" Asher asked roughly, trying to keep himself contained. "I would never wish for you to be afraid, least of all afraid of me. What would you have me do?"

Ellanden's eyes flashed up, full of feeling. Then he bowed his head. "I don't know."

THE NEXT MORNING THE entire camp rose with the dawn, determined to start the day in better spirits. They were on the verge of a great and terrible fight. They didn't know how many dawns they had left to salvage. They wouldn't be wasting a single one.

"Hey!' Evie crammed her arms into the sleeves of her cloak, running down the beach to find the others. "I've been looking everywhere for you!'

The rest of their group was still sleeping—they rarely took those revelatory 'make the most of each day' moments to heart—but to her surprise Ellanden and Seth were walking along the beach together. Rather, they were standing at the edge of the water...holding hands?

She came to an abrupt stop.

"Well, this is new..."

The men startled and took a step back—dropping their hands with a simultaneous flush. It was only then she realized they honestly hadn't heard her coming. Despite her obnoxious shouting and the general clamor coming from the camp, the two had been lost in their own world.

Seth recovered first, squaring his shoulders. "So now you know everything."

Ellanden glanced back in alarm. "...what?"

Yeah—what?!

"I *love* him," Seth replied gravely, reaching for the fae's hand. "I'm tired of hiding it."

There was a beat of silence, then the two shifters burst out laughing—shaking even harder when the prince kicked a splash of water towards them with a reluctant grin.

"We were practicing a form of meditation my gran taught me," Ellanden explained, instantly regretting the water soaking his boot. "Seth's been struggling...with the bond."

The smile vanished from Evie's face.

"Because they're so close?" she guessed quietly, glancing towards the trees. She hadn't put it together, but since the arrival of the vampires Seth had been staying as far away as possible from the forest. "Is it more difficult to tune them out now that they're so close?"

The shifter tensed in spite of himself, raking back his hair.

"It shouldn't be," he said lightly, trying hard not to act as rattled as he felt. "I was speaking last night with Aidan, and he said proximity shouldn't be a factor. I suppose seeing those specific faces just brought it all back again."

The princess' heart broke a thousand times.

And Ellanden was helping you? Meditation by the sea?

Sometimes she underestimated her friends. Not only the difficulties they found themselves facing, but the steps they took to overcome them. She was about to say as much, then—

"Do you not have a mirror in your tent?" Ellanden asked, looking her up and down.

...and we're back.

The princess smoothed down her hair.

"I was actually looking for Asher," she answered tightly. "Have you seen him?"

The fae shook his head. "Not since the beach. I went straight to bed."

Liar!

She raised a finger between them, about to jam it into his chest, when there were sudden footsteps behind her and she turned to see the vampire walking towards them across the beach.

Despite his rather disastrous evening, it looked as though Asher was trying to embrace that fresh start just like all the rest. His skin was flushed with the taste of fresh blood, he'd already visited the blacksmith, and a determined smile was playing about his lips.

"Good morning!" he called, waving above his head. "Was I seeing things this morning, or were the two of you holding hands?"

Ellanden merely shook out his shoe as Seth greeted him with a smile.

"Landi was helping me meditate. Your father seemed to think it might help calm things down—what with the clan of vampires camped out in the forest."

"That's right," Asher replied thoughtfully. "He told me this morning."

"He told you," Evie repeated in surprise. "...you spoke with him?"

The vampire hesitated, then inclined his head.

"I went to him last night, apologized for...well, for a lot of things." His eyes flashed ever so briefly to Ellanden. "It was brought to my attention that I've been holding an unwarranted grudge."

It might have been a touching moment if the fae hadn't been abruptly distracted.

"When did you get that?"

Evie followed his gaze to the brand new sword sheathed in the vampire's belt. It was a stunning piece, even from a distance. She was surprised she hadn't noticed it from the start.

The fae had noticed. He couldn't tear his eyes away.

"It's exquisite," he murmured as Asher held it between them. "Edged lining along the cross-guard, rose-silver and Demascan steel." He squinted for a better look. "Is that a custom—"

"I'm giving it to you."

The fae lifted his head in astonishment. "...are you serious?"

Asher flipped it gracefully in the air, pressing the grip into the prince's hand.

"That's twice-spun oressta on the blade, with rubies inlaid on the hilt. Perfect balance, forged in the halls of Nestor himself. It belonged to a Knight of the Rose...or so I'm told."

Ellanden took it in reverent hands, eyes shining with excitement. "How did you...?"

The vampire shrugged with a little smile, looking pleased. "Every craftsman and warrior in the five kingdoms is gathered in one place. You know how I like to wander..."

"It must have cost a fortune," the fae murmured, giving it an experimental swing.

Asher merely shrugged. "About as much as a ship."

...how convenient.

The princess rolled her eyes, watching with an amused smile as the two passed it back and forth—forgetting their existential reckoning as they promptly regressed to about five years old.

"Is this about last night?" Seth murmured, watching them as well.

"It's far more pathological," she replied. "I've seen this kind of thing before..."

Since they were children, the boys could never just make up and be done with it. They needed to prove their apology through material things. Absurdly *extravagant* material things.

"It's an aggressive gift-giving campaign," she explained. "Highly competitive and wildly expensive, as they need to keep one-upping each other. It only ends when one of them dies."

It had happened four times over the course of their lives. The last iteration had cost Ellanden a castle. A castle that wasn't technically his to give.

"Well that's sweet," Seth replied, eyes twinkling with amusement. "Some guys buy each other a drink, or just...aren't arseholes to begin with. But the two of you aim right for the heart."

They turned in perfect unison, those flushed smiles gone cold.

"Ellanden," Asher finally replied, "the dog is speaking to you."

The fae tilted his head. "Does it expect me to speak back? Hard to say from that improbable height."

"Perhaps you could make it a bit smaller," Asher coaxed, gesturing to the sword. "Christen the blade with a bit of Belarian blood."

"Pauper's blood," Ellanden scoffed. "Couldn't afford the grip. But I suppose I could be persuaded. There's nothing wolves like more than silver..."

Evie stifled a smile, gazing up at them.

My boys...

She sometimes forgot how intimidating they were together. That careless beauty and those flashing eyes. When you spent all your time among the same people, you grew used to such things.

Unfortunately, it took a bit more to intimidate Seth.

"That's adorable," he mused, "you even speak in tandem. Tell me, I know that Freya was teasing about the marriage, but have you actually considered..."

He trailed off, staring over their shoulders.

Evie looked at him a moment, then turned to follow his gaze. At first she couldn't tell what he was looking at, then she saw a group of men walking slowly up the beach. Not men, she realized, but shifters. *Hundreds* of shifters. All following in the shadow of an enormous man.

"Isn't that...?"

She caught herself with a gasp as Seth's face went pale.

"My uncle."

Chapter 12

The Red Hand.

There hadn't been a single day since that first encounter that the gang of shifters hadn't crossed Evie's mind. She could still feel that burst of initial shock when they'd kicked open the door to the tavern; could still see the fear and resignation in the other patrons' eyes.

And all that was before it got personal.

All that was before she met Seth.

"What in seven hells is he doing here?" Ellanden asked in bewilderment.

"My father must have sent for him," Evie breathed, unable to tear her eyes away from the pack. "He was speaking to Atticus about something before we left. This must have been it."

Most wolves belonged to smaller packs scattered through Belaria, but there were a few larger factions as well. Mercenaries, for the most part. A few traders and settlements. They lived freely, but were called upon in times of need the way other monarchs summoned their bannermen.

They were certainly needed now.

Except—

"Seth?"

The man in front stopped with a look of sheer astonishment, staring as though he couldn't believe his eyes. The last time he'd seen his nephew the boy had been bruised and bleeding, dragged away by slavers with a salcor around his neck. Now, he was standing with a strange yet distinguished assortment of people just a stone's throw away from the royal tents.

"I can't believe it..." he murmured. "Is that really you?"

Seth took a step back without thinking, pale and unable to speak.

There was a second of silence, then the man threw open his arms with a cry of delight. The shifters behind him picked up the cue, flashing obligatory smiles as he crossed the distance between the two groups—catching the young wolf in an unexpected embrace.

What the—?!

Evie shared a stricken look with the others, but they were at a similar loss. For his part, Seth seemed to be in a state of shock, his body simply locked down—waiting for the hug to be over.

"Look at you," the man said, pulling back and clapping the tops of his arms. "New weapons, new clothes. Must have put on ten pounds of pure muscle. That time in the arena served you well!"

Excuse me?!

"Or perhaps someone's merely feeding him," Ellanden said stiffly, wrapping a casual arm around his friend's shoulders and pulling him back. "Unlike some of the rest of your...recruits."

It was true, they were a rough-looking bunch. Not so much in demeanor, but the obvious circumstances from which they'd been selected. Most were under the age of thirty, and most of those had experienced only a handful of hot meals in their entire lives. Sickness and injury were apparent at only a glance—medicated by a thick stench of whiskey and the fierce will to survive.

The pack-leader took a step back, assessing the friends for the first time. A look of vague recognition flitted across his face at the sight of both a fae and a vampire before it suddenly clicked.

"You were in the tavern that night," he murmured. "Along with that witch and the pretty girl with the white hair—the one who enchanted our young Seth."

He lowered his voice, looking the boy in the eye.

"She ended up costing you quite a bit."

Enough!

"Why are you here?" Evie asked sharply, stepping between them.

She might have only come up to the man's chin, but the people in those tents answered to her call and she'd be damned if this brute added even another second of misery to Seth's life.

The man's lips curled back in a smile.

"I'm here, sweetheart, because I was summoned by the King of Belaria."

Her eyes flashed as she smiled sweetly in return. "What a coincidence. I happen to know him."

Right on cue, there was a flood of movement in the camp as the scouts who'd seen the wolves approach sent word that reached the ear of the king. Only a few seconds later, Dylan himself strode out from the encampment—the entire Belarian Council at his side.

His eyes swept over the unruly pack before landing on his daughter.

"I see you've started without me."

She smiled again as the shifter glanced between them in alarm.

"You...you are acquainted with the king?"

One could say that.

Dylan joined them a moment later, and she slipped under his arm.

"He's my father."

This produced a far greater effect.

The man's face stilled with instinctual dread before he sank into a sudden bow, awkward and clumsy—the bow of a man accustomed to other people bowing to him.

"Your Majesty," he murmured, eyes locked on the ground. "I received your message."

Dylan stared at the top of his head, but didn't motion for him to rise. He'd seen enough of the exchange and felt enough of his daughter's tension not to welcome the shifter now.

"He wasn't difficult to find," Atticus remarked tightly, standing at the king's side. "Wherever his pack went...they seemed to draw a lot of attention."

Each of the shifters standing on the beach tensed at the same time, bent in the same position of deference as their leader. Attention was a generous way of putting it. The pack was run with a mantra both simple and vain: The greater the trail of wreckage, the greater the acclaim.

Dylan nodded quietly, taking in the smallest of details.

"And you still wear the insignia," he remarked with a hint of surprise. "Those who pledge themselves to Belaria serve no higher cause. I was under the impression you came to seek a pardon."

What?!

"A pardon!" Evie exclaimed before she could stop herself. "For him?"

The pack had been in the process of tearing the emblem from their cloaks, but their hands froze at the princess' words. Even the man who led them flashed a quick look—his head still bent in an unending bow until his king saw fit to release him.

Dylan glanced at her in surprise before looking a bit farther to the wolf at her side.

In the short time since they'd met, he'd seen the young shifter throw himself in front of monsters and demons. He'd survived the fighting pits at Tarnaq. He'd survived a sparring session with the king himself. He'd made a solemn vow to forever defend his daughter's life.

In all that time, he'd never seen him freeze.

Not the way he was doing now.

"You claimed to come from a small pack in the mountains, yet the course of your journey led you somewhere quite different. Is this the group you spoke of? The ones you were with before?"

Evie sucked in a quick breath, waiting for the wolf to respond.

It was a subject he'd danced around since the moment they reunited with their family, never telling an outright lie but never volunteering a complete version of the truth.

He didn't volunteer it now, either.

Even though his king had asked him a direction question. Even though the ghosts of his past were literally standing in front of him and there was nowhere left to hide.

He simply let out a breath and turned on his heel, vanishing into the camp.

IT WASN'T HARD TO FIND the shifter. There weren't many places he could go. With the vampires on one side and the ocean on the other, it was simply a question of picking the right tent.

The princess made it even easier than that. She followed the smell of the whiskey.

"Thought I'd find you here."

Seth jumped in his skin when she pulled back the flap, but had already resigned himself to the fact that he'd soon be found. It was a childish impulse, one he'd grown out of long before. But something had crumbled deep inside him the moment he found himself locked in his uncle's gaze.

"Have you come to arrest me?" he queried with a humorless smile, waving the bottle in her general direction. "Or simply to join me for a drink?"

She sank down at the table beside him. "What do you think?"

He procured another glass, filling it to the brim.

They drank for a while in silence, taking measured sips, both pretending it was a normal morning and a gang of cutthroat shifters wasn't gathered somewhere outside. Ironically enough, it was a habit he'd picked up from the pack. New recruits were all initiated in the same way, and at some point or another they learned self-medication was the easiest way to keep the demons at bay.

"Cosette will be looking for you," Evie finally murmured, staring at him over the rim of her glass. "She will have heard what happened."

He started to raise the bottle, then set it back on the table.

"Then she'll know it's over," he said simply, staring without blinking at the floor. "I enlisted in the Belarian army under false pretenses. I hid my involvement with a notorious gang, and now those sins have literally shown up at my door. My time here is finished. Cosette will move on."

He reached again for the whiskey, but Evie caught his wrist.

"Do you think any of that matters?" she asked fiercely. "Do you think the rest of us forgot the circumstances under which we met? The sacrifice you made? The only reason you were in that arena in the first place was because you *saved* our lives—"

"My uncle didn't toss me in that arena because of you," he interrupted, eyes never leaving the table. "He was already looking for a way to be rid of me. That was simply a convenient excuse."

She shook her head blankly. "What do you mean? Why was he—"

"Family problems," Seth murmured, yanking himself free. He drained the whiskey in a single gulp, setting down the glass. "That's what my mother would call it...family problems."

With a deliberate swipe of her arm, Evie knocked over the bottle. The two friends watched as it emptied slowly onto the grass. When it was finally empty, they looked at each other instead.

"Tell me what you mean."

He stared at her a moment longer, then drew in a breath. "I never wanted to join the Red Hand. Not when I was a kid, not when I got older. Not even when my father died and I knew my mother needed the help. I tried to help in other ways—hunting, fishing, random repairs around the village. I tried to do everything my father might have done, but it wasn't enough. Then two weeks after Violet was born, my uncle came back to town."

His eyes hardened with an expression the princess had never seen.

"He was loud and unsettling, and everything about him rubbed me the wrong way. When my mother cooked him dinner he got drunk and overturned the table, frightening my sisters so much they cried. But he had money. The wolves that ran with him had money. And the next morning I found myself leaving with the rest of them, promising things would be different when I returned."

That expression hardened into a wry smile.

"But the only thing different was me. Jack might be family, but he'd been running the pack a long time and he knew how to get what he wanted from new recruits. If you hesitated before kicking down some tavern door, you'd be the first one pushed through the frame. If you tried to spare some poor villager, he'd think of a worse punishment for the next one you passed. It was a never-ending cycle, one that deepened so quickly that, by the time you realized just what was happening, it was too late to get out. But I *wanted* to get out. And Jack knew that."

He reached for the bottle, only to remember the puddle on the ground.

"That was good whiskey, Everly."

"Just keep telling the story."

He raked his hair back with a sigh.

"In one of the towns we raided, there was this boy. A *young* boy, about the same age as my sisters. Jack was tormenting him. It was just teasing at first, but the kid was frightened—kept trying to run back to his mother. In the end, he suggested that the boy come with us. Said it was bound to happen sooner or later, and he might as well just get it over with and take the plunge."

His eyes fixed on the table, caught in a daze.

"The men were laughing, the boy was crying...I punched Jack in the face."

Seven hells.

Evie leaned back in her chair, pale and shaken. Whether it was the effect of the whiskey, the shifter's dreadful story, or the flat monotone in which he told it, she would never know.

"He laughed it off to the pack," he continued quietly. "Said that I was drunk. In public it was all smiles, but he beat me that night, so hard I was barely breathing. He threatened my family, ranted about loyalty. Then the next night we went to that tavern...and I met all of you."

Just like that, the story was finished. The princess leaned back in her chair, blinking dazedly.

"Like I said...family problems."

A throat cleared outside and Dylan stepped through the doorway.

He didn't seem angry about the abrupt departure. He didn't even seem all that surprised. He simply looked at the empty bottle of whiskey then at the boy in front of it.

"Jack is your uncle?" he asked quietly. "The one who sold you as a slave?"

While the children would never know, he was already quite clear on the answer. Having followed in his daughter's footsteps, he'd heard the entire story from the other side of the canvas.

Seth bowed his head.

"I'm so very sorry," he murmured, wishing he wasn't half-drunk. "I should have told you from the beginning. The first time I met your daughter wasn't in Tarnaq. I was a member of the Red Hand. I should never have enlisted with the Belarian army. I do not deserve to wear its colors."

He let out a quiet breath, watching the dream vanish forever.

"I can only beg your forgiveness."

A ringing silence fell over the tent as Dylan gave the boy a long look—the kind that made his daughter nervous. After what felt like an eternity, he nodded his head.

"I refuse your commission," he said quietly.

"What?" Evie sprang to her feet, grabbing his arm. "Dad—"

"Now come...we have business on the beach."

NOT MUCH HAD CHANGED when the trio went back outside. Time had a way of moving at the leisure of kings, and the pack was still waiting exactly where Dylan had left them.

His eyes swept over each one, so many as to block out the rolling sand.

"The wolves of Belaria are raised to follow a certain code. It's passed down to us from mother to daughter. From father to son. It's a guiding sense of honor, a moral compass that's embedded beneath all the rest." He paused, staring over the pack. "I see no such honor here."

A ripple of unease filtered through the wolves, a pleading kind of whine that was even easier to see because of each of them was still kneeling in the sand with heads bent in respect.

"You travel to this place searching for absolution, yet how can I ignore the cries of the people you've left in your wake? Men, women, and children. Shifters and non-shifters alike. You have disgraced yourselves to a point where you can sink no further, making a fine mess of my kingdoms and tarnishing the very magic the runs inside your veins."

...not good.

Evie sucked in a breath, but stood next to Atticus beside him. Seth cast a frightened look at them both, but kept his head bowed and his arms at his sides.

Dylan was immune, already decided. He stared once more over the pack, eyes sweeping atop all those bowed heads before narrowing his gaze to a single man.

"But such a thing doesn't happened naturally. It is fostered and bred."

He snapped his fingers, motioning for Jack to rise.

"What have you to say for yourself?'

The man stood tall for only a moment, then half-bowed again on trembling knees. He tried to hold the king's gaze, but his attention kept retreating to all corners.

"My king," he finally managed in a low and rasping voice, "this isn't..." He took a breath and started again. "I'm not sure what rumors you might have heard, but I can assure you—"

Dylan held up a hand, silencing him on the stop.

"Such behavior is abhorrent," he spat. "A stain upon all Belaria. And if any of you is lucky enough to leave this beach today, *I* can assure you...you will be making amends."

He paused ever so slightly, staring at the men trembling before him.

Some of them were already so battered it was unlikely they could hold a sword. Some of them were scarcely older than his daughter.

"It is a sacred calling to lead a pack," he continued softly. "To be entrusted with the blood of our people, there is no greater privilege. No greater honor. In this, you have failed."

His eyes fell upon Jack.

"...you will be leading this pack no longer."

Another agitated murmur swept through the wolves, a feeling of anticipation that was mirrored by all those who had gathered to watch beside the tents. A few of them had simply drifted over from breakfast, wondering at all the commotion. But those who already served in the Belarian army had a keener focus. Some had removed their cloaks. Some looked preemptively grave.

Jack glanced over his shoulder, then pushed to his feet. A kind of recklessness had come over him; the wild look of a man who could stoop no further and had nothing left to lose.

"Do you mean to fight me?" he rasped in a loud voice.

There was no other way to claim ownership of a pack. Such a thing must be sealed in combat and blood—even the words of a king would not suffice.

Dylan took a hard look at his face, relishing the idea. Then he turned to the boy at his side.

"Not I..."

Seth had been watching every moment of the exchange with bated breath, finding all those familiar faces in the crowd and terrified that he might see them be put to the slaughter. When he heard words of mercy instead, such powerful relief had washed over him that he was able to see nothing past it. He was still nodding along in contented agreement when he registered the king's words.

"Wait—me?" he gasped, pressing a hand to his chest. "No, that's not—"

"I don't want to execute all of these people," Dylan said quietly, angling him away. "That's a lot of graves. But I will if I have to...or you can fight him yourself."

"But I'm not...I am *nothing* to these people," Seth stammered. "I come from a hovel in a forgotten range of mountains. I am but a foot-soldier in your great army. This is a borrowed blade."

"You are no longer a foot-soldier in my great army," Dylan replied calmly. "I refused your commission. Try to keep up." His lips twitched with what might have been a smile as he lay a steady hand upon the boy's arm. "And to say you are nothing...?"

The king waited patiently until their eyes met.

"You protected your family when you were but a child. You travelled the realm when there should have been people looking after you. You *saved my daughter's life* and have been safe-guarding my people ever since—defending a cause that wasn't your own, yet still think yourself unworthy."

He stared deep into the boy's eyes, seeing futures yet to come.

"You are *nothing* to these people?" he repeated, shaking his head. "You are *every single one.*"

They stood a moment in perfect silence before he gestured to the wolves.

"...will you answer the call?"

It was a large, unruly pack. Poorly disciplined, lacking the trust and foundation that bound most others together. It would take a quite a man to lead them. Seth was only seventeen.

But his king had spoken. And the boy's blood was on fire.

"I will."

A cheer erupted from those on the beach, startling the young man with surprise as the rest of the pack scrambled to their feet. He hadn't yet realized they were watching. Hadn't yet realized they had chosen a side. They blurred together as a young woman made her way to the front.

Eyes shining with the fiercest hope, waves of crimson hair tumbling beside her.

Yes...you will.

"I'll do it," he said a bit louder, lifting a hand to acknowledge the crowd. They swelled to new heights as he began removing his cloak, repeating it to himself more softly. "I'll do it."

That confidence remained until the second his back was turned.

"What if I *can't* do it?" he whispered in a quiet panic, unheard by the rest. Those dark eyes caught hold of the princess. "It isn't like...it isn't like I haven't tried."

In spite of her best efforts, her eyes drifted past him to the savage pack-master pounding his fist in the air. He looked even bigger than the last time she'd seen him, with the scars of a thousand failed challenges gleaming like trophies across his brutal face.

...piece of cake.

"You're going to beat him," she said simply, picking up his cloak and folding it over her arms. When he faltered, she tilted her head—catching his gaze with a smile. "Don't quote me on this, but it seems a bit like your entire life has led you to this moment. How can you turn back?"

He met her eyes for a moment, then slowly returned the smile.

"...I won't be your beta."

"Nonsense," she scoffed. "You'll always be my beta. You don't have to live in the palace for that. And it doesn't really matter until we find a way to force my father off the throne."

Atticus cast a pained look towards the heavens. "I really wish you'd stop speaking like that, Your Highness. At least not in front of the rest of the Council..."

Evie flashed a grin, mouthing words behind his back.

Ignore him.

The pack stomped in anticipation, ready for blood.

"This is your proxy?" Jack threw back his head with a cruel laugh, one that was echoed by several of the wolves behind him. "I have been leading this pack for years—he is but a boy!"

"Then a *boy* will beat you," Dylan called in return, intercepting that borrowed blade before Seth could cast it to the ground. "Don't throw that. Hand it to someone."

The shifter flushed as Ellanden took it with a grin.

"How about I hang on to it for you until you come back." Their eyes met in a moment of silent acknowledgement as the blade passed between their hands. "...you *will* come back."

Seth drew in a breath, then nodded.

"He'll come back as something more than a beta," Asher added lightly, eyes flickering across the sand. "What is the title, Uncle? For a pack of this size?"

Dylan tilted his head appraisingly. "I'd say...it makes him something like a general."

Evie warmed with a secret smile.

"A general and a princess. Sounds about right."

THE CAMP WAS STILL celebrating the young pack leader until late into the night, toasting his success and calling out the highlights of the fight. There were many to choose from: the moment two men crashed together into the water but two wolves rose up out of the sea, or the moment Seth had defied all odds and broken his uncle's unceasing momentum by pushing him back across the sand.

But Evie's favorite moment had come at the end, when the fighting was all but finished and the transformation had broken—the moment Seth said those final words in the voice of a man.

"That girl you mentioned before, the one with the white hair," he'd murmured, pressing a weathered blade deep into his uncle's heart, "She didn't cost me a thing...she set me free."

The old leader had died a moment later, passing the wolves into new hands.

"These men belong to you now," Dylan had announced, lifting the shifter to his feet and draping his own cloak across his bloody shoulders. "It is a privilege. Lead them well."

Seth gazed out across the beach, slowly shaking his head.

"These men belong to themselves," he replied softly. "But I would be *honored* to lead them."

A heavy silence followed the declaration.

Then, one by one, each of the men watching sank into a bow.

...and proceeded to drink.

"To our new alpha!" the cheer rang out in the night. "To the Red Hand!"

The princess snapped back to the present, raising her glass with a grin as the scores of wolves toasted her friend's victory, blending with the existing packs of Belaria and the other companies that had gathered from across the realm. It was a celebration as much as a reunion.

The calm before the storm.

"An interesting choice," Diana murmured, raising an empty glass in salute. "To keep the name that struck fear in the hearts of so many..."

In a move that had shocked those around him, one of the first things Seth declared as alpha was that the vampires were invited to attend the celebration as well. When Atticus wryly informed him that offer wasn't his to extend, he'd settled for the lieutenants and Diana.

"A rather ironic observation," Leonor replied innocently. "Are you considering changing the word *vampire* as well?"

The elder statesman had little interest in the internal affairs of wolves, but when he'd been told that members of the clan would be attending the bonfire he'd claimed a seat for himself at the table as well. It was a stiff reception, but one that got considerably easier at the bottom of each glass.

"We cannot move forward as the Red Hand," Seth conceded, rubbing his eyes. "There are too many connotations. Too many memories to bury. We must find something new."

He instantly regretted opening his mouth.

"*The Less-Red Hand.*"

"*The Other Hand.*"

"*The Unrelated Hand.*"

"*How about the we're so sorry for taking things that didn't belong to us, look at all the ways we're going to make it up to you...hand.*"

The shifter looked at each of his friends in turn.

"No more whiskey for you."

"Let me name it!" Freya insisted. "I almost died!"

"You *did* die," Ellanden corrected with a subtle shudder, pressing a kiss to the top of her head. "And we're not making jokes about that yet."

"You should name it yourself," Cosette murmured in contentment, leaning back in the shifter's arms. "Don't force something, it will come in its own time."

She alone hadn't stayed to watch the battle. The second the wolves made contact, she'd turned with a little smile and walked straight to her parents' tent—informing them with her signature pragmatism that she'd fallen in love with a general in the Belarian army and would be pledging herself to him forthwith. She'd allowed them until the bonfire to come to terms.

Kailas still hadn't arrived.

Because he's killed himself.

That being said, the night was progressing in fine fashion.

Eleazer had taken the opportunity to lead the rest of the clan further into the mountains to feed. News had been received from the southern tribes that another contingent of Kreo, along with the queen mother, was soon to be arriving. And the old pack-master had been buried and almost as quickly forgotten—as soon as the loose sand had settled upon his grave.

Even the addition of two additional vampires wasn't enough to dampen spirits. Even though not everyone had been warned ahead of time that they were coming. Or that they had arrived.

"Hello again, angel."

Ellanden glanced up with a start as Andrei appeared in front of him, looking like one of his secret nightmares had come to life. His hand slipped from his glass with an involuntary curse, and it took him a moment to recover—one that felt all the longer under the vampire's unnerving stare.

"What...what are you doing here?"

"I came at the invitation of your friend. To celebrate his success, and to escort my queen." Those dark eyes twinkled with a smile. "And perhaps to see you again."

The fae paled then gestured behind him. "Allow me to introduce my guards."

Andrei laughed quietly, raising his hands. "Haven't you understood yet? I have no wish to harm you."

"Yes, well...that still leaves several options on the table." Ellanden fidgeted needlessly with his tunic, trying to regain his composure. "Good luck in the battle. I sincerely hope no one kills you."

"And you as well." The vampire was at least sincere. "What a tragic waste that would be."

He vanished without another word, securing himself a permanent place in the fae's darkest dreams. Ellanden stared after him, jumping a mile when Asher clapped him on the back.

"You all right, buddy?"

The fae opened his mouth to answer, then merely shook his head.

"Drink," Seth advised wisely, pressing a fresh goblet into his hand. "It helps."

For the next few hours, the friends did exactly that.

AS THE FIRES BURNED low and the celebration came to an end the princess leaned back in her chair, staring at each of the couples backlit by the glow of the flames.

Freya was nestled in the hollow of Ellanden's shoulder, chattering excitedly about the new sword they'd 'both' been gifted and stealing sips of his wine. Cosette was perched on Seth's knees, pointing to things around the table and teaching him to say them in Fae.

The shifter could not have looked any happier, matched only by the prince at his side.

Then her eyes drifted a little further...to the vampire sitting alone.

Why must it always be different for us? Why must things always be hard?

She remembered the first time he'd kissed her—seconds after escaping a giant. She remembered the first time they'd made love—seconds after forming a bond.

All her life, she'd dreamed of adventure. But if she had ever slowed down enough to dream of romance she would have wanted something steady, something certain. Something that would be there day after day, night after night. The first thing she saw each moment when she woke up.

Why can't it be that simple? Why can't that be you?

He glanced up a second later, almost as if he'd felt her gaze. For a suspended moment, their eyes met in the dancing flickers of light—full of silent questions, full of silent promises.

That's when they heard the first of the screams.

THERE WAS NO NEED TO run outside, all the friends needed to do was get up from the table. It buckled beneath the weight of so many people, tipping over into the sand.

"What is it?" Evie asked with a gasp, squinting into the dark. "What's happened?"

It wasn't immediately clear. The only thing she could tell as she gazed at the distant harbor was that something wasn't quite right with the ships. They seemed over-crowded, over-wrought, tipping precariously, then righting themselves just as fast. Over and over and over.

"Estien. Neirae."

The names flew from Cassiel's mouth like arrows, summoning the two fae who appeared at his side. They stood there only a moment, receiving his murmured instructions, then streaked forward into the darkness—moving so quickly their feet barely left imprints in the sand.

But they'd only made it halfway down the beach before they came to an abrupt stop.

What the HELL is going on?!

Evie leaned forward, pulling against her father's restraining hand. It was almost at the end of her vision, even though the eyes of a shifter could manage so well in the dark. But when the moon slipped out from behind a cloud, she managed to see their faces—pale as ghosts and staring into the night.

"What is it?" Cassiel called aloud, unable to await their return. "Tae nuen mos..."

But he trailed off as a third person joined them, trudging in strange, disjointed movements through the sand. His skin was mottled and grey, but he wore the remains of a royal uniform.

And there was something familiar about his face.

Seven hells.

Evie let out a quiet gasp, hands lifting to her mouth.

"...Hastings?"

Chapter 13

Old enemies prowl, for the dead never die.

Since stumbling into that carnival tent all those years ago, the princess had often wondered after those words—turning them over in her head, inserting new names and possibilities. Trying even to rearrange them in an effort to force a bit of sense.

Never in her life would she have guessed something like this.

Hastings.

She'd known that her childhood protector had died the moment she set foot in the High Kingdom. Never once had he not been there to greet her when she walked through the door. When Mace had confirmed it, she hadn't been surprised. The man was gone, lost to some nameless peril in the ten years she'd been away. Like so many others, he was buried in an unmarked grave.

So how in the world is he here?

"Stay away from him!" Petra shouted suddenly. "Don't touch him!"

The pair of fae glanced back towards the others, their faces blank with confusion as the man continued lurching forward. He didn't appear to have a destination, and he wasn't moving at great speed.

Then all at once he stumbled.

What happened next was pure reflex. The man was grievously injured, the man wore the uniform as a friend. And though the Kreo general's warning still echoed in his ears Estien's hand flashed out of its own accord, catching his shoulder and steadying him.

As if a trance had broken, Hastings slowly lifted his head to stare into the fae's eyes.

"Caroset ni monia—" The fae caught himself quickly, searching for the words in the common tongue. "Are you all right?"

The legendary knight stared for a split second, then plunged a dagger into his side.

NO!

The fae let out a cry and collapsed to the ground, blood soaking into the sand. His companion raced forward to catch him, slipping a hand beneath his neck as a sudden shadow fell over them both. The fae lifted his eyes just as Hastings lifted his sword.

But the fae was faster.

A second later his bow was drawn, and from the height of a child he fired three arrows between them— each one burying itself somewhere deep inside the knight's skull.

In theory, that should have stopped him. But he simply lifted the sword again.

What the...?

"Get out of there!" Cassiel shouted, straining against the arms of half a dozen guards as he tried to get to them himself. "Get off the beach—NOW!"

The fae didn't need to be told twice.

Neirae released his bow and picked up his friend's body, backing away from the knight with a look of genuine fear before racing back to the crowd at the other end of the beach. They opened ranks as he approached, closing behind him just as fast.

Because the fae wasn't the only one running. The knight had started running as well.

And he appeared to have a singular target in mind.

"Protect the princess!" Dylan cried, unsheathing his sword.

It didn't matter that he and his wife had hand-picked the same man to defend their infant daughter. The creature tearing across the sand bore no resemblance to the person they used to know. It was nothing but flesh and bones, cursed with some dark reanimation.

No fewer than fifty knights of the High Kingdom moved of one accord, drawing their weapons as their old comrade barreled across the sand. A vicious noise ripped through the air as they were quickly joined by fifty Belarian wolves. Mace was among them, tears in his eyes.

But none of them turned out to be necessary. Because at the last possible second Katerina Damaris stepped in front of the line, shooting a wave of pure dragon fire from her hands.

...and that was it.

There were no last looks. No final goodbyes. In a flash, a man the princess had known forever was simply gone—nothing left to bury, nothing to remember but a name.

She let out a faltering breath, placing a hand on her father's back. "...is it over?"

Why did I have to ask?

It started as nothing more than a rumble, as though the earth was shifting in a storm that no one could see. Then the ground began truly quaking, enough to frighten the cages of ravens; enough to buckle the princess' knees. She grabbed hold of her father once again, peering into the night.

Only to freeze with a look of pure horror.

In a kind of daze, the beach vanished and a sudden memory flashed through her mind. Of all things, it was the giant who'd captured them in his garden—stuffing them like pets into a cage.

He'd delighted at their tiny movements, thrilled to have found them alive.

"Nothing can stay dead for long!"

As it turned out...he was absolutely right.

"That's..." Aidan took a step back, then another. His entire body was in rebellion as his mind flat-out rejected the sight. "That's not possible."

A second later he called out again.

"Where's Asher?"

The boy appeared at his side—white-faced and trembling. His father grabbed hold of him, hard enough to break bone, but the vampire hardly noticed. His eyes were trained on the beach. Of all the nightmares he and his friends had faced, this was without question the absolute worst.

Because Kaleb had not gathered an army. He'd raised one from the dead.

There were creatures the princess had never imagined—mutilated and deformed from whatever had killed them in their previous life. Gaunt-faced harpies with their wings cut off. Herds of skeletal kelpies so bereft of skin she could see right through to the other side. There were manticores and demons. Things the princess had read about but never dared to ask their name.

But worse than the monsters were the men. Some of them had faces she recognized. All of them bore emblems she recognized. Some looked as though they'd just risen from a grave.

"Your orders, Sire?"

Evie never knew who summoned the breath to ask the question, but Dylan was certainly in no state to answer. While she might have recognized several of the faces, he was familiar with quite a few more. At one point he lifted a hand to his mouth, tears shining in his eyes.

After a few seconds, the order came from Cassiel instead.

"Archers!"

In a single movement two companies of fae appeared from nowhere, lifting their bows with an arrow already notched in the string. They stood in perfect stillness—bright eyes piercing through the darkness, fingers keeping light tension as they awaited their lord's command.

As if on cue, the army marching towards them broke into a run.

"Hold!"

They were closer now, already halfway across the sand. A host of chilling noises came with them—choking snarls, splintered wails.

Evie clamped both hands over her ears, but she could still hear it—boring its way deep inside her. Slowly driving her mad—

"FIRE!"

The archers released their arrows in a single breath, watching as they curved gracefully over the sand. For a few seconds, they seemed to hover—a shimmering veil protecting the people on the ground from those watching in the stars. Then, with immortal precision...each one struck its target.

This time, Evie wasn't the only one covering her ears. Dozens of the shifters were doing the same thing as that keening chorus soared to eye-watering heights. But there were heavier sounds interspersed now as well. Deep grunts and low impacts. The sound of flesh pounding into flesh as the faes' bright arrows ripped through whatever had been left of the creatures that came before.

Like a sweeping tide a sea of bodies fell to the ground before them, leaving not a single creature standing, making Evie wonder how each fae knew where to take aim. Her heart soared as particles of sand and blood settled around them, actually daring to pull in a breath.

Then, at the same time...they picked themselves back up.

A hush swept through the royal battalions. There was no way to shake it, no words would suffice. Even the fae stepped back with a look of uncertainty, breaking that flawless formation as those celestial arrows failed them for the first time.

"The fire," Dylan breathed, squeezing his wife's shoulder. "It was the only thing that worked against..." He couldn't bring himself to finish. "How close must you be? Are you able to shift?"

But even as he said the words, the enemy spread their formation—vanishing like shadows as they continued ever-closer beneath the cover of a dark and starless night.

Yes, the fire might stop them. But it could stop them only one at a time.

And each of their own fallen soldiers would soon rise up to join them.

Even sooner than we thought.

There was a gasp from somewhere near the water, causing the people standing closest to stumble back in alarm. A spray of sand shot skyward, followed by a grasping hand.

Followed by a recently buried pack-master out for blood.

...Seth.

She reached instinctively for her friend, but he was frozen to the spot—staring with a look of childlike horror as the man crawled out of the dirt and headed towards him, still leaking brackish blood from the gaping wound the young wolf had stabbed into his chest.

"Get down!" someone called.

But the wolf couldn't move.

"Get down!"

A few people drew palsied blades, but the shock was too great and the vengeful shifter was already upon them. With a wild cry he launched himself towards his stricken nephew, reaching for the boy's throat with his bare hands...only for someone else to flash in between.

When Cosette had first ventured into that cave, Evie remembered being truly astonished by the sight of her. The speed, the skill, the fact that she seemed to flit through the air like a graceful bird despite the fact that her cousin was the one who'd been granted wings.

She didn't have time to feel the same way now. The fight was over too fast.

With the quick slice of a blade, Jack's head detached from his shoulders—falling with a sickening thud to the ground at the Cosette's feet. She stared at it with a lingering caution, a sword still raised by her side, then nodded briskly.

"That will kill most things."

When she raised her eyes a moment later, the entire army was staring back.

"Are you waiting for something? Our enemy has arrived."

THE THINGS THAT HAPPENED over the course of the next hour could easily be described as some of the worst moments of Evie's life. Again and again, the royal forces drove back the army of corpses that charged towards them. Again and again, that army stitched itself back to life.

A flaming log swung by an undead warlock had scorched the skin on the right half of her body. A desiccated hand of what might have been a djinn had nearly choked her. Things spiraled even farther when their own dead began to rise with the others, turning blades toward the people they'd been fighting with just moments before. In the illuminated smoke of a distant fire, Evie saw two brothers reunite in that precise situation. The living couldn't bring himself to raise a hand against the dead. A few seconds after that fateful decision, they were fighting together once again.

How much longer can we keep doing this?

She threw up her hands reflexively, showering the banshee that had been tearing towards her in a burst of flames. There were similar explosions of fire deeper inside the battlefield, evidence that her mother was still alive and fighting, though she'd lost track of her father in the crowd.

"Evie—get down!"

She dropped without thinking, watching as a hyena that had been leaping towards her came down onto nothing but sand.

It took a second to recognize it as the same kind of creature that had attacked them in the grassland. It took another second to recognize her boyfriend's voice.

"Stay down!"

He streaked over her like a wisp of shadow, tearing straight through the monster as if there wasn't anything there. Dark clumps of blood and rotten fur exploded into the air, coating the young vampire from head to toe—leaving only his bright eyes roving wildly in the dark.

"Are you okay?" he cried, spotting her on the ground. In a flash he was kneeling beside her, running a tentative hand along her back. "You ducked in time, didn't you?"

She straightened up slowly, relieved to be at the edge of the fight.

"Yeah...I ducked in time."

Asher sank down beside her, truly exhausted for one of the first times in his life. His eyes swept over the battlefield, catching only glimpses in the murky night. A burst of flames as his aunt claimed another victim. The tip of Petra's spear as it whirled above her head.

"I've been trying to reach you for a long time," he panted, wiping a smear of blood from the top of his ear. "Your father's been trying, too. I heard him shouting."

Evie's eyes shot towards him. "He's okay?"

The vampire nodded wearily. "Yeah, he's okay."

For now.

It was one of the strangest things about a battle—something the princess had never known until she'd been in the thick of one herself. Despite the danger, despite the chaos, despite the fact that you never knew where exactly you stood in relation to the people you loved...you got *tired*.

There was only so much the body could withstand before needing to rest.

Living bodies get tired, she corrected herself. *The dead have all the time in the world for that.*

She and Asher watched as a Belarian wolf was torn apart by the spears of two deceased warlords—both in a state of such disrepair they could barely manage a grip. They both tensed their legs to rise and help before realizing at the same time that it was already too late.

"How's your arm?" she asked softly, throwing him a sideways glance. It was hard to tell how much of the blood staining his body was his own, but he was holding it delicately, cradled against his chest. "Can you move it?"

He startled slightly, still looking at the remains of the wolf. Already it had started to pull itself up from the sand—shaking itself clean and throwing itself back into the fight.

"...what?"

She was about to ask again, then realized it didn't matter in the slightest. No, it probably wasn't okay. No, he probably couldn't move it. And there was nothing to be done.

"I keep trying to shift, but I can't," she confessed, pulling what looked like a claw from the leather of her boot. "Ever since the baresmain, I haven't been able—"

"Hang on."

Asher squinted into the darkness, then his face went still.

"Ellanden."

How he could spot him from such a distance the princess would never know. It looked as though the fae had been racing towards them, but he couldn't make it over the sand in time. As he was running two hyenas leapt upon him from either side, felling him to the ground with a cry.

"LANDI!"

His friends were sprinting towards him a second later, watching in horror as the creatures let loose a shriek of beastly laughter as they clawed at the flesh on his back in tandem. He tried at first to fight them off, crying out blindly for help, then he went frighteningly still. The feet scrambling in the sand stopped moving. The arms covering his head tensed with a shudder, then went abruptly limp.

NO!

The princess let loose a wave of fire—incinerating the first creature as the vampire tackled the other one straight off the fae's back. They tumbled together in a violent circle, leaving a wide smear of blood in their wake before there was a sudden crack and the hyena stopped moving.

Evie sprinted towards that one as well, burning the body before it could come back.

"...Ellanden?"

By the time she turned around, Asher was already there—kneeling helplessly in the sand and staring at the massive tears in the fae's shirt. He took him gently by the shoulders, perhaps to turn him, then stopped himself in the same moment—afraid the motion would cost too much blood.

"Is he alive?" the princess whispered, freezing in her tracks. "Asher, is he—"

The fae let out a sudden cough, choking on the sand.

"Of course I'm alive," he muttered, gasping for breath. The vampire lifted him immediately, and he let out an involuntary cry. "I've been trying to find you—we need to get to the ships!"

Both friends stared as though he was crazy. Then they realized he was waiting for a reply.

"Get to the ships?" Evie repeated incredulously. "We need to find my parents and find out why in seven hells they haven't called for a retreat!"

"What's the point in retreating?" Asher asked quietly. "The dead will follow either way."

"But the ships—"

"It's a ridiculous idea, so stop asking!" Evie snapped. "They were the first things to be overrun, we cannot leave the others, and I truly could not care less about—"

"Evie, they are *sinking* the ships!"

THE THREE FRIENDS DARTED forward in a low crouch—leaving the main swarm of the battle behind as they neared the harbor. There were still plenty of nightmarish creatures to keep them occupied, but they tried as best they could to avoid them. While the army of the dead maintained every bit of strength from their former lives, they were slightly lacking in higher thought.

"Do you see?" Ellanden panted as they hid behind a rock. "They're lighting them aflame!"

His friends peered towards the water, squinting blearily in the smoke.

In all likelihood, it wasn't their enemy's intention. Ships were full of lanterns and kerosene, and in an attempt to destroy the people aboard those things tended to overturn and collide. That being said, they'd already lost four of the vessels intended to take them to the Dunes. The royal troops upon those that remained were still fighting fiercely, but were cut off from the rest of the group.

"So this is what I'm thinking," the fae whispered, pointing over the edge. "I'll take the first three and secure them myself. You two can work on liberating that little dinghy by the—"

Look out!

The princess whirled around with a silent scream as a resurrected Carpathian barreled towards them, inadvertently impaling himself on the fae's quickly-drawn blade. It stuck out of the very center of his chest, buried almost completely to the hilt.

The Carpathian looked down at it. The fae looked down at it.

Then both lifted their eyes to each other.

"Are you, like...okay?"

"Ellanden!"

"Right—sorry!' The fae ripped out the sword, beheading the man for good measure, then raced with his friends up the remainder of the beach. "On second thought, let's stick together!"

It was a good thing none of the teenagers looked back. The sight of the man's body reaching blindly for its head would have given them nightmares for years to come.

THE FIGHTING WASN'T easier when they reached the ships, it was merely in closer quarters. Neither were the friends able to stay together. From the moment they sprinted up the gangplank on the first vessel a pack of undead shifters leapt upon them, and they were funneled off in separate ways.

Evie slammed the hilt of her sword into a head of blond hair, then let out a sharp cry when she was immediately kicked down a rickety staircase. Her fingers clawed desperately to slow her momentum, but the wood was already slick with a coating of salt and blood.

It wasn't until she reached the bottom that she realized it wasn't actually a terrible place to have ended up. There was no one else within sight. If she could just locate her missing sword—

"Caros."

She turned with a gasp to see the fae they'd met earlier, the one who'd smiled at their enthusiasm and offered to give them a tour of the ship. He was standing in the shadows, half-shadowed in the dim light. It wasn't until he took a step closer that she saw the giant tear in his neck.

"Oh shit," she gasped, abandoning the search for the blade and hurrying towards him, ripping a piece from the bottom of her skirt at the same time. "It's all right, we can fix this. Just hold this tightly to keep the pressure—"

He backed away just as fast, a strange expression flickering over his face.

"*Caros.*"

The word was whispered again between them, the fae asking for help.

The princess stopped in the center of the floor, staring with confusion. It's what she'd been trying to do, he couldn't have thought she meant him any—

Then all at once, those tiny details she'd missed before burned brightly in her eyes.

There was too much blood on the floor—the fae had been there for a while and he couldn't possibly have enough left. Then she saw the severity of the wound. The greyish tint to his skin.

...you are dead already.

She backed away, staring up at him in dread.

"But you're speaking to me," she panted. "How are you still speaking to me?"

The fae lunged toward her then caught himself just as fast, staring without comprehension at the strange sluggishness to his hands. Breathing quickly, though he didn't seem to be getting any air. His gaze rose once more, and the help for which he'd been asking suddenly made sense.

"I can't..." she whispered, tears spilling down her cheeks. "It isn't a certainty, it's only a spell. You are breaking through it already. You need to fight. You need to..."

...but he is dead already.

The fae lifted his head, still touched with an eerie beauty though the ethereal light that had once illuminated his features had faded into dusk.

"Milady." He said the word with great effort, looking into her eyes. "*...please.*"

A wave of fire poured between them, vanishing quickly into the dark night.

Evie backed away as soon as it was finished, trembling uncontrollably as spirals of smoke drifted up from her hands. She was lucky the flames hadn't spread—there was a reason she and her mother were being so careful. She was lucky the fae hadn't simply murdered her the moment she'd fallen down the staircase. It would have been so easy. She hadn't even seen he was there.

But she didn't feel very lucky. She felt like she was going to be sick.

"Evie?!" Asher's voice echoed down the stairwell, tight with panic. "Are you—"

"I'm here," she murmured shakily, then a bit louder, "I'm down here. Just a moment, I'm coming...I'm coming to you."

With a final look the princess dragged herself back up the stairs, collapsing with a silent whimper against the vampire's chest. He was sporting fresh wounds of his own, but none of them appeared to be serious. He grabbed hold of her with unnatural strength, eyes roving the deck of the ship as he took stock of the rest.

Two more vessels had sunk in the harbor, but the chaos enveloping the harbor seemed to be winding down. Most of the creatures on their own ship had already been dealt with—thanks in large part to the efforts of Ellanden, who was still tearing wildly across the deck.

That inevitable fatigue touched them all differently, but the fae's immortality had protected him from the worst of it thus far. The tears on his back were already in the process of healing, and he slashed and battled his way across the deck with an almost feverish light in his eyes.

But he never saw the Carpathian rising up behind him, no more than he heard his friend's frantic cry. He didn't realize what was happening until a savage blade flew straight towards his face.

—only to be caught with the flash of a hand.

The prince stepped back with a gasp as Andrei appeared between them—watching with wide eyes as the vampire dispatched the brutish warrior with a flick of his hand. He kept the blade a moment longer, giving it a cursory twirl before dropping it to the ground.

It clattered between them.

"Hello again, angel."

He lifted a hand to the others in acknowledgement, who were still clutching each other in belated panic as the terror slowly subsided.

"You fight well," he commended, picking a piece of mottled flesh from the fae's shoulder. "I tried to get to you sooner, but I was securing the rest of the ships."

The three friends glanced towards the harbor in shock.

Of course you were. All by yourself.

Ellanden stared at him in the darkness, trying to catch his breath.

"Still offering your protection?"

"What—this?" The vampire nudged the Carpathian with his boot, then flashed a bloody grin. "This is just good fun."

The fae stared a moment longer, then a slow smile spread up his face. "I'm clearing the upper decks, should be heavily guarded." He paused ever so slightly, before extending a blade. "Up for some more fun?"

The vampire's eyes twinkled in the dark. "Always."

The two were gone a second later, vanishing up the stairwell and leaving the others standing in stunned silence on the deck. They remained there a few seconds longer, fatigued to the point of delirium and unable to reconcile the image to the point of it making any sense.

Then they shared a quick look and drew blades of their own.

"It's not the strangest thing that's happened," Asher assured her. "If we live through this, we can hire some coven to expunge the memory from our minds."

"Agreed."

They were off a second later, battling monsters and demons of their own.

THE FIGHT CONTINUED raging long after the friends had reached their limit, stretching into the early hours of the morning as they worked in tandem—clearing ship, after ship, after ship.

Evie and Asher were never more than a heartbeat away from each other—one of them massacring whoever dared cross them, while the other incinerated the bodies before they could rise again. It was a dangerous pairing—one that was matched only by the vampire and the fae.

After their alliance had been struck, they drifted in and out of the picture—moving with a synchronicity and intuition that defied the fact they were technically strangers and spoke to a history that neither actually shared. Like a pair of twin spirits they flitted up and down the ship, dipping between light and shadow and leaving a trail of utter destruction in their wake. Until suddenly—

"No!"

The princess raised her head at once, turning in fear towards the captains' quarters only to see the door burst open a second later. Two men had gone inside. Only one of them had returned.

"He took a hit for me," Ellanden panted, carrying the vampire towards them. The front of his tunic was drenched in blood, but none of it belonged to the fae. "There was a shifter I didn't see in the corner. And by the time I turned—"

"It's all right," Asher steadied him, blurring across the remainder of the deck. The final ship had at last been cleared, and they'd been preparing to head back. "Few wounds can prove fatal for a vampire. I'm sure we can heal him. The only thing he'll need is a little..."

He peeled back the cloak and trailed into silence.

Whatever blade the shifter had been wielding had clearly left a mark. It looked as though something had torn the vampire straight up the middle, slicing a gaping ravine into his chest.

"Blood?" the fae asked frantically. "The only thing he'll need is a little blood?" He yanked up his sleeve with his teeth. "He can have some of mine. The two of you can steady him—"

"Ellanden," Asher interrupted softly. "A wound like this can't heal. No matter whose blood we give him. No matter how much he's able to drink."

The fae stared back in silence before shaking his head.

"No, we can fix this. We just need to get back." He shifted the fallen vampire higher, already racing towards the gangplank, pale as a sheet. "We need to find the others—"

But at that moment there was a sudden shift upon the battlefield. One significant enough to be felt in the harbor. One that made everyone still fighting on the sand turn at the same time.

The sound of the battle had travelled far across the forest, reaching immortal ears.

The vampires had returned.

For one of the first times in memory, that eternal poise had fractured. The clan was staring across the battlefield with a look of collective shock. Death wasn't something new to a vampire, but even they were unfamiliar with this version of it. A version that kept coming back again and again.

"Thank the gods," Ellanden panted, the vampire still draped across his arms. "We're saved."

Evie's heart lifted at the words before freezing just as fast.

No, death wasn't something new to a vampire.

Some might say their entire existence hovered right on the edge, blurring the line between light and shadow, between day and all that endless dusk. Some might say that they had already crossed it. That their hearts were no longer beating. That they already belonged to the dead.

One way or another, it was about to be put to the test.

Wait...what's happening?

The change was both slow and subtle, like an icy breeze stirring amongst the leaves. While all of the vampires continued to stare, some were finding their gaze to be newly directed—falling on royal targets while drifting straight over the army of the dead.

It was only then Evie realized a chilling truth.

There would be no more welcome a sight to a necromancer than the arrival of a thousand vampires. He would simply raise his hands and command them. All that terror and talent and cold inhumanity they'd seen crush an army of Carpathians would be leveled against their own side.

"Seven hells," she gasped, turning to the others. "What can we...?"

She trailed off a second later, staring in fright.

"Ash?"

Her boyfriend was gazing towards the vampires as well, but his entire body had gone rigid. A whispered chill swept across his skin and he winced suddenly, as though he'd heard a loud noise.

Ellanden took a single look and backed away.

"Everly...walk to me."

She stood there trembling, tears blurring her vision.

"Evie—*now*," the fae insisted, suddenly grateful the vampire he was holding had drifted out of consciousness. "Get away from him."

"He's right," Asher breathed, staring down at his body with a detached curiosity as if it no longer responded to his commands. "Go to him, Evie. Run to the trees."

She wanted to. Every instinct was screaming to. But some part of her held back.

"You can fight this," she whispered instead. "This is not who you are. This is not *what* you are. You can fight this, Asher Dorsett. You just need to try."

Another shiver swept over him, causing his hands to ball up at his sides.

"*Run*," he panted, baring his fangs. "Get away from me—"

That time Evie did run. but towards him instead.

"Please!" the vampire cried as the fae shouted something behind them. His dark eyes were flashing, torn between different worlds. "I don't want to hurt you! I can't—"

A steady hand settled upon his heart.

"I know you can feel this," the princess murmured, gazing up at him. "I know you are more than this. I've known it since the first moment you stepped into our lives, and every moment since."

Their eyes locked beneath a starless sky.

"Stay with me."

He stared back in silence, overwhelmed by the feeling—overwhelmed by the conflict. Finding nothing to which to tether himself besides the quiet, trusting smile in her eyes.

After a small eternity, his own cleared as well.

"Always."

The two came together as the fae let out a silent breath behind him—releasing the secret grip on his blade. Exactly what he'd intended to do, there was no answer. But it was a question the rest of the realm found themselves facing as each of the vampires splintered inside.

It held them first in stillness, then fractured some of them apart.

Evie watched from afar as a dozen or so raced towards a coven of witches—hands reaching forward and fangs bared—only to find themselves dragged back again just as fast. For as many of the clan found themselves weakening to the necromancer's command, even more of them hardened against it with a fresh burst of resolve. Subduing and restraining, killing only when necessary, forcing their brethren back from the brink as that deathly call found itself falling on deaf ears.

The three friends stared in silence before Evie flashed a little smile.

"Looks like vampires have a soul after all."

Some of them. Others had strayed too far over the line.

"Release me!" Eleazer's voice rang over the sand as he threw off those who'd been trying to restrain him with a wave of his hand. "Too long have I waited...the blood is mine to take."

Evie followed his gaze in horror, only to find Leonor standing in the crowd.

The immortal councilman looked up in the same moment, meeting the vampire's hungry gaze. His arrows were spent so he lifted a sword from his belt, bracing for whatever was to happen next with a weary lifetime of experience that somehow translated into perfect calm.

But as it turned out, he would not be fighting that particular battle.

"Eleazer."

At first, there were only the two of them. Then Diana appeared beside them, speaking in a low murmur as she walked slowly across the sand.

"Eleazer," she repeated softly, "will you not look at me?"

She stepped towards him cautiously, the way one approached wild animals. The way one approached most vampires. Slipping between him and the fae without a hint of fear.

"Listen to me, old friend. Focus on the sound of my voice."

His head jerked to the side, pulling in different directions.

"It is too much," he hissed between gritted teeth. "You have always asked too much."

She shook her head slowly, eyes on his face.

"I have never asked anything more than what you are capable of. It is nothing but a choice that I ask of you now. Look into my eyes. We will return to the forest together—"

But there wasn't time to say anything more. Because the vampire leapt towards the fae a second later, and the queen who loved him tore him in half.

There wasn't a sound on the beach after. Nothing but the quiet settling of sand.

Then Diana threw back her head with a deafening cry.

It was echoed at once in the forest. It was echoed by those standing on the beach. It was answered by each and every person left standing in the royal army.

An army that stood united. An army that threw itself upon the dead with fresh vengeance.

Tearing them to pieces until nothing was left.

Chapter 14

Evie stood at the crest of the forest, watching the piles of bodies burning on the beach.

Her mother and grandmother had been at it for hours, never faltering and never saying a word in complaint as the foot-soldiers of the five kingdoms scoured every inch of the shoreline—wearing scented scarves around their faces as they brought back piece, after piece, after piece.

She should probably have been helping. But there were apologies that needed to be made.

"Is he awake?" she asked quickly, turning as an immortal healer made his way out of a nearby tent. She'd been waiting for the last hour, hardly daring to pull in a breath. "Please say—"

"He's awake," the fae replied with a slight frown. "But I don't know why you're—"

"Thank you," she gasped, pushing inside before abruptly freezing in the doorway.

When her beloved Hastings had lifted his sword, she thought the fae he'd struck was gone forever. It was a devastating blow, in a dangerous location. But Estien was lying upon a makeshift cot—tired, but most definitely breathing. When she burst through the door, he lifted his gaze.

"Princess...?" he trailed off in confusion. "Why have you—"

Her cheeks flamed with a blush. "I wanted to apologize for what happened."

The fae blinked in a daze. "I don't understand...are you going from tent to tent?"

She ventured a few steps closer, then perched on the edge of his bed. A second later she leapt back to her feet, thinking it might aggravate the wound. In the end she tried to compromise, fussing unnecessarily with his covers before dropping her arms uselessly back to her sides.

Estien watched in perfect silence, convinced he must be in a fevered dream.

"The man who stabbed you," she finally began, unable to stall any further, "was the knight assigned to protect me back at the palace when I was a child."

The fae's eyebrows rose ever so slightly, but he didn't speak.

"I've known him all my life," she continued, wringing her fingers together, "and I just wanted to...the thing is, he would have been horrified to learn that he..." She drew in a quick breath, not realizing she'd begun to cry. "I understand this doesn't do anything to ease your condition, but I know that if he were standing here today he'd want me to apologize—"

"*Peace*, child." The fae's eyes softened, understanding for the first time. "Is that really why you've come? To make amends for those lost to enchantment?"

She bit down on her lip, unable to meet his eyes.

"It was a curse, dear one," he continued gently. "You would no more have to apologize for the changing of the seasons, or for the rain falling from the sky."

He tilted his head, catching her gaze.

"Treasure the memory you have of him, and let that be the end." His lovely face warmed with the hint of a smile. "I'll do my best to forget mine."

She let out a breath of laughter then threw her arms around him in a sudden embrace, never seeing the rush of pain that swept over him or the look of exasperation as he raised his eyes to the sky.

"Thank you," she murmured, wiping her eyes. "I'll be back to check on you soon."

The fae smiled tightly. "Only if you must."

She was gone a moment later, feeling considerably brighter. And completely oblivious when the healer returned and the two fae stared after her with the same puzzled look in their eyes.

"What a strange girl..."

UNWILLING TO STAY ON the beach, the rest of the camp had moved into the forest—where the vampires had been staying in the nights before. Since the two groups no longer had any boundaries between them, there was no reason not to cluster together for protection—though it did make for a befuddling labyrinth of tents. Evie walked twice into the wrong one before finally slipping inside the one she'd been looking for.

"I've been looking for you," she announced, watching as Asher set down his satchel and slipped a fresh shirt over his head. "Where's Ellanden? I thought we might get some lunch."

"He went to see Andrei."

"Andrei," she repeated in surprise. "But I thought he was—"

"He is," Asher interrupted. "There are some wounds from which even a vampire can't heal."

She shook her head blankly.

"So what is Ellanden doing?"

The vampire hesitated before answering, as if he couldn't believe the words himself.

"He's giving him a vial of blood."

...he's what?!

Asher held up his hands, shaking his head. "I know, you don't even have to say it."

"Well, that tops my news," she said dispiritedly, plopping onto his bed. "The most I was going to share was that I *thought* I saw two pieces of an undead kelpie dragging themselves back together...but it turned out to be a log."

Asher snorted with laughter, but it faded quickly from his face.

"He was terribly upset about it," he murmured, sinking onto the bed beside her. "Came to my tent an hour before dawn, started pacing back and forth, grilling me on vampiric anatomy. At first, I thought he was just flirting. But then he mentioned what happened on the ship..."

The two of them bowed their heads in silence, staring at their hands. It wasn't until a few seconds had passed that Evie shot him a quick look. "You thought he was flirting?"

The vampire shrugged. "A little joke to lighten the tension."

"How did Ellanden take that?"

"...he punched me in the jaw."

The two friends laughed again, leaning subconsciously together—then quieted abruptly as the sound of footsteps approached the tent and the fae himself ducked into view.

"Hey," Evie said tentatively, pushing to her feet, "we were just talking about you."

Asher got to his feet as well. "How's Andrei?"

"He's nearly there," the fae replied, fiddling with the flap on the tent. He looked strangely unsettled, refusing to meet their eyes. "I might go back and see him this evening."

His friends shared a look, but kept their silence.

"They had a meeting of the High Council without us," Ellanden continued, unhitching his bow and propping it against the wall. "Just our parents, along with Diana, Leonor, and Atticus. They decided without contestation to officially recognize the accords." The corners of his lips twitched in a wry smile. "At some point since last we spoke, it seems my people had a change of heart."

Evie let out a burst of laughter, unable to believe it was true. "Perhaps they were simply waiting for the vampires to acknowledge their own."

"*Very* diplomatic," Asher commended with a wink.

"Yes...and they did it all without rings, or flowers, or a pretty white dress," Ellanden added sarcastically. "Let's not forget they said I was *crazy* for suggesting they do this weeks ago."

Evie laughed again as Asher rolled his eyes with a grin.

"You're ahead of your time, Landi. A virtual prophet—"

He stopped himself quickly when a shadow loomed on the other side of the door. A second later, a throat cleared apologetically as the voice of one of the healers drifted inside.

"Pardon the intrusion, but you had asked after the vampire?"

Ellanden took a quick step forward. "Yes, I had planned to check on him—"

"There's no need, Your Highness. The vampire passed away."

There was a beat of silence.

"He died?" the fae repeated in shock.

It *couldn't* have been a shock. He had to know that it was coming. Yet it struck him all the same. He recovered quickly, blushing as the princess squeezed his shoulder.

"Thank you for telling me," he intoned, dismissing the man. He stared a moment at the door before casting a quick glance at the others. "Sorry, I just wasn't expecting..."

In a flash, Asher was beside him.

"Don't apologize," he said softly, resting a hand on the fae's arm. "You were kind to look in on him. I know it wasn't always the easiest relationship, but the two of you ended things well."

The fae stared back at him with a strange expression, as if the vampire had put voice to the exact things he'd long been thinking himself. There was a moment when he simply stared, then another when he hesitated—held back by tide of feeling so immense it would have been hard to describe.

Then he drew in a deep breath.

"I need to ask you something."

Asher leaned back, surprised by the change in tone.

"I'm not angry about the ship," he guessed, trying to interpret the fae's expression. "You hadn't commissioned one yet, and we lost the sword anyway. At any rate, Evie's probably right about the whole gift-giving campaign. Over the years, it's gotten a bit out of control. And seeing as I don't technically have any money of my own, we should probably stop before it—"

The fae reached into his pocket, extracting a crystal vial.

"I would like for us to bond."

Asher's lips parted as time itself seemed to pause.

"...you win."

TEN MINUTES LATER, the conversation had not progressed.

"You wish to bond," the vampire repeated for the tenth time, staring at the vial of blood still resting in the fae's palm. "You already had this in your pocket."

"I was preparing one for Andrei," Ellanden hesitated shyly, "...then I decided to make two."

Asher stared a moment, then shook his head—laughing a bit hysterically.

"Because you wish to *bond*."

"Yes, I—"

"Since when?"

The fae pulled in a quick breath, flustered by the speed of the conversation.

"You've spoken of it before, but I dismissed it on impulse out of—" He caught himself, unable to see past that eternal pride. "Not fear...but something not unlike it."

If Evie hadn't been so astonished, she might have laughed.

In a way, it made perfect sense. While theirs wasn't a connection required by prophetic decree, they had grown up together and were far closer than their parents had been at the time.

But Asher couldn't wrap his head around the fae's decision.

Long had he imagined such a thing himself, but on the few occasions he'd been either brave or careless enough to bring it up the fae had dismissed the idea in a burst of thoughtless laughter.

Needless to say, he'd stopped bringing it up. And instead of embracing the idea, now that the moment was upon them he found himself inexplicably stalling.

"Your father wouldn't—"

"My father did the same thing himself."

"Your council wouldn't—"

"Leonor has run the table for long enough," Ellanden interrupted wryly. "And while I may have apologized for striking him, I did not surrender the point. All my life people have worked so hard to create a distinction, building this up into some kind of..." He shook his head in frustration, dismissing it. "But it's only blood. It's mine to give to whom I wish. That's if you still..."

For the first time, a look of uncertainty flashed across the fae's enchanting face.

"...if you still want to."

Asher took an actual step back, his mind spinning beyond all rational thought.

There were too many currents at play. A lifelong friendship, a political entanglement, the ego and possible heartbreak of a man he'd loved since they were boys. It was critical to navigate each of the waters carefully, imperative not to misstep. But all he could do was be surprised.

"Yes, I want to," he admitted, raking back his hair. "I have since the moment the three of us left. It's just...you are *impulsive*, Ellanden. And this is not an impulsive thing. I would never..."

He caught himself quickly, realizing all at once there were two delicate egos on the line.

"I would never want it to be something you'd come to regret."

The fae stared at him, then tilted his head.

"But it's just *you*, isn't it? This bond...it's merely a connection with *you*."

The vampire nodded uncertainly, watching as his face went clear.

"Then I won't regret it."

Evie stared between them with a little smile.

My boys...

Before the vampire had a chance to process, the fae pulled in a determined breath.

"I'll go first."

"Right here?"

"Where else?"

"Right now?"

"There *is* only—" Ellanden caught himself, glancing towards the sea. "There is only right now. The army may be defeated, but the stone remains. And if Kaleb has truly embraced the path of necromancy, he will never run out of dead. One of us is doomed not to return from this adventure, and while I'd give my last breath to ensure that person is *me* such things are beyond our control."

He looked at the others, lingering on each one.

"We have only this moment. We have only each other. The two of you have already bonded, and I would not like to leave this world without doing the same. I would like it to be all three."

A tear slipped down Evie's cheek. Asher cleared his throat, then glanced away.

"...all right, then."

WHILE THE ORATORY HAD been both poetic and odd, the act itself was somewhat of a mystery.

"Our parents," Asher began uncertainly, "they cut their hands—"

"My blood isn't pure like my father's," Ellanden interrupted. "There's a chance I could tolerate yours. There's a chance it could even heal me." A flash of that signature curiosity danced in his eyes. "If you don't mind...I'd like to try."

"All right," Asher replied softly.

He picked up the knife and nicked the tip of his finger, holding it out to the fae. Knowing him as she did Evie could tell Ellanden was disappointed not to partake the traditional way—in a blur of fangs—but he kept this graciously to himself and did not demand the vampire cut himself twice.

"So now I just..." He trailed off into silence, staring at the blood dripping down his friend's hand. "...drink that."

Evie bit her lip, trying *very hard* to keep from laughing while a look of irritation flashed across Asher's face. "Since this was your idea, and I've already gone through the trouble of cutting open my skin—*yes*, that's the general idea."

Ellanden nodded, looking vaguely sick. "Perhaps we could just—"

"Landi, I'm not going to sedate you. Do you want to do this, or not?"

"Of course I do, it's just—"

"*Hurry*, then. The wound is already closing."

"Well if it's already closing then maybe we could try a more theatric approach," the fae suggested innocently, reaching for a blade of his own. "Perhaps if it felt more incidental—"

Evie shoved him forward.

"*Drink.*"

Ellanden shot her a glare, then swiped his finger along the vampire's skin. It came away wet, but when he lifted it to his mouth a lifetime of deep-rooted instinct took over.

"This is disgusting," he muttered, turning his face. "I don't understand how you—"

Asher shoved his finger into the fae's mouth.

At last…silence.

"That was beautiful," Evie murmured from the sidelines, clasping her hands.

Ellanden froze in surprise, making a conscious effort not to gag. Then he turned discreetly to the side, gagging anyway. "Seven hells…I'm going to be sick."

"Just take a breath," Asher soothed, growing abruptly serious as the fae swallowed it down. He stilled a moment in anticipation before brightening with a sudden smile. "You did it."

The fae lifted his eyes with a petulant glare.

"That would never *heal* me."

I should be writing this down. Start a comedy hour to cheer the troops.

"Now for mine."

The second the fae extended the vial, the vampire was the one who froze.

"Ellanden…you don't *have* to do this," he said softly, though his eyes remained fixed on the blood. "No one's forcing you—"

"But I can choose it," the fae replied.

Yes, he could choose it. To ensure, above all things, empathy. Asher was connected to all vampires, and the fae would be connected to him. Never could you destroy one without harming the other. Never could the alliance break without the devastation of not one, but two lives.

They would be tied together, bound by their very souls.

If they don't end up killing each other…

"I don't know why," Evie started nervously, "because I was weirdly okay with the finger, but *this* part seems strange to me."

"It's not strange," Asher said innocently, reaching for the vial at the same time. "It's actually rather sweet—"

She intercepted it. "Give us assurances you won't kill him."

The vampire rolled his eyes. "Oh—what do you care?"

Ellanden glanced between them. "Wait—what?"

"Give us assurances!" Evie demanded.

"I solemnly swear not to kill him," the vampire chanted sarcastically, raising a hand in the air. "But I make *no* such promises concerning you, if you don't give me that blood."

All that bravado disappeared the second it was in his hand.

His lips parted ever so slightly and his eyes flashed to Ellanden's face—seeking endless permission, and suddenly worried that perhaps the fae should preemptively leave.

Then, with prompting looks from his friends, he drained it like a shot.

Wait for it...wait for it...

"SEVEN HELLS!"

Both of the others jumped a mile as Asher's eyes shot open—his gaze flying around the room like he'd never seen such a thing before. The colors were brighter, the air was sweeter. His very body felt as though part of it might be floating—reading to take off and fly.

It only took a moment to find the fae.

"Come here," he panted, reaching at the same time. "I want to...thank you."

Ellanden stayed right where he was, fighting a hesitant smile.

"You can thank me from over there."

"No, seriously—come here." The vampire made a sudden grab for him, laughing innocently when the fae stepped out of reach. "I just...I have something for you. Come see what it is."

The princess and the fae shared a quick look.

I honestly can't tell if he's joking.

"An embrace," Asher insisted, stumbling a few steps closer. "We are bonded now, and I simply want to embrace you like a brother. It will be fine. I promise. Close your eyes."

Close your eyes?!

"I'm...going to head out." Ellanden flashed a shaky smile, backing towards the door. "Have a good night, you two. I'll be sleeping somewhere different than before."

The vampire flashed a manic smile, eyes twinkling in the light. "...I'll find you."

Ellanden laughed under his breath, ducking beneath the flap. "Wow, you're scary..."

He vanished a second later, presumably to spend the night camped out in the center of the garrison, leaving the princess and the vampire alone in the tent.

In hindsight...that's a bit of an ask.

"Should we go and find him?" Asher asked immediately, those luminous eyes widening to take up his entire face. "Or should we stay here and sing a little? I could go for a swim..."

She cocked her head. "In the blood-soaked ocean?"

"Just *look* at this..." he continued obliviously, abruptly thrusting his entire hand into her hair. "The softest thing in the world—and it smells of lilacs," he added suddenly. A dreamy look came over him as he sank onto the bed with a sigh. "I think of it often."

You. Are. So. Adorable.

"Everly...please make me a promise," the vampire murmured, running his fingers through each crimson wave. "Never cut your hair. But if you do...give it to me. I'd like to keep it."

She laughed softly, settling down beside him. "I'm going to remember you said that."

They stayed down there together for a while, not speaking much. Not even really thinking about anything in particular. Just sitting quietly in each other company, arms curled into arms.

"There is no more betrothal," she finally murmured. "Why are things still so strange?"

She didn't expect him to answer. She didn't even really expect him to hear. But he sat up abruptly, gazing down at her in concern. "What do you mean?"

She debated keeping it to herself, then abruptly realized the fae was right.

We only have this moment.

"Ellanden is my brother once again," she said quietly. "The two of you have bonded. There are no further requirements of us. We're free to do as we please. And yet...it's strange."

His eyes clouded over, feeling the same thing himself.

"We made promises of eternity, and one of the first things we did was break them," he answered softly. "Is it really so strange? It will only take a while...for things to settle."

But we don't have a while.

She twisted around in his arms, turning to face him. "I love you, Asher."

He waited for more, then nodded. "...I love you, too."

Then why is that not enough?

❧

THE PRINCESS MIGHT have stayed longer but Asher had promptly fallen asleep 'in the hopes of dreaming of butterflies', and the mood had taken a decided turn. She wandered around the camp for a while, watching smiths and the soldiers, watching the healers roam back and forth.

Then her eyes caught with a sudden movement.

"Uncle Kailas?"

He was striding with purpose through the center of the trees and didn't hear her. For a split second, she turned to look where he was going. Then realized the larger question was from where he'd just come. The usual lines of worry that aged his handsome face had all but vanished, and there was a lightness to his step where there hadn't been one before. Not since that first moment by the portal, before they'd set foot in the High Kingdom, had she seen him so relaxed and unconcerned.

Must be the recent...army of the dead?

She stared after him in bewilderment, then turned again to follow his steps. He'd come from a line of tents along the edge the treeline. Not much else was there, except—

It struck her all at once.

Where he was coming from. What he had done. A rush of feeling swept through her, lifting her to the tips of her toes. Then she found herself darting through the trees as well.

To a specific tent that housed a specific lady.

"Aunt Tanya," she gasped, sweeping back the door, "I need your help."

"ARE YOU SURE ABOUT this?"

The two women sat in the middle of the floor, knees touching and hands resting lightly upon their legs. After getting over the initial shock, it had only taken the Kreo priestess a few moments to understand what the princess was asking and consider the request.

She studied her carefully, taking in every inch of her face.

"Journeys like this aren't always easy—"

"I'm sure you can do it!'

"I mean they aren't always easy for *you*," Tanya corrected, leaning back with a sigh. "And, for the record, I hate talking like this. It makes me sound like my grandmother."

Evie's eyes flashed up before she chanced a little smile. "There are worse people to sound like."

The shifter's lips twitched. "Yes, there are. But the fact remains, this isn't an easy journey. Not because of what you might see, but because of how it might change you coming back on the other side. Ellanden asked me to do the same for him not long after you got back. I refused him cold."

Evie's mouth fell open in surprise. "You did? Why?"

"Ellanden is highly immature," Tanya explained patiently. "And it does far more good for his particular character to deny him things than to grant every request."

...that's a good point.

"I was also afraid of hurting him further," the shifter added suddenly, looking at the ground. "I could not bear the thought of...him seeing things he didn't really want to see."

The princess hesitated a moment, then took her hands. "Aunt Tanya...I need to do this. I need to see what happened for myself." She weighed the queen's expression. "If you don't help me I'll just stomp through the forest, looking for snakes."

Tanya snorted with laughter, reaching for her hands. "If I didn't know your mother was currently outside burning corpses, I'd swear you were the same person..." Her fingers wrapped around the princess' wrist before she suddenly looked into her eyes. "You won't be able to see the entire thing. Your mind wasn't aware of most of what was happening. The most you'll be able to get is flashes. A general mood to set the tone."

Evie nodded quickly, heart fluttering with anticipation. "That's fine. That's all I'm going to need."

It happened without a hint of warning. Not a single breath of transition to ease the princess along. Just a hard tug around her stomach and then the tent vanished.

A cave rose up in its place.

She was right...I shouldn't have done this.

The princess straightened up slowly, staring into the gloom.

The smell was the first thing that struck her. Damp stone, with a faint dusting of herbs from the wizard's spells. It was enough to turn her stomach. How long had she breathed it before?

Just a few steps further, and then she saw it. The cage on the far side of the room.

The wizard was there as well, as he always was. Humming to himself and bustling cheerfully around the kitchen, but never in exactly the same place at exactly the same time. She realized as she drifted closer that time was the real factor. She was seeing none of it. She was seeing all of it.

Ten years condensed into a single, shifting image. Yet one thing remained the same.

There we are.

She pulled in a breath, staring down at the three sleeping figures lying on the ground. It was almost hard to make out their faces—each was cloaked in shadow and so still, it might have been carved in stone. But it wasn't the figures themselves that concerned her. It was how they slept.

Together. Always together.

Asher had once told her he'd fallen in love when he was dreaming. Ten years of dreaming with the same girl curled up in his arms. She saw now that it was true.

Trapped in a cage. Lost to the rest of the world. Yet there was something inexplicably peaceful about the two of them together. As if time had stopped by intention, just to let them sleep.

She pulled from the vision with a gasp, clinging tightly to her aunt's hands.

The room swayed but Tanya steadied her, rubbing circles on her knees then pushing to her feet and murmuring something about a calming draught of tea.

But Evie sprang to her feet as well.

"No—it's fine," she said breathlessly. "I'm fine. I...I saw everything I needed to see."

A quick kiss to her aunt's cheek and she was racing back through the forest. Weaving through the maze with unlikely confidence, her mind still spinning from everything she'd seen.

She remembered her talk with Kailas, the certainty he'd felt with Sera—more than a guiding light in the darkness, the woman had become a kind of faith.

And that's exactly what I have with Asher.

She'd wanted something steady? Something certain?

For *ten years* the vampire had cradled her in the darkness. Day after day, night after night. His was the first name she called in times of danger, the face she looked for in the wreckage, the smile that pieced it back together. His was the hand she always reached for, always reaching back for hers.

Ten years...he'd never left her side.

"IT *is* enough!"

The princess burst into the tent without a hint of warning, startling the vampire right out of bed. He landed on the ground with a gasp, putting a trembling hand to his chest.

"...what?'

"It's enough," she said again, kneeling beside him and taking his hands. "Whatever becomes of us at the end of this journey, whatever things might happen, whatever people we might turn out to be...it is enough that I am with you."

She paused for breath, staring into his eyes.

"It has always been you, Asher. And it always will be."

He stared back at her in a daze before pressing her hand to his chest, just as she'd done just a few hours before—when he'd heard death's call echoing from the forest.

"You saved me," he murmured, placing his hand upon hers. "Even when I didn't know I needed saving. You brought me back to life."

A tear slipped down her face as she kissed the tips of his fingers.

Time stopped again for the young lovers. It was a courtesy only awarded to some. But the princess had no intention to linger. She had other plans for the night.

"That's right...I saved you." She gazed up at him in the light of the candles, biting her lip with a secret smile. "Have you remembered to thank me?"

A look of surprise flitted across his face, followed by a devilish grin.

"That's a very good question..."

He slowly crawled forward, lowering her body to the ground.

"We might be here for a while," she whispered, closing her eyes as he pressed kisses down the length of her skin. "I'm not sure you can ever thank me enough."

He blew out the candle...and decided to try.

Chapter 15

The princess stood the next morning at the edge of the water, gazing out over the distant waves. She felt strangely calm, if not particularly well-rested. Though the clouds rolling on the horizon made it feel as though the tides themselves were shifting, drawing them closer to an end.

Long will they travel, for deep does it dwell...

All night she'd been tossing and turning, plagued with the feeling that she was on the verge of something important—the answer to some question hovering just out of reach.

To recover a stone from a land that won't burn...

She looked over the water then lowered her eyes to the waves.

A land that won't burn.

Her lips parted with a silent gasp.

"We're looking in the wrong place."

The sound of chattering voices drifted up behind her as her friends ventured out of the forest themselves and joined her at the crest of the beach. Considering what they'd been through the night before, they were sated and an unlikely kind of happy.

This battle was finished. They would worry later about the stone.

"Good morning." Asher came up behind her, wrapping his arms around her waist. "You're up early... I didn't even hear you get out of bed—"

"We're looking in the wrong place!"

She whirled around to face them, ignoring their looks of surprise.

"What are you—"

"Guys, listen to me! Kaleb's had ten years to look for the stone. We went to the same library, read the same inscription. It took the three of us less than a minute to decide it was referring to the Dunes. It was the obvious answer. *Ten years* he's had to look...but he didn't find it there."

The smiles froze, then vanished from their faces. After a few seconds of claustrophobic silence and uneasy glances, Ellanden finally cleared his throat.

"So, what are you saying?"

She stood there a moment, then pointed to the waves.

"...it's in the water."

Like something out of a dream, a chorus of unearthly voices started ringing in her ears.

The men exchanged a worried look. The girls wondered if she'd been drinking. Then, as it happened so often in situations such as these, Asher was pushed to the front.

"Honey, I don't think—"

"It's not just floating around, Ash. It's at the bottom of the sea." She threw up her hands, like it should have been obvious. "A place covered in sand? A land that won't burn?"

She stood there with a smile, waiting for them to fill it in.

"It's at the bottom of the ocean!"

Five blank faces stared back.

...probably not the best time to mention the voices.

"You're serious with this?" Cosette asked with a touch of amusement. "You think whatever great power sent these stones here in the first place dropped one of them into the sea?"

"Perhaps it was clumsy," Seth whispered conspiratorially. "You know how these great powers can be."

"You *are* being serious," Asher murmured, staring into her eyes. "Is that why you came out here this morning? You've been thinking how to search beneath the waves?"

She bit her lip, worried she might lose them. "Actually, I had an idea about that..."

"THIS IS YOUR FAULT," Ellanden said stiffly, shooting the vampire a glare. "I don't know how or what it was, but you did something to break her."

Asher threw a quick glare as the princess waded out into the surf.

"I'm not broken," she muttered. "I'm just testing out a theory."

The cool water streamed around her legs, misting against her cheeks and filling her nostrils with the scent of salt and brine. She pulled in a deep breath, hyper-aware of the dubious people standing on the beach behind her, then she lowered her lips to the surface of the waves.

"...hello?"

Ellanden threw up his hands as Asher's eyes snapped shut.

"Seven hells, Everly."

She ignored them, hovering just over the water.

"Can anyone hear me?" Her voice lowered to a whisper. "If you *can* hear me, you should know that you're really starting to make me look bad."

"Maybe you should stick your head under!" Freya called helpfully from the beach.

The princess couldn't tell if she was joking or not. But with a furtive glance over her shoulder, she leaned forward and decided to give it a shot.

An explosion of bubbles burst from her mouth.

"Hello?!"

"Up here, my darling."

The princess yanked up her head, sputtering and coughing up bits of salty foam. As Ellanden would tell her later, it looked a great deal like she'd developed a case of rabies.

It could not have proved a greater contrast to the woman in front of her. And it was the last manner in the world in which she'd have wanted to meet the mermaid queen.

A pair of golden eyes twinkled in the sun.

"You are utterly adorable."

She hiccupped once again, then turned in waterlogged triumph towards the beach.

Told you.

THEIR PARENTS WERE summoned quickly as the friends watched the mermaid in fascination from the shore. Several others had surfaced to join her—each of them wild beyond comparison, colored like rainbows and flashing coy smiles at the mortals with little flicks of their tails.

Some were wearing jewelry. Most were naked from the waist up.

Are you looking? Evie shot a sideways glance at Asher. *I can feel you looking.*

"Your Majesty." Katerina froze upon leaving the forest, staring with surprised recognition at the woman lounging atop the waves. "Well this is...unexpected. Evie—get back on dry land."

The queen merely flashed a pearly smile. Cassiel seemed oddly familiar with a few of the mermaids as well. Tanya's arms were folded stiffly across her chest.

It didn't take long for Evie to share her suspicions, ones that were confirmed almost as fast.

"You are right about the stone; it was left here for safe-keeping many years ago. We built our palace around it for protection, but our years of stewardship have come to an end," the mermaid queen explained.

"Why?" Cosette asked sharply, keeping her distance. "Why have they come to an end? If the stone was left with you, it was done so for a reason. We may not be able to reach it, but it's out of Kaleb's grasp as well. We should leave it where it is. Why take the risk—"

"Because your Kaleb has spent the last ten years mastering the art of necromancy," the queen replied softly. "He has raised an army of the dead. And we can no longer keep them at bay."

Evie stared at her in wonder. "You tried to warn me. You've been sending me dreams."

The others looked at her sharply, but the queen only smiled.

"For some time now. But the human mind is a tricky thing, and I couldn't speak to you directly. I had hoped when we sent the storm—"

"I'm sorry," Seth interrupted, "*you* sent that storm?"

"We did it to help you," another mermaid chimed in—one who'd been eyeing him from the waves. She peered up beneath watery lashes as Cosette's hand tightened around her bow.

The queen seemed oblivious to how the news was received. Either that, or she simply didn't care. What was one shipwreck to a people who'd seen thousands? What was another violent storm?

"The seas did just as I wanted," she continued in that lyrical voice, "breaking your vessel and spilling you into the waves. But before I could reach you the necromancer sensed you as well, taking you away on a dark current before stranding you on distant shores."

Evie thought back to her vision in the Kreo camp—the cold tide that had swept them away from the grip of the sea. She also remembered a shadow always lurking in the distance, and suspected the queen was keeping a few things to herself.

"You could have come to us sooner," the queen added in sudden accusation. "Your mortal squabbles have wreaked havoc on my kingdom."

Mortal squabbles?

"You could have been *slightly* more clear," the princess snapped defensively. "I dreamt of the ocean, but there wasn't any water. There were just bones. And all of my friends were dying. And the hands of the dead were dragging them downward—into the depths of the sea."

A profound silence fell over the beach.

"Don't let that put you off," she added quickly, "because that's probably where we should go next."

Dylan's eyes snapped shut. "She is *your* daughter, *not* mine."

"Why must we go anywhere?" Asher asked plainly. "Why can't you just bring us the stone?"

The queen opened her mouth to answer, then looked him slowly up and down. Not until he was flushed with color, unable to meet her eyes, did she deign to respond.

"Because I cannot touch it," she answered. "None of my people can. When it was flung into the water all those years ago the enchantment was sealed. Only someone marked by the fates may lay hands upon it. The ones chosen by the prophecy. The three of you...or him."

A faint shiver swept over Evie's body as an invisible line appeared in the sand—separating her, Asher, and Ellanden from the rest. They turned to each other, feeling it at the same time.

"We could get it right now," Ellanden said in a lowered voice. "*Right* now. Bring it back to the beach and destroy it with dragon fire."

"What if dragon fire doesn't work?" Evie asked in panic. "It doesn't destroy my mom's."

"They we'll figure something else out," the fae said impatiently. "But it's not like Kaleb doesn't know we're here—"

"He's right," the queen interrupted with sudden urgency. "Our defenses have already started to crumble, and the enemy remains at our gates. It's why I summoned you to the sea."

Evie looked at her in surprise. "You didn't summon me."

The queen smiled.

"It's more of a feeling."

...I like you.

"So we'll go down together," Asher declared, "just us three."

His father's hand appeared on his arm. "You are absolutely out of your mind."

"Take who you like, but you are right to hurry." The queen's eyes drifted out of focus, as if she was no longer seeing the beach but things happening far in the depths of the sea. "The enemy is upon us. And he's decided to bring his pet..."

"A *kraken*?!" Ellanden exclaimed for the fifth time. "An actual *kraken*?!" He glanced around at the others, seeing the same blank look. "Why am I a little excited?"

"Because you're certifiably insane," Asher replied. He turned to his girlfriend for help, but had never found much sanity there either. At present, she was chatting with a mermaid.

"You've got it wrong, it's pronounced—" at that point, the mermaid made a sound like a dolphin being raked across hot coals, "—but people from your world call me Lydra."

"Lydra," Evie repeated, warming with a shy smile. "I like it."

The mermaid shrugged. "To each their own."

It had been less than an hour, but news of their underwater adventure had already spread.

Diana was on the beach, along with Aidan and Petra. The rest of their parents would be taking the remaining ships out of the harbor to use as bait. While that would normally qualify as the most dangerous part of the mission, the young friends somehow had them beat.

"Are you ready?" the queen asked briskly. "My people can protect you for the journey, but once we get below the water things will happen quickly. You will not have time to linger or waste."

The friends shared a quick look.

"We're ready."

Weapons were checked a final time. Sweet goodbyes were murmured between parent and child. It had seemed impossible that so few of the adults would be going with them, but the queen had cryptically refused them entry. Petra had supported her, and in the end only the two vampires had been allowed safe passage as well.

"You'll get the stone, you'll bring it back, then we'll figure out what comes next." Dylan kissed the top of his daughter's head, fighting hard to keep steady. "We'll do that together. *Promise?*"

She nodded shakily, grabbing him in a hug. "I promise."

She could have held on forever, but her mother pried her loose.

For a few seconds, the two women just stared. Each one a vague reflection of each other, representing different moment in history, a different moment in time.

Then Katerina tucked her daughter's hair behind her ear with a smile.

"Trust your instincts," she murmured. "They'll never lead you astray."

Then it was over. The time had arrived.

The mermaids came as close as they could to the shore while the friends ventured out into the water, finding their balance and gripping cold hands. Evie ventured out after them, but at the last moment she turned to Asher—grabbing the corner of his sleeve.

"I'm scared," she whispered. "I don't know what comes next."

He cupped the sides of her face, staring deep into her eyes.

"I'll find you."

Then they pulled in a deep breath...and vanished into the depths.

OVER TEN YEARS, THE friends had been searching for the stone. Waiting for that precise moment, dreaming each night. However, like all long-awaited things, it happened in the blink of an eye.

The descent into the sea was something Evie would rather forget.

She hadn't known exactly how it would happen, as mermaids weren't exactly forthcoming, so when Lydra pulled her closer for a gentle kiss the princess let out a watery gasp.

A stream of bubbles trailed from her mouth, but the beautiful creatures were already carrying her and her friends swiftly downward, cupping a hand round the back of their heads the way a mother cradles a newborn, leaning down occasionally to breathe into their mouths.

She didn't know where they were going. There was no longer any light. At one point, the water got distinctly colder. So cold that her bones began to rattle. But the mermaids swam quickly past it, kissing another burst of oxygen before the picture suddenly brightened into light.

Evie blinked in astonishment, unable to believe her eyes.

She'd always imagined the kingdom of the mermaids to be a transient kind of place. As though all the treasures of the ocean were dumped carelessly upon a random stretch of seabed, until the creatures eventually forgot them and drifted on to someplace new. She hadn't expected a city.

A breathtakingly *beautiful* city.

The sculpted towers reminded her almost of Taviel, but everything had come from nature and these spiraled up like shells. Streets of iridescent gemstones wound like ribbons through the entryways, and strands of brightly-colored sea glass hung from the windows like chimes. Sharp etchings depicting violent disasters laced together in sprawling mosaics, and there wasn't a single building that didn't sport one of the stricken-looking maidens torn straight from the hull of a ship.

It was absolutely enchanting. It was also under attack.

Even from such distance, Evie could see the armies of the dead toiling slowly beneath the water. She realized now only a small fraction had been sent to greet them on the beach. It wasn't until they got closer that she realized what it was they were struggling against—the same stroke of enchantment that she was desperately hoping was going to allow them to breathe.

...it's like a bubble.

The princess could think of no better name for it, yet the simplicity fell insultingly short.

For around the entrancing city there rose an iridescent dome—almost translucent, save for the occasional rainbow flickers when it caught the light. While schools of mermaids were slipping in and out without problem, it was acting as a kind of shield against everyone else who'd arrived.

A truly magnificent protection, but it was beginning to crack.

With a burst of speed the mermaid carrying her shot towards the far side, away from the advancing tide. Scores of men and shifters, glassy-eyed sailors lost at sea, all raised their heads in unison as the friends shot past before attacking the dome once again.

Faster and faster they moved. So fast, the princess sincerely hoped the mermaid hadn't forgotten she was carrying her. Then without a hint of warning, they broke through the strands of light and came tumbling out into the open air on the other side.

When she lifted her head, it was only her friends beside her. The mermaids were gone, but as they swam away they pointed towards the dome and the message was clear.

You don't have much time.

"We need to move quickly," Evie panted, rising to her feet. "Come on!"

Like a city under siege, the street were abandoned—with no one left to tell the friends where to go. Even if they'd been full, Evie didn't know how the mermaids would have managed. The premise of an underwater city having streets in the first place was almost too laughable for words.

Yet with just a single glance the friends started sprinting for the palace. The queen had said the stone was at the very heart of the foundations. It was the first and only place to start.

About halfway there, a shadow streaked above them and Evie lifted her gaze to see a massive creature aiming for the ships in the harbor—large enough to black out the skies.

"...*Mom*."

There was a hitch in her momentum and she almost froze where she stood, staring in horror as a host of tentacles ribboned across the sky. It was over twice as big as a dragon. Even with the help of her uncle, she didn't see what chance they would possibly—

"Don't think about that now," Aidan commanded, taking her arm and forcing her back into stride. "The only way you can help her is by getting that stone."

With a fresh surge of energy, the princess raced to the front of the group—rushing through the deserted palace just as another splinter cracked its way up the dome like the shattering of glass.

A quick glance through a window and she saw the problem. The mermaids in charge of said fortified defenses were being picked off one by one. Even as she watched, another was impaled by an insectoid-looking demon and a trickle of monstrous creatures began leaking inside.

Without a single word, half of their party reversed momentum—throwing themselves backwards into the fight. Seth and Cosette were the first to leave, with Freya racing in between them. Diana and Aidan got a little farther before another part of the dome started to crack.

There was a suspended moment where Aidan looked at his son then he vanished as well, leaving only the three friends racing up the palace steps.

"Come on—hurry!"

With a burst of speed, they pushed themselves even faster—the soles of their boots slipping on the wet stone. They had just reached the inside of some kind of cathedral when there was a groan from somewhere in the foundation. Deeper than the foundation, coming from the earth itself.

"What the hell was that?!" Asher gasped, racing to a window.

In a single moment, his face turned white as a stone.

The others joined him a second later, watching as the dome shattered completely. Falling away in shards of broken light as the breathtaking city became submerged.

"Would you look at that," Ellanden murmured. "The sky is falling."

The princess would never forget the expression on his face while he backed away from the window. Amidst the screaming mass of chaos he closed his eyes with a look of perfect calm.

Then as the world crashed down around him, the fae lifted his arms.

Fulfilling his long-awaited vision. Holding back the sky.

"Ellanden," Asher gasped, his face awash with celestial light.

The dome was holding, but even as he spoke the door to the palace crashed open beneath a tide of shrieking monsters. It took them only a moment to locate the fae.

The vampire's face whitened in panic as he turned to the girl he loved.

"I can't...I can't leave him! They'll rip him to pieces!"

She nodded once then sprinted in the opposite direction.

Get the stone! It's the only way you save them! Get the bloody stone!

The hallway grew twisted and narrow, slanting sharply downward though there weren't any stairs. She ran as long as she could before her legs gave out beneath her, and she slipped across the freezing stone with nothing more than a whispered scream.

She tumbled out into a simple chamber. And that's when she saw it.

...there you are.

Her mother's was blood-red, a suitable color for a dragon. But this one was dark. Flat. Like the eyes that find you in nightmares, so cold they seem barely alive.

All that momentum but she approached it cautiously, scared that at any moment something would jump out and grab her. Scared that it couldn't be so simple as to just reach out and take.

But the prophecy was finished. The journey had been fulfilled.

And the second her fingers closed around the stone...the world turned to black.

EVIE DIDN'T REMEMBER being carried out of the water. By the time she opened her eyes, Lydra was laying her gently upon the shore. Her friends were nowhere in sight. The stone was in her hand.

She lifted a hand to shield her eyes, squinting blearily down the sand. There were figures in the distance, moving gradually towards her. She recognized tiny faces and cloaks.

"Nice aim," she mumbled, pushing weakly to her feet.

The mermaid slipped back into the water, pale with fear.

"I didn't carry you here, milady."

Evie nodded vaguely, then lifted her head.

"...what?"

That's when she saw him, a tall man slowly walking along the beach.

His hands were in his pockets, and though he was standing alone just few short miles from the royal army the worry of it seemed not to have crossed his mind. Neither was there anything particularly menacing in his approach. He could have been just any man strolling along the sand.

Kaleb.

"You destroyed my army."

He was conversational, almost friendly. Yet somehow detached. The princess unstuck her tongue from the roof of her mouth, trying her best to answer.

"I noticed you didn't stick around to watch." She studied him further. "Why is that?"

He flashed a cheerless smile.

"Well, they were new. I wasn't very attached. At any rate, I can always make more." He stopped a few paces away from her, tilting his head. "So that's the stone? Rather small, isn't it?"

He lifted a hand and it flew towards him.

No!

The princess stumbled forward on weak legs, but there was no point. The man had access to worlds she couldn't imagine. Dominion over the very shadows. And now he had the stone.

My uncle, she forced herself to remember. *This man is my blood.*

"I wasn't sure who was going to find it," he murmured, turning it over in his palm. "You or me. My guess was actually on me, but I've always had a problem with over-confidence."

She unsheathed a tiny dagger. The only thing that had survived her watery flight. It glinted in the air between them, and he glanced up from the stone with a bland smile.

"Have you forgotten your fire, Evie? Or are you simply too tired to use it?"

Let's find out!

With a wild scream the princess raised her hands, but only a second before she could test her fledgling magic against powers of a wizard she was suddenly tackled from behind.

"Seth?!"

The two tumbled together before he came out on top—eyes shining with apology as he pulled a slender coil of rope from the pockets of his cloak.

"I'm sorry," he breathed, lashing it around her wrist. "I can't let those dreams of yours come true. *Forgive me* and *take care of yourself.*"

With each whispered command, the salcor glowed upon her skin.

He was gone before she could register what had happened, racing towards the wizard with a wild cry. A pair of blades shot from his hand, released without warning. Fast and true. But it had been many years since Kaleb had anything to fear from things as common as a blade.

When he lifted his hand, they changed course—flying back towards the shifter and burying themselves deep in his side. He lifted a hand just as Evie reached him, staring down in surprise.

"...that was fast."

NO!

She screamed as he collapsed beside her, quickening the pace of those still running to meet them up the shore. One girl in particular stood out from the crowd. A pair of ivory braids flying behind her. A look of tear-stained terror written across her face.

Seth saw her at the same time, managing a wistful smile.

"I was going to marry that girl..."

Then his eyes fluttered shut.

"SETH!"

Evie screamed again as Kaleb watched in silence from a short distance, not even bothering to move when the rest of her friends joined them as well. For a suspended moment they hardly even noticed him—circling around the fallen shifter as he died quietly on the sand.

"No!" Cosette gasped, pulling his body towards her. "*Please*...don't leave!"

She didn't have wings to get there faster. She didn't know how to call down the power of some distant star. She was just a girl with a wooden pony, crying on a beach somewhere.

Wondering why she always ended up alone.

"You bastard!"

Ellanden leapt towards the wizard, but was batted away with a flick of his fingers. Asher streaked towards him a second later before finding himself lying flat on the sand. A kind of paralysis came over the rest of them, anchoring them where they knelt. Not that the lovely fae noticed.

She had broken with the shifter's death. All that remained was a girl weeping in the sand.

A strange look came over Kaleb as his fingers tightened around the stone.

"You're Kailas' daughter," he murmured. "The one who was left behind."

She gripped Seth's tunic harder, shaking with silent sobs as a torrent of bitter tears rolled down her porcelain cheeks. It was hard to tell whether or not she'd heard him. But the wizard froze with a curious expression before fluttering his fingers in the breeze.

There was a sudden gasp, followed by a breathless scream.

...then Seth opened his eyes.

"What did you...?" Evie trailed off in astonishment as the rest of her friends froze perfectly still. A second later her eyes flashed to her uncle. "Not like one of those—"

Kaleb shook his head.

"He was not far gone. He is how he was before. That's how he shall remain."

The shifter was slowly sitting up, looking confused as to why he was there in the first place. A look of belated fear shivered across his face when he saw the amount of blood on his shirt, but a second later his vision was obstructed with a cloud of ivory hair.

"They're gone," he murmured aloud.

Cosette tightened her grip. "What's gone?"

"The vampires," he answered in a daze. "The ties between us...they're gone."

A bond that ends only in death.

The others gathered around him, too stunned to do anything else. However, the princess took a step forward—staring at the man across the sand. "But...why?"

He hesitated a moment, almost like he was debating whether to tell the truth.

"It was easier to see you all from a distance. It's why I haven't strayed so close. It's why I couldn't stay with my mother—" He caught himself quickly then flashed a sad smile. "Sometimes it's easier to read about these things in stories."

Then he slipped the stone into his teeth, and leapt into the sky.

The princess staggered backwards, staring at the dragon. Despite its incredible size, it was already a fading shadow—heading east towards the rest of the realm.

She stared after him a moment, then lowered her eyes to the beach.

The rest of her friends were still gathered around Seth, oblivious to the subtle change that had come over her, but she and the vampire were bonded closer than blood.

He pulled himself immediately away from the others, running towards her in what felt like slow motion—a look of absolute terror on his face.

"Evie?!"

She blasted a wave of fire between them, burning a line into the sand.

"It was always going to be me, Ash. It was always going to be me."

He leapt through the flames just as the transformation started—reaching desperately for a girl before a dragon sprang up in her wake. Ellanden caught him a second later, frantically dousing the flames, but still the vampire was reaching towards her, his scream echoing across the sky.

"EVIE—NO!"

She looked down on them from above, immortalizing the image forever.

My boys...take care of each other.

Then she headed into the eastern sky.

EVERYTHING THAT HAPPENED next happened very quickly.

Evie flew after the dragon in a way she'd never managed to in her dreams—keeping pace despite the impossible distance, streaking like a crimson arrow across the sky. When they reached the snow-capped mountains he turned abruptly and streaked towards her, colliding with the force of a meteor, tussling together in a scuffling of wings.

She had no plan, other than already knowing the outcome. These were to be her final moments. This is when she was supposed to die.

But no matter how long she waited, it didn't seem to happen.

Faster and faster they spiraled, ripping and gnashing with claws. The only way she managed to stay in the game was to simply keep herself out of reach—constantly ducking, constantly writhing, constantly evading the strength of his claws. A single targeted blow and it would all be over.

But when she got close enough for it to happen, something different happened instead.

Kaleb opened his mouth to bite her...and inadvertently dropped the stone.

The game changed. The princess' direction shifted.

With a piercing cry, she dived straight towards the earth—chasing that tiny fleck of onyx, trying to incinerate it for good measure—then when that didn't work, catching it in her teeth.

Vague half-formed thoughts began racing through her brain. In a slow-motion parade, she saw the different steps she had taken to get there. The twisting adventure that had led to that point.

There was the basilisk that had driven them towards Freya and the library, the sorcerer's enchantment that had kept them suspended long enough for the rest of the friends to grow up. The vampires that sent them to the hyenas. The hyenas that sent them to the witch. And the witch that made a portal to send them towards her resurrected grandmother—

She caught herself suddenly.

Or perhaps the point of the portal wasn't to find Adelaide.

Perhaps the point was to find something else.

In a flutter of wings, she abruptly changed direction—hurtling her body back towards the distant peaks. There was a screech behind her as Kaleb turned to follow. But she didn't stop when she reached the mountains. Neither did she stop when she reached the fort. She dived straight inside.

...and into a terium mine.

The world exploded into a spray of silvery powder. The only reason it didn't kill her on the spot was that she entered not as a girl but as a dragon. But the power of the drug was overwhelming and she couldn't maintain the transformation for long. No sooner had she scrambled towards the entrance than the wings vanished and she found herself on two legs instead.

The dragon was circling above her, preparing for the dive himself.

She didn't think. She started to run.

⁂

WITH HER LAST BIT OF strength, the princess raced through the forest. Unable to understand how things had changed so quickly, unable to comprehend how far she was from the place she'd started. When the dragon cried in fury behind her, she pushed even faster.

Past the drawbridge where she'd defeated the hellhound. Past the bell-tower where she and Asher had made love. Past the trees where she and Ellanden had been attacked by slavers. Over a month since it had happened, but there were still scorch marks burned into the ground.

The drowsiness was wearing off, but the terium was still strong in her system. She couldn't use that fire now. The most she could do was force herself on to the remains of her grandmother's house, hoping there was something there to help her—hoping she could hide the stone before...

"He must have eaten the hemlock...that's what broke the spell."

Evie slid to a breathless stop, staring across the charred remains of the garden gate. She'd never understand how, but Kaleb had actually gotten there before her. He was standing quietly in the wreckage—not looking for her, not looking for the stone—but staring at his father's grave.

"I had wondered if she'd still be here," he murmured, glancing towards the ruins of his childhood home. "She was always here. We both were. We were never able to leave."

The princess' heart pounded as she took a step closer—unable to look away.

"You managed to leave," she finally managed. "You came to the party at the palace."

His lips twitched up in another humorless smile.

"That's right, your little celebration. Another night that didn't go as planned."

Run!

Every instinct was screaming. Though they were hundreds of miles away, she imagined that her friends were probably screaming the same thing.

But a part of her didn't see the point. She got closer instead.

"Your mother said that your plans had changed," she prompted. "What happened?"

His gaze rose from the grave.

"I saw you," he answered with the hint of a smile. "I was going to kill them all. Poison. It's a specialty of mine, the chill and shadow that grow beneath the ground. But when I saw this young girl with red hair walking amongst the tents, so much like the one in the pictures I grew up seeing on the wall... I decided to follow you. I saw you get the prophecy. Saw that you'd been given the same chance as your parents. A chance that was never given to me."

He broke off quickly, catching his breath.

"But I saw a chance of my own...so I took it."

It wasn't enough just to rule. You wanted to be better. You wanted to win.

But when he looked back at the headstone with the same expression as when he'd seen Cosette on the beach, the princess thought that maybe he wanted a bit more than that.

"I found this in the forest," he said abruptly, holding up Ellanden's bow. It was the one the villagers had given him. The one he'd lost when they were attacked. "Not the most sophisticated instrument, but it will get the job done."

She took a step back, staring in a daze. "We're still family, beneath it all. Do you really intend to kill me?"

He glanced across the fence. "I intend to take the stone. Will you give it to me?"

Their eyes met.

"Then, yes, I intend to kill you."

She took another step back and something snagged on her wrist. She glanced down to see a tiny golden ribbon. One that had stayed magically with her during the transformation.

One that had gone loose the moment Seth died.

She twisted her fingers and unwrapped it, coiling it loosely in her hand. Her uncle was looking in the other direction, fluttering his fingers as he conjured a shadowy arrow for the bow.

"I am sorry," he murmured, never noticing when she tossed it over the fence. "In a perfect world, it would never have ended this way. We could have gotten to know each other, you and I."

He lifted the bow.

"The way real families should."

It was over before he released the string. The enchantment had already taken hold. The moment he released the arrow it changed direction, protecting the life of his master.

...burying itself deep in his chest.

He let out a gasp and fell to the ground, sinking into the princess' arms. She held him as he convulsed and bled, the look of shock slowly fading as a stain of blood blossoming over his chest.

"I just wanted to be there," he panted, gazing up at her. "I just wanted..."

She squeezed his hand, tears slipping down her face.

"I know."

They held on a moment longer, both strangely intertwined.

Then he let out a quiet breath and died.

Evie stayed there a good while longer, staring into the distance, then looked down at the stone in her hand. It sat on the fence as she buried her uncle. It tucked into her fingers as she peered up at the starry sky. The constellations burned bright above her, the way she'd first seen them when she was just a child. Like something in a dream, her father's voice floated through her mind.

"In case you ever get lost, you can find your way back."

With a quiet breath, she found the ones she needed and started the long journey home.

"I CAN'T BELIEVE YOU'RE making me do this."

Evie, Asher, and Ellanden trudged up the last of the mountain, panting for breath as they finally neared the peak. It had been over two weeks since the death of the wizard. Over two weeks, and their parents had finally chided them for procrastination and insisted they destroy the stone.

It was a task they would have delighted them, but there was something particularly difficult about Mt. Grace. It's the reason Petra had selected it. The reason the stone was to go to the very top.

"Remind me again why we didn't just fly."

The princess stifled a grin, sharing a quick look with the vampire.

Since 'single-handedly saving the world', the fae had been rather reluctant to engage in any activity that didn't directly involve him and his bed. His friends would have been happy to scold him, but they'd found themselves sharing a delightfully similar inclination as well.

"Because it builds character," Evie replied. "Because the mountain is protected by some ancient sprits and you can't just *get* to it, Ellanden. You have to be worthy. You have to climb."

Another reason they were leaving the stone. Even if someone managed to make it all the way to the top, they would be ensured at least to have character.

And they would die shortly after of a cardiac event.

"Why in the world did Petra climb this in the first place?" Ellanden muttered.

Asher shook his head in agreement. "She's absolutely deranged."

They'd expected to find something of note at the top. Perhaps an enchanted fountain, or a pair of unicorns, or at the very least a flask of whiskey to make it worth the trip.

But there was nothing but a pile of rocks and a scattering of flowers.

"Do we just...leave it?"

The friends shared a look, then Evie dropped it in the grass.
Hurray.

"We did it," Evie said haltingly. "The prophecy is complete."

It seemed almost anti-climactic. There was nothing left to do but walk down the mountain.

Then all at once the weight of those words sank in.

We did it. The prophecy is complete.

A second later they came together.

The fae was too dignified, the vampire was too restrained, but the princess was pure fire. She brought them all together, crushing each other in a fierce embrace.

The feeling of it lingered as they headed down the mountain.

"Prophecies are tricky things," Ellanden murmured a while later as they weaved their way slowly towards the bottom of the mountain. "In the future, it's probably best to ignore them."

Evie glanced over with a smile.

"How do you mean?"

"All this time I've been torturing myself," the fae explained, "wondering which of us was meant to be lost. I tried to take control of it. Set up little traps for myself around the palace just so one of you morons wouldn't end up dead. And look at this, we're all still standing."

They considered this for a while, walking in silence.

"They're also lyrical," Asher finally offered. "More poetry than fact. Perhaps it just meant there are *more* of us that return. Three shall set out, though six came back."

"That's true," Evie agreed. "We couldn't have accomplished anything without Cosette and Seth and Freya. Then there're our parents. I suppose we'll never know."

They walked a bit farther, then the vampire turned to the fae.

"You set traps for yourself around the palace?"

"Small ones," Ellanden admitted. "I supposed my heart wasn't in it."

Asher looked at him incredulously, then draped an arm around his shoulders with a grin.

"I think the shifter's right. We need to find someone to examine your head."

They continued walking together, the princess lingering a step behind. A strange feeling had come over her. A kind of warmth she wasn't yet able to explain.

Three shall set out, though three shall not return.

She went suddenly still, pressing a hand to her belly.

"...seven hells."

Epilogue

Ellanden stood in the courtyard, looking at a reflection of himself in the glass.

It was hard to find much that was familiar. His hair was tied back with a band of leather, his fair skin was swirled with amber henna, and his usual clothes had been replaced with robes of a shimmering auburn. All this was overlaid with a headdress he had yet to acknowledge, even to himself. When he lifted his arms, the feathers of a dozen red-tailed hawks fluttered in the breeze.

...perfect.

He shook his head with a little smile, wondering what his life had become.

"Are you nearly ready?" Cassiel's voice echoed up the stairwell as he jogged lightly up the steps. "The covens are almost finished with the backdrop and the other priests—"

His voice cut short as he stared across the terrace.

Ellanden turned around quickly, fidgeting with a nervous smile. "How do I look?"

Cassiel stared a moment longer, then smiled in return. "Like my son."

Time moved quickly in the five kingdoms, especially considering it had *stopped* moving for the monarchs altogether. But the seasons waited for no one, and there were traditions to be upheld.

The realm was crying out for stability. A great deal had already changed.

Diana had never returned from their journey into the ocean. In a moment of bravery that would be spoken of for many years to come, she had thrown herself straight into the path of the oncoming army—giving the rest of the friends the opportunity they needed to escape.

She had entrusted the safety of her new kingdom to the hands of her oldest friend. Even now he was making one of his first addresses to the Council, but they expected him to return soon.

As one queen faded into memory, another made herself a home.

Adelaide had been unable to decide where to build her new life in the five kingdoms. The land of her son-in-law was a bit wild for her tastes, but there were too many painful memories to make the High Kingdom suitable as well. In the end, she'd decided to spend her time in the adopted land of her eldest son—travelling with him and his lovely wife across the sea to the Ivory City.

She still visited often. She had flown back that very morning.

As for the rest of the five kingdoms, that mending would be done incrementally, guided on occasion but mostly allowed to play out naturally over time. Progress had been slow yet steady, and ironically enough this was thanks in large part to the efforts of the warlocks after the war.

While the remains of Kaleb's army had sunk back into the grave with the dissolution of his spell, the darkness he'd been fostering lingered heavy in certain parts of the realm. But what dark magic had worked hard to build a lighter magic helped restore.

Within months, crop rotation and migratory patterns had returned to normal. People who'd fled into the larger cities for protection had the courage to venture home and rebuild.

The world fell once more into balance, guided by the warlocks' careful hands.

But they were not the only magical creatures to be welcomed back into the fold. Even the mermaids had done their part—forging a connection between the kingdoms of the land and sea.

Tired of their perpetual isolation, the mermaid queen had sent message to the rest of the ruling families— demanding a seat at the next meeting of the High Council. For obvious reasons, she also demanded that the Council be situated somewhere more convenient than at a table indoors.

When they had broached the subject of the Dunes—endlessly debating what might be done to contain the darkness—she suggested they eliminate the troublesome place altogether. A few days later the tides themselves had rose up against it, cleansing the parched land in the waves of the sea.

But the greatest hope of the future was yet to come...

"Ellanden, hold very still...something's got you."

Both fae turned around as the King of Belaria stepped onto the terrace, drawing a blade for good measure as he approached with raised hands.

"That's hilarious," Ellanden replied with a rueful grin. "I'll have you know, the Autumnal Equinox is a day of great importance to my people. I was *honored* they should ask—"

"Seven hells!" Seth stepped out the same door as the king, freezing with a look of the utmost astonishment as his eyes travelled over the prince. "I'm going to ask you a single question and you'll need to be very clear: how often are your feedings and when do they begin?"

Ellanden removed the headdress with a flush. "This was a mistake—"

"I suppose that was two questions."

"There you are!" Dylan greeted the shifter with a clap on the back. "We thought you weren't going to make it!"

There had been some question as to where the young wolf would settle, given the immense size of his newfound pack. Fortunately, the fortress the friends had liberated from the slavers was large enough to accommodate everyone in question. He'd spent the last few weeks with a team of wolves and rangers—clearing the surrounding forests of any lingering monsters whilst rebuilding all the damage the dragons had caused upon crashing into the mine.

"Have you already cleared the western trails like we discussed?" Dylan asked before he could answer, fidgeting uncomfortably in his heavy robes. "Did you start with the Altrean Pass?"

Cassiel glanced between them with a slight roll of his eyes. "You cannot trade lives with the shifter."

"I was never going to suggest—"

"Yes, you were."

Seth let out a sparkling laugh, shaking back his hair.

"Of course I made it," he replied, avoiding the rest of his king's micromanaging. "I couldn't miss this one dressing up like a molting bird...or the arrival of the baby."

For the last few weeks the kingdoms had been in a state of heightened anticipation, eagerly awaiting the first child of the crown princess and her husband—the newly-crowned vampiric prince.

"Do not make jokes, dog." Ellanden straightened with as much dignity as he was able. "This is a sacred rite of passage, a blessed day for every Kreo—"

"A blessed day for the rest of us as well!"

The others turned as Aidan jogged quickly up the steps, shrugging out of his heavy cloak and tossing it carelessly onto the table. His skin was flushed with excitement and he threw constant looks towards the tower rising above them, one foot bouncing uncontrollably on the stone.

"Has it happened yet? I heard it was nearly time."

"*Nearly* time," Cassiel soothed him fondly, glancing towards the tower as well. "And I can promise, when it happens—you'll know."

Dylan sauntered up beside him, flicking the vampire's crown with a grin.

"So...king, huh?"

Aidan lifted an involuntary hand. "More like the thug in charge."

The men shared a smile, when a servant burst into the courtyard.

"My lords, it's time!"

ELLANDEN WAS THE FIRST to enter, having shoved violently past all the rest. He burst into the room in a cloud of feathers, then froze when he saw the little family settled on the bed.

"Oh...he's perfect."

He slipped inside and joined them, staring at the newborn prince with a look of tender adoration. A tiny smile curved the corner of his mouth as he ran a finger along the baby's soft cheek.

"He is the most beautiful child in all the kingdoms. He will remain so until mine."

Asher's eyes twinkled as he shifted on the bed.

"Wait until you see his sister..."

The fae looked up in shock as another baby was suddenly presented. A girl to complete the package. The young prince's twin. Both shared the vampire's fair coloring, but they were of Damaris blood through and through. A dark-haired boy, and a fire-haired girl.

Part vampire, part shifter, part human.

"*Two*!" Ellanden gasped, as if they'd somehow planned it. "You would make me have *three*?"

Asher laughed under his breath, unable to tear his eyes away from his children.

"Close your mouth and hold my son," he commanded, passing the baby prince into the fae's arms. "When you're quite finished, you may hold my daughter as well."

The words were curt but the men shared a warm smile, one that reflected down onto the infants as the fae rocked the prince gently in his arms.

"He's perfect," he said again, pressing a kiss to the boy's dark hair. "He looks just like me."

Asher smiled to himself, playing with the child's toes. "You look like you're about to carry him off to your nest..."

A second later the door burst open again, and three more men appeared in the frame.

Cassiel lingered there, watching from a distance with a glowing smile—patiently awaiting his turn to hold them while Dylan went straight to his daughter.

Aidan made it halfway, then froze with a look of shock.

"Am I misunderstanding...?" he asked in astonishment, making a point to count them although there were only two. "...twins?"

Katerina flashed a smile, smoothing her daughter's hair. "What did you expect? When you marry into this family..."

Asher took back the newborn prince, carrying him to his father. "This is my son. This is your grandson."

Aidan's arms rose of their own accord, cradling the boy as though he was made of glass.

"Such a thing is so rare for our kind," he breathed, peering down in quiet wonder. "Ellanden was the first baby I ever held. I had never seen another."

Asher smiled in spite of himself, guiding his father's hands. "Well, don't let that put you off..."

Dylan gave his wife a kiss, then settled down beside his daughter—cupping a gentle hand around the princess' tiny head. Fiery crimson tendrils curled around his fingers as she lay in peaceful slumber, sucking voraciously on her thumb. "She's a treasure...have you thought of names?"

Evie gazed down with a tired smile, playing with the baby's hair. "I was planning on naming them both Everly, but Asher just told me he didn't like that idea."

"It's up to you," Katerina whispered conspiratorially. "From now on, *everything's* up to you."

The family came together in laughter, then settled back on the bed—circled in a gentle crescent around its newest members, wondering what else the future had in store.

"MOMMY?"

Evie looked down with a start at the children on her lap. The little boy was dozing, but the girl was staring up with wide eyes—tiny hands still wrapped around the book of fairytales.

"I'm sorry, my love. What did you say?"

The girl shifted impatiently, eyes flickering in the light of the candles.

"I asked if the story was really over. Is there nothing left to say?"

Evie smiled as she pushed gracefully to her feet—tucking a child under each of her arms as she carried them off to bed. The blankets were turned down, and the candles were extinguished. Still, the little princess waited for her answer. She could wait for hours. Her questions never ceased.

"If there's one thing I've learned about adventures, it's that they're never really over. The heroes may change and the stories may vary, but the adventure itself remains the same."

The child absorbed this as the final candle was extinguished.

"But how do you know?" she pressed. "How can you be certain more will come?"

Evie made her way to the window, gazing at the constellations shimmering high above.

"It's in the stars..."

THE END
... till you start reading
BEGINNINGS ...

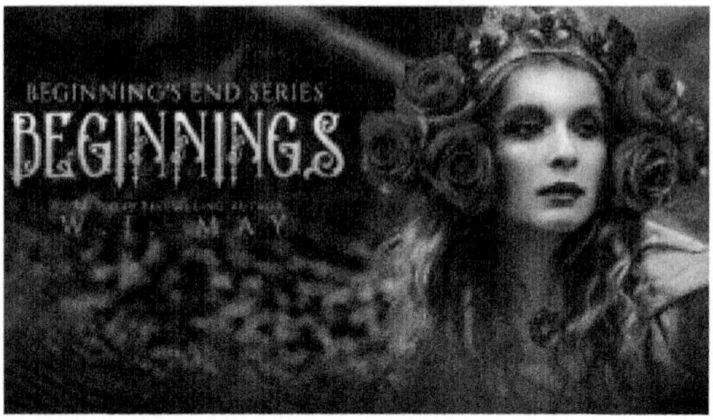
BEGINNING'S END SERIES
BEGINNINGS
W.J. MAY

The Queen's Alpha Series

Eternal
Everlasting
Unceasing
Evermore
Forever
Boundless
Prophecy
Protected
Foretelling
Revelation
Betrayal
Resolved

The Omega Queen Series

Discipline
Bravery
Courage
Conquer
Strength
Validation
Approval
Blessing
Balance
Grievance
Enchanted
Gratified

The Beginning's End Excerpt

Excerpt included

BEGINNING'S END SERIES
BEGINNINGS

USA Today Bestselling Author
W.J. MAY

BEGINNING'S END SERIES
BEGINNINGS
USA TODAY BESTSELLING AUTHOR
W. J. MAY

Beginnings Blurb

Book 1 of the Beginning's End Series

You've read the ending, but there is a beginning to every story...

Centuries before the creation of the five kingdoms, when the great houses were still forming and the realm was ruled by the fae, a small band of companions set out on a journey.

Kiera had never left her village. It was a stroke of luck that she wasn't there when the dragon attacked. Without any friends or family, without a shred of hope that anyone might believe her, she strikes off alone into the forest, looking for people that can help.

The world is new and untamed. The people are leaderless and wild. There has never been an alliance to unite them, but an alliance is exactly what the realm needs.

Because a darkness is coming. One that threatens to consume them all...

Chapter 1 Beginnings

"Those fish heads aren't going to chop themselves!"

The girl stared down at her hands. Pale from too little sunlight. Scarred from cooking over an open fire. Beneath the grease stains were callouses reserved for those who gripped reins all day, or devoted their lives to the swing of a sword. She'd gotten hers from decapitating fish.

"Kiera!"

She startled back to the present as a door swung open and the sounds of a crowded tavern filtered inside. A discordant chorus of voices, punctuated every few seconds with a deafening shout for *more ale*. Those two words haunted her dreams. It didn't help that she slept above the tavern.

"Nice of you to join us."

The man scowling in the doorway could hardly be counted as a man at all. While the general shape was there, he was sporting an extra three feet in every direction. It made him invaluable as the proprietor of such a rowdy establishment, and somewhat difficult when it came to stairs.

"The fish," he repeated slowly, as if she couldn't be counted on to remember. "I needed that stew to be ready ages ago. The people are hungry."

That stew will make them ill.

Instead of voicing this opinion aloud, she gave a sarcastic salute and poured a bucket of freshly caught trout upon the counter, grabbing a cleaver as the man slipped back through the door.

I shouldn't have done that.

Her cheeks flushed with belated guilt, as she gave the blade a cursory rinse.

She was lucky to have a job. So many people didn't. Since scraping its way through an especially bleak winter, work in the tiny village had been scarce. Fortunately, for all his menace and bluster, the proprietor was actually a good man. He kept her on staff. And no matter what might be happening in the rest of the world, there remained a universal truth: people always needed a drink.

With the skilled hands of one who'd done it many times before, she positioned the fish and swung the blade fiercely, imagining each one to be the face of a recent patron. A goblin who tried to walk out on his bill. A shifter who'd grabbed her around the waist as she tried to pass by.

There were more than enough to keep her occupied, and before long, she was hacking merrily away—dreaming now of bigger things: ogres and giants and trolls. Some people might fend them off with swords and spears, but she didn't need anything more than her handy cleaver. They fell, one after the other, crumbling to the ground in a revolting display of blood and gore. Some tried to flee in terror, before feeling the kiss of her deadly blade. Some were screaming for—

"More ale!"

She paused with the cleaver still raised above her, a ribbon of amphibious blood trailing up the inside of her arm. The fish were quickly abandoned, dumped into a large pot, as she hurried out of the kitchen and back to the main bar—grabbing two pitchers as she went.

Marcel, her fellow bartender, was in the corner with some fishermen, trying to settle was quickly escalating into a violent dispute. Talbot, the proprietor, had taken his place behind the bar, watching the crowd with one eye, as the other measured the drinks.

"Busy night," he murmured, unfazed by the general clamor as he continued to pour. "Did you finish with the fish?"

She swept up beside him, tying back her hair.

"I annihilated them..."

He chuckled under his breath, flicking a piece of tail from her shoulder, then quickly easing the frothing pitchers from her hand. "It's too festive out there tonight. Why don't you stay behind the counter? Pour the whiskey. Let me handle the ale."

Festive. Tavern code for: dangerous. It was the word they used when it was a little too full, tempers were a little too heated, and the men had already been served a little too much whiskey.

Marcel had no such codes, but he didn't need them. The man was part shifter.

"Are you sure?" she asked, trying to hide her relief. "It's no problem."

The man nodded, squinting slightly, like he'd gotten something in his eye. It was a dance they'd done many times. A brusque series of grunts and deflections, hiding the affection beneath.

He was gone a moment later, leaving her alone behind the bar.

END OF EXCERPT

Find W.J. May

Website:
http://www.wjmaybooks.com
Facebook:
https://www.facebook.com/pages/Author-WJ-May-FAN-PAGE/141170442608149
Newsletter:
SIGN UP FOR W.J. May's Newsletter to find out about new releases, updates, cover reveals and even freebies!
https//www.wjmaybooks/newsletter

More books by W.J. May

Hidden Secrets Saga:
Download Seventh Mark part 1 For FREE
BOOK TRAILER:
http://www.youtube.com/watch?v=Y-_vVYC1gvo

Like most teenagers, Rouge is trying to figure out who she is and what she wants to be. With little knowledge about her past, she has questions but has never tried to find the answers. Everything changes when she befriends a strangely intoxicating family. Siblings Grace and Michael, appear to have secrets which seem connected to Rouge. Her hunch is confirmed when a horrible incident occurs at an outdoor party. Rouge may be the only one who can find the answer.

An ancient journal, a Sioghra necklace and a special mark force life-altering decisions for a girl who grew up unprepared to fight for her life or others.

All secrets have a cost and Rouge's determination to find the truth can only lead to trouble...or something even more sinister.

RADIUM HALOS - THE SENSELESS SERIES
Book 1 is FREE

Everyone needs to be a hero at one point in their life.

The small town of Elliot Lake will never be the same again.

Caught in a sudden thunderstorm, Zoe, a high school senior from Elliot Lake, and five of her friends take shelter in an abandoned uranium mine. Over the next few days, Zoe's hearing sharpens drastically, beyond what any normal human being can detect. She tells her friends, only to learn that four others have an increased sense as well. Only Kieran, the new boy from Scotland, isn't affected.

Fashioning themselves into superheroes, the group tries to stop the strange occurrences happening in their small town. Muggings, break-ins, disappearances, and murder begin to hit too close to home. It leads the team to think someone knows about their secret - someone who wants them all dead.

An incredulous group of heroes. A traitor in the midst. Some dreams are written in blood.

Courage Runs Red
The Blood Red Series
Book 1 is FREE

WHAT IF COURAGE WAS your only option?

When Kallie lands a college interview with the city's new hotshot police officer, she has no idea everything in her life is about to change. The detective is young, handsome and seems to have an unnatural ability to stop the increasing local crime rate. Detective Liam's particular interest in Kallie sends her heart and head stumbling over each other.

When a raging blood feud between vampires spills into her home, Kallie gets caught in the middle. Torn between love and family loyalty she must find the courage to fight what she fears the most and possibly risk everything, even if it means dying for those she loves.

Daughter of Darkness - Victoria
Only Death Could Stop Her Now
The Daughters of Darkness is a series of female heroines who may or may not know each other, but all have the same father, Vlad Montour.
Victoria is a Hunter Vampire

HUNTRESS SERIES
USA TODAY BESTSELLING AUTHOR
W.J. MAY
LOOK BACK
MASTER
PERMISSION

PROPHECY SERIES
• W.J. MAY •
PROPHECY
PROPHECY
PROPHECY

The Chronicles of KERRIGAN
W.J. May
RAE OF HOPE
DARK NEBULA
HOUSE OF CARDS
ROYAL TEA
UNDER FIRE
END IN SIGHT
W.J. May
KERRIGAN

THE HIDDEN SECRETS SAGA
W.J. MAY
W.J. MAY
THE HIDDEN SECRETS SAGA

Don't miss out!

Visit the website below and you can sign up to receive emails whenever W.J. May publishes a new book. There's no charge and no obligation.

https://books2read.com/r/B-A-SSF-UJVRB

BOOKS 2 READ

Connecting independent readers to independent writers.

Did you love *Gratified*? Then you should read *Beginnings*[1] by W.J. May!

USA Today Bestselling author, W.J. May, brings you the story of how the prophecies began--before Evie, before Katerina--starting from the very beginning. The Beginning's End Series is a prequel and continuation of the bestselling YA/NA series about love, betrayal, magic and fantasy. Welcome to W.J. May's world of paranormal, full of shifters, fae, fairy, witches, dragons, dark magic... and did I mention the vampires?

Learn to fight, it is the only option

You've read the ending, but there is a beginning to every story...

---

1. https://books2read.com/u/mvo9BV

2. https://books2read.com/u/mvo9BV

Centuries before the creation of the five kingdoms, when the great houses were still forming and the realm was ruled by fae, a small band of companions set out on a journey.

Kiera had never left her village. It was a stroke of luck that she wasn't there when the dragon attacked. Without any friends or family, without a shred of hope that anyone might believe her, she strikes off alone into the forest, looking for people that can help.

The world is new and untamed. The people are leaderless and wild. There has never been an alliance to unite them, but an alliance is exactly what the realm needs.

Because a darkness is coming.

One that threatens to consume them all...

Be careful who you trust.

Even the devil was once an angel.

BEGINNING'S END SERIES

Beginnings

Curiosity

Scrutiny

Foresight

Disavow

Trickery

Wisdom

Decree

Influence

Prevail

Dignified

Honored

QUEEN'S ALPHA SERIES

Eternal

Everlasting

Unceasing

Evermore

Forever

Boundless
Prophecy
Protected
Foretelling
Revelation
Betrayal
Resolved

OMEGA QUEEN SERIES

Discipline
Bravery
Courage
Conquer
Strength
Validation
Approval
Blessing
Balance
Grievance
Enchanted
Gratified

Read more at www.wjmaybooks.com.

Also by W.J. May

Beginning's End Series
Beginnings

Blood Red Series
Courage Runs Red
The Night Watch
Marked by Courage
Forever Night
The Other Side of Fear
Blood Red Box Set Books #1-5

Daughters of Darkness: Victoria's Journey
Victoria
Huntress
Coveted (A Vampire & Paranormal Romance)
Twisted
Daughter of Darkness - Victoria - Box Set

Great Temptation Series
The Devil's Footsteps
Heaven's Command
Mortals Surrender

Hidden Secrets Saga
Seventh Mark - Part 1
Seventh Mark - Part 2
Marked By Destiny
Compelled
Fate's Intervention
Chosen Three
The Hidden Secrets Saga: The Complete Series

Kerrigan Chronicles
Stopping Time
A Passage of Time
Ticking Clock
Secrets in Time
Time in the City
Ultimate Future

Kerrigan Memoirs
Chronicles of Devon
Chronicles of Angel

Mending Magic Series
Lost Souls
Illusion of Power
Challenging the Dark
Castle of Power
Limits of Magic
Protectors of Light
Mending Magic Box Set Books #1-3

Omega Queen Series
Discipline
Bravery
Courage
Conquer
Strength
Validation
Approval
Blessing
Balance
Grievance
Enchanted
Gratified
Omega Queen - Box Set Books #1-3

Paranormal Huntress Series
Never Look Back
Coven Master
Alpha's Permission

Blood Bonding
Oracle of Nightmares
Shadows in the Night
Paranormal Huntress BOX SET

Prophecy Series
Only the Beginning
White Winter
Secrets of Destiny

Revamped Series
Hidden
Banished
Converted

Royal Factions
The Price For Peace
The Cost for Surviving
The Punishment For Deception
Faking Perfection
The Most Cherished
The Strength to Endure
Royal Factions Box Set Books #1-3

Royal Guard Series
Guardian

The Chronicles of Kerrigan
Rae of Hope
Dark Nebula
House of Cards
Royal Tea
Under Fire
End in Sight
Hidden Darkness
Twisted Together
Mark of Fate
Strength & Power
Last One Standing
Rae of Light
The Chronicles of Kerrigan Box Set Books # 1 - 6

The Chronicles of Kerrigan: Gabriel
Living in the Past
Present For Today
Staring at the Future

The Chronicles of Kerrigan Prequel
Christmas Before the Magic
Question the Darkness
Into the Darkness
Fight the Darkness
Alone in the Darkness
Lost in Darkness
The Chronicles of Kerrigan Prequel Series Books #1-3

The Chronicles of Kerrigan Sequel
A Matter of Time
Time Piece
Second Chance
Glitch in Time
Our Time
Precious Time

The Hidden Secrets Saga
Seventh Mark (part 1 & 2)

The Kerrigan Kids
School of Potential
Myths & Magic
Kith & Kin
Playing With Power
Line of Ancestry
Descent of Hope
Illusion of Shadows
Frozen by the Future
Guilt Of My Past
Demise of Magic
Rise of The Prophecy
Deafened By The Past
The Kerrigan Kids Box Set Books #1-3

The Queen's Alpha Series
Eternal
Everlasting
Unceasing
Evermore
Forever
Boundless
Prophecy
Protected
Foretelling
Revelation
Betrayal
Resolved
The Queen's Alpha Box Set

The Senseless Series
Radium Halos - Part 1
Radium Halos - Part 2
Nonsense
Perception
The Senseless - Box Set Books #1-4

Standalone
Shadow of Doubt (Part 1 & 2)
Five Shades of Fantasy
Zwarte Nevel
Shadow of Doubt - Part 1
Shadow of Doubt - Part 2

Four and a Half Shades of Fantasy
Dream Fighter
What Creeps in the Night
Forest of the Forbidden
Arcane Forest: A Fantasy Anthology
The First Fantasy Box Set

Watch for more at www.wjmaybooks.com.

About the Author

About W.J. May

Welcome to USA TODAY BESTSELLING author W.J. May's Page! SIGN UP for W.J. May's Newsletter to find out about new releases, updates, cover reveals and even freebies! http://eepurl.com/97aYf

Website: http://www.wjmaybooks.com

Facebook: http://www.facebook.com/pages/Author-WJ-May-FAN-PAGE/141170442608149?ref=hl *Please feel free to connect with me and share your comments. I love connecting with my readers.* W.J. May grew up in the fruit belt of Ontario. Crazy-happy childhood, she always has had a vivid imagination and loads of energy. After her father passed away in 2008, from a six-year battle with cancer (which she still believes he won the fight against), she began to write again. A passion she'd loved for years, but realized life was too short to keep putting it off. She is a writer of Young Adult, Fantasy Fiction and where ever else her little muses take her.

Read more at www.wjmaybooks.com.

Printed in Great Britain
by Amazon